A THOUSAND FALLING CROWS

ALSO BY LARRY D. SWEAZY

See Also Murder

A
THOUSAND
FALLING
CROWS

LARRY D. SWEAZY

SEVENTH STREET BOOKS®
AN IMPRINT OF PROMETHEUS BOOKS
59 JOHN GLENN DRIVE • AMHERST, NY 14228
www.seventhstreetbooks.com

Published 2016 by Seventh Street Books, an imprint of Prometheus Books

Cover design by Nicole Sommer-Lecht
Cover image © Valentino Sani / Arcangel Images

Inquiries should be addressed to
Seventh Street Books
59 John Glenn Drive
Amherst, New York 14228
VOICE: 716–691–0133 • FAX: 716–691–0137
WWW.SEVENTHSTREETBOOKS.COM

20 19 18 17 16 • 5 4 3 2 1

Library of Congress Cataloging-in-Publication Data

Sweazy, Larry D.
    A thousand falling crows / by Larry D. Sweazy.
        pages ; cm
    ISBN 978-1-63388-084-9 (paperback) — ISBN 978-1-63388-085-6 (e-book)
    I. Title.

PS3619.W438T48 2016
813'.6—dc23

                                                                    2015030324

Printed in the United States of America

To Matthew P. Mayo and Jennifer Smith-Mayo

"The crow wished everything was black, the owl, that everything was white."
    —William Blake, *The Marriage of Heaven and Hell*

"From childhood's hour I have not been
As others were—I have not seen
As others saw—[. . .] I could not awaken
My heart to joy at the same tone—
And all I lov'd—I loved alone."
                    —Edgar Allan Poe, "Alone"

CHAPTER 1

JUNE 11, 1933

The farm-to-market road was vacant, the day's traffic settled and tucked away as the big red sun dropped below the horizon. The hard days of summer had set in early. The few clouds that had showed promise of rain in the past month had pushed east, rushing by in a hurry like there was some place better to go, like the stink of dry Texas ground had offended them. Tender young crops succumbed to the heat and lack of water quickly, and the farmers, who'd had a bad year the year before and the year before that, knew that things were only going to get worse.

Soft pink light reached up with long fingers from the west, poking at the coming darkness like there was a victory to be won. But that was not the case. Light never won over darkness. At least at this time of day.

A lone crow sat on the telephone wire looking down at the road. Blood never escaped the eyes of a crow, but the smell of death was a vulture's quest. A kettle of six curious vultures glided down to a dead oak tree that had stood next to the road for a hundred years, its gnarly branches offering a perfect roost for the coming night. The big black birds were not attracted to the spot for rest, but by the rage, the loneliness, and the empty heart that had fulfilled nature's cycle of life and death. The smell of blood had piqued their appetite. The prospect of drought offered them abundance, reason to celebrate their way of living. There would be even more vultures this time next year.

The vultures and the crow looked at the blood without judgment. That was better left to humans and their laws, their ways of setting things straight. There was no justice to a hungry bird. There was only the now, the knowledge of hunger, and the need to fly. Blood and decaying flesh offered an opportunity, the concept of evidence and law foreign, useless. The crow was not disturbed by the vultures' presence.

The girl hadn't been there long. Her blood still pooled on top of the road and had yet to soak into the thirsty dirt. The blood glowed in the dusk, the pink fingers of the dying day reflecting off it like a mirror held up to the sky. There was no life left in the girl. She had been killed just before she was dumped from the speeding car, tossed out like an extinguished cigarette butt, left behind without worry or care. Her clothes were ripped and torn, and her face—what was visible of it— was plump with bruises and covered in blood. She was fresh. Not stiff. Flies had already found her. Joyful in the bounty, like the vultures.

Curiosity propelled the crow down to get a closer look. It didn't worry about the others. They were the least of its concerns. Coyotes would come soon. But for now the crow would claim the girl as its own. A feast to enjoy before darkness fell and the world turned black, black like itself, a twin without wings, but with far more secrets than it would ever tell.

The glass exploded out of the back window of the Chevrolet sedan like somebody had thrown a brick from the inside out. Once he saw the muzzle flash, it only took Sonny Burton half a second to realize that someone had taken a shot at him.

There was no question who was doing the shooting. Less than a year before, back in August, they'd killed a deputy in Stringtown, Oklahoma, launching a killing spree that had captured the nation's attention and made the pair as famous as the dead actor Rudolph Valentino.

Sonny had been alone, coming off duty in the small Panhandle town that had been his home for as long as he could remember. He was surprised at his luck, recognizing the two of them walking arm-in-arm to their car like they didn't have a care in the world, like nobody would know, or give two shakes, about who they were. Or maybe they just didn't give a rat's ass.

It didn't take them long to figure out that they were being followed by a Texas Ranger—the Cinco badge emblem and announcement that it was a Ranger's car was plastered across the side of the black 1932 Ford in hard-to-miss six-inch white letters. Thankfully, the duo had turned off on a nearly deserted dirt road when the shooting started.

With no way to communicate with anyone back at company headquarters about his lucky find, Sonny was on his own to bring the pair of lawless gangsters in for justice—if that was possible.

The shattering of his windshield sounded like a bomb had gone off directly next to Sonny's ear. He was pelted with stinging shards of the broken glass, and it felt like he'd fallen face-first into a hornet's nest. But that didn't stop him. His fingers tingled as he gripped the steering wheel; the thrill of the hunt never got old. The skin above his chest burned like it was going to rip open, and his heart was racing a mile a minute. Blood trickled down from his brow, but his eyes were safe, not hit, the blood not blinding him. He could still see the Chevrolet swerving in front of him, trying to get away or to get a better shot at him—one or the other, he wasn't sure.

A bullet whizzed by Sonny's right ear, just a couple of inches away from its intended target: his forehead. Luckily, he had tilted his head in the right direction. The wrong way would have put him directly in line with the shot and it would have been lights out. Game over. A Texas Ranger added to their growing collection of law enforcement kills.

It was a sobering thought, dying this close to the end of his career. Sonny wasn't sure what the future held for him, but up until a few minutes prior, he hadn't been too concerned about living to a satisfactory old age. He just wanted to finish what he had started—being a proud Texas Ranger and alive to boot.

The duo's older-model Chevrolet was no match for Sonny's newer Ford. The '32 Model B had a flathead V-8 engine and was fast off the start with sixty-five horsepower under the hood—an amazing thought considering Sonny had been born long before the invention of automobiles—when all of the Texas Rangers, including his own father, had ridden horses across the great state of Texas, pursuing the worst of the worst outlaws, like King Fisher and John Wesley Hardin. As a boy, Sonny wouldn't have been capable of imagining so much power in one vehicle. Times had changed all too quickly as far as Sonny was concerned.

He pushed the accelerator as far to the floor as it would go. His gun was loaded and in his hand almost magically, like a magnet had drawn it to his fingers. He aimed his Colt .45 Government Model automatic pistol with confidence at the busted out window of the Chevrolet and returned fire.

The Chevrolet swerved again, fishtailing on the gravel road and spraying the hood of Sonny's car with hundreds of pebbles—little pings and thuds that sounded like gunshots finding their target but posed no real threat.

A rifle poked out of the rear window, and a hot, orange flash exploded from the end of the barrel and did not stop at one. This was no riot gun or deer rifle, but a Browning automatic rifle, a fierce weapon that could empty a twenty-shot magazine in three seconds.

The noise was excruciating, metal piercing metal, ripping into the fenders, then shattering what little remained of the car's windows. Sonny could hardly take a breath or gather his wits about him. He wasn't ready to die.

The radiator exploded, sending a geyser of steam spraying upward to the heavens, clouding Sonny's vision. Bullets whizzed by his ears as he pulled the trigger of his .45, not stopping until every bullet had been fired.

He thought for certain he heard a tire explode, thought he saw a sign to his left warning that the road ahead was closed, under construction, that the bridge was out, but thoughts no longer mattered. He had been hit.

A bullet ripped into his shoulder, sending white-hot pain screaming though his body; blood sprayed out of the wound like a dam had been breached, an artery severed.

Another bullet hit him, not far from the other, and Sonny screamed with pain, with frustration and fear, as reality left him and his fingers slipped from the wheel, sending the '32 Ford careening into a ditch. He felt like he had been hit twice by a sledgehammer.

The last image Sonny saw before the car rolled and he blacked out was Bonnie Parker laughing like a maniacal child.

CHAPTER 2

JUNE 14, 1933

The volume of the radio was turned down low, the voices distant but decipherable. "The Nazi Party was made Germany's only legal political party today. Any political opposition is punishable by law . . ." the announcer said in a droning voice.

Sonny reached over with his left arm and was about to turn the radio off when he heard the announcer go on to say, "And in local news, the manhunt for Clyde Barrow and Bonnie Parker continues after their car was found wrecked and abandoned just outside of Wellington. They are to be considered armed and dangerous. If you see the duo, or know anything of their whereabouts, contact your local police or the Texas Rangers. Bonnie Parker is reported to be injured." The announcer stopped for a brief second, allowing the radio to buzz, then continued, "The identity of the girl found on the farm-to-market road leading out of Wellington is still unknown. Funeral arrangements are being postponed until a positive ID can be made. If you have any information concerning this case, please contact the Wellington Police."

Sonny took a deep breath as he struggled to turn the radio off. His right arm was bound and unmovable. He was right-handed, and any coordination and strength in his left hand was lacking, to say the least. He really wasn't supposed to move, but he didn't want to hear any more news, even though he was reasonably interested in hearing about Bonnie and Clyde and what had happened to them after he had been shot.

It was the first time he'd heard they'd wrecked, too.

The idea that he had something to do with that settled easy on his shoulders, but it didn't make the pain, or the uselessness of his arm, go away. All he really wanted was silence.

He didn't know anything about the dead girl found on the road, and he let the information flitter away. On any other day, he would have been interested, probably involved in the case, but now his concern was distant, difficult to hold onto. He resigned himself to that fact, eased down onto the hospital bed, and stared out of the second-floor window.

Summer had set in with a vengeance.

The windows were cracked open, but there didn't look to be a breeze outside. Every tree he could see was still as a statue, their leaves droopy. The sky was clear, the color of a roan mare he used to know, and the sun was a red hot plate, beating down relentlessly on the earth, scorching everything in sight; the grass had already given up all of its green and browned out. The landscape out the window was desolate, hopeless, but familiar. Hot, uncomfortable summers were just part of the deal when you lived in Texas. Sonny knew nothing else.

The door to the room was ajar, and a murmur of low voices found its way to Sonny's ears. He couldn't make out the words. It was like a small group was consulting three or four doors down, all whispering in soft, professional tones. The hospital was nothing more than a large two-story house with an operating room in the basement and patient rooms, at most four beds to a room, on the top floor.

Sonny closed his eyes. He had a room all to himself and hoped for sleep to come and take him away from the reality he'd woken up to, but that wasn't to be.

The door pushed open slowly, along with Sonny's eyes at the noise. A Mexican man, his black shiny hair just starting to turn gray, entered the room. His skin was as brown and leathery as a hundred-year-old holster, and though the man was probably in his late thirties, early forties at the most, he looked much older. He'd pushed a mop and bucket into the room, trying to be quiet. He was unsuccessful in the attempt. The wheels on the mop bucket squeaked like fingers slowly scraping down a chalkboard when he pushed it inside the room.

The man wore a blue short-sleeved work shirt with a pack of Chesterfields poking out of the pocket. He had the largest collection of keys dangling from his belt that Sonny had ever seen.

It was tempting for Sonny to close his eyes again and let the man do his job, but he couldn't keep himself from acknowledging the janitor's presence. "*Hola*," he said, his voice weak but steady as he stared directly at the man. The patch on the Mexican's work shirt said his name was Albert, but Sonny doubted that was really the case.

Sonny had startled the man. His shoulders jumped back, then he looked up, glancing over at Sonny sheepishly, then back to the floor, as he pulled the mop out of the water. "*Hola*," he answered. "*Hablas Español?*"

Sonny nodded and tried to pull himself up. "Yes, I learned to speak Spanish a long time ago," he said, speaking fully in the Mexican's language.

The janitor smiled, relaxed a bit, then pulled up the mop and let it drain through the ringer. "You speak very well."

"I was raised by a Mexican woman."

"Really?"

"Yes. She was with me every day until I grew up and left home."

"What happened to your momma?"

"She died about a year after I was born," Sonny said, looking away from the man, out the window. At sixty-two years old, Sonny should have been long past the sadness of losing his mother and his nanny, if the woman who raised him could be called that, but Sonny still thought about Maria Perza every day. She had taught him everything he knew about being a decent, Anglo man, living in Texas. "What's your name?" Sonny finally asked.

"My name is Aldo," the Mexican said. "Aldo Hernandez."

Sonny smiled. He knew it wasn't Albert.

"And what is your name, *señor*?" Aldo said.

"Lester. Lester Burton. But everybody calls me Sonny. They have ever since I was four or five."

Aldo returned the smile. "You are that Ranger that was shot by Bonnie and Clyde aren't you? You are lucky you are not dead, *señor*."

"Yes, I know."

"Your arm, will it get better?"

Sonny shook his head. "I'll be lucky to feel anything or be able to use my hand ever again."

"Then you are done working. It is all over for you?"

"Seems that way. Times are tough all over. Another man can take my job. I've had my life, and it's been pretty good up until now."

"Yes, yes, times are very bad. This Depression seems like it will go on forever. I, too, am happy to have a job, happy that the doctor has kept me employed through this dark time. I have hungry mouths at home who depend on me. What about you, do you have children?"

Sonny nodded. "A son. He's a Ranger, too, down in Brownsville. He's married with a couple of little ones of his own." A smile crossed Sonny's face, then quickly flittered away. He hardly ever saw his grandchildren. The distance between them was too far to encourage closeness, and that seemed just fine with his son, Jesse. They never seemed to see eye to eye on anything. It had always been that way, and Sonny didn't expect it to ever change.

"You are lucky then. You will have someone to help you when you go home."

Sonny didn't answer. He looked away and stared up at the ceiling. There was no use telling Aldo that he'd be all alone when he left the hospital. The house was empty, a collection of dusty furniture and a clock that ticked for no one but him. Martha, his wife, had been dead for ten years, struck down in a single, unforeseen blow by a massive heart attack while she'd been out weeding the garden. The emptiness of the house was his sadness to bear and no one else's.

Aldo didn't broach the silence. He let it hang in the air knowingly.

Like his father, Sonny had always been tall and rangy, and he could only imagine how he must look to the Mexican—skeletal, gaunt, each breath a rattle on death's short chain. He closed his eyes then, the strength not in him to push away the memories of the past. Maria, Martha, Jesse, his father, the good times and the bad.

When he opened his eyes again, it was dark and chilly in the room. Aldo was gone.

It was a slow ride from the morgue to the funeral home. No one had claimed the dead girl. She was lost in a world of darkness, with no name, no family, no one to love her as she was prepared for her final rest. More important news had drowned out the cry of the injustice of her death. A small corner on the front page, otherwise loaded with images of Bonnie and Clyde and the Texas Ranger they'd shot, was all the notice the murder had garnered. On any other day in Wellington, the discovery of the girl would have been great cause for speculation, fear, and locked doors.

Only the crows worried over her now. The crows and her killer. The crows watched from close by, then flew away as the hearse passed. They went on with their day, always watching, always listening. Would the killer offer the world more carrion? More of what it deserved?

CHAPTER 3

AUGUST 12, 1933

Bonnie and Clyde's Chevrolet was sitting inside a barn. Three bullet holes had pierced the rear fender. Both of the tires on the driver's side were flat. Straw and dust covered the roof of the car, and a red tabby cat lay sleeping in the backseat, the coils poking up through the brown velvet material that was slowly being carted away, one mouthful at a time, by a herd of opportunistic mice—when the cat was away, of course.

Sonny stood back staring at the car. Hard afternoon light filtered in through the barn walls, and the August heat was so stifling and humid it made him sweat just at the thought of walking the rest of the way inside.

"Been chargin' a nickel a peek," Carl Halstaad, a dairy farmer the size of a bull himself, said, as he chewed a big wad of Red Man tobacco in his right cheek. "But I 'spect I won't charge you a penny since you're the man who put them bullet holes there."

"I appreciate that, Mr. Halstaad."

"Carl. You can call me, Carl, Ranger Burton." He spit a long stream of brown liquid from his mouth, splashing, respectfully, a good two feet from Sonny's boots.

Sonny nodded. "My Ranger days are behind me now. Most folks just call me Sonny."

"Ah, heck. I can see you got a bad limb, there, but once a Ranger, always a Ranger, right?"

"Well, yes, I suppose so." The doctors had wanted to amputate the arm. They feared gangrene would set in, but so far it hadn't. The arm just hung there, useless and numb, an annoying reminder of the time when he had felt whole and young. Most days he kept busy, didn't allow himself to feel sorry for the loss or grow too angry.

He walked up slowly to the driver's door and peered inside the window. The windshield was shattered, and the battery lay on the floor in front of the passenger's seat.

"People say Bonnie's got a limp now," Halstaad said. "Clyde carries her around a lot. The acid burned her bad, but maybe not bad enough."

"Maybe not," Sonny said.

"Some folks up in Dexter, Iowa, seen them at an amusement park a couple weeks back. Bonnie was bandaged up pretty good. They was surrounded, but somehow they managed to get away again. Must be magicians, or blessed with the dark skills of Houdini's lost spirit. The one they called Buck died after surgery for a gunshot wound. And they just left him, ran from him like thieves in the night. There are no true friends to those two."

"What are you going to do with it?" Sonny asked, pulling himself from the window, ignoring the news about the Barrow gang's whereabouts. The inside of the car smelled like cat urine, pungent and sour, mixed with acid and dried blood. His stomach lurched.

"The car?" Halstaad asked.

Sonny nodded.

"I suppose I'll just hang onto it, keep gettin' my nickels from it for as long as I can. Why? You want to buy it?"

"No, I've seen all I need to." Sonny turned and pushed past Halstaad. He knew about the incident in Dexter, Iowa. He followed Bonnie and Clyde's every move on the radio and in the newspapers. He'd been practicing shooting left-handed, just in case another chance at them ever came his way.

No grass grew on the grave. No name had been given to the dead girl. She was a wanderer, a ghost now with a sordid past, her wicked ways most likely the cause of the sad end she'd found in the middle of some farm-to-market road in the Panhandle of Texas. Newsmen forgot about her. The sheriff misplaced her file, stuffed it in the bottom of a drawer in a room that was rarely visited. Her flesh fell away from her skin in the bottom of a grave in Potter's Field. It was like she had never stepped a foot on the good earth, had never existed at all.

The crows went about their summer business. Families were raised and fledged, the promise of winter certain but distant. What corn had survived the drought was hardly worth eating. For now there was a bounty of dead things to feed on. But hunger would come soon. The desire and hunger for fresh meat, already dead or just dying, would be unbearable. Grain or meat, sustenance would come from wherever it could be found. Only survival mattered. The hand of death provided the crows the opportunity to continue to fly.

CHAPTER 4

MAY 1, 1934

Nine months later, there was no ache to warn Sonny that something was wrong. He could see it coming, though. The tips of his fingers were turning black. His arm was useless, had been since two bullets had blasted through the top of his shoulder, slicing the arteries, and exploding his flesh into a mess that was left beyond repair. Part of his body was dying, a quarter of an inch at a time. It might be weeks, or months, before the poison took him—if he did nothing, if he ignored the darkness and pretended his life was normal. The lack of pain was a contributor to denial. He could look away and not feel a thing.

The doctors had said there was no hope in saving the limb at the time of the shooting, but Sonny had resisted, remained stubborn in his stance to live out what remained of his life whole and intact.

He had been right-handed all his life and couldn't imagine having to depend on his weaker, less reliable, left hand. That hand seemed to have a mind of its own, often ignoring his commands recklessly—or on purpose, he wasn't sure which. Even in his clearest moments, Sonny couldn't see himself with only one arm, a sleeve pinned to his side, a constant reminder of what he once was. That seemed to be an unimaginable way to live, with part of your body lost, incinerated, not even saved, like a rare diamond, to be buried with you.

Oddly, in those moments Sonny remembered when he was a little boy and his father, who had fought for the Confederacy, would stop along the street and talk to men he saw without a leg or an arm.

They whispered, lowered their voices, looked away distantly to the past, to some unseen place. It was like they spoke a secret language or belonged to some secret fraternity. At the end of the whispers, his father would pull away from the amputee solemnly and push Sonny forward, reminding him of what to say: "Thank you for your service to the cause." The wounded man would normally nod with glistening eyes, offer a sad smile in response, wordless in his gratitude but certain in his loss when he looked to where a leg or an arm once had been.

The words echoed deep in Sonny's memory as he stood, an old man himself, fully dressed in front of the mirror, staring at himself, separating his story from the legion of dead Confederate soldiers who lived in his mind. Somehow, he thought he was going to will a miracle and save his fingers and arm from rotting off.

If he screamed, no one would hear him. He was alone. The nearest neighbor was a mile and a half to the east. Sometimes, he went to the basement. It was dark and dank down there, the walls built into the earth with planks, bound with roots from above. The smell was old, musty, organic. When he turned off the single bare light, it was like standing in a giant grave, a grave he could dance in, cry in, scream in, then walk up the stairs and out into the waiting sunlight, like he was well, whole, and resurrected from his nightmare.

He never believed it for a second. There was no question what path lay before him—he had seen it before.

Sonny had fought a different war than his father, on the soil of a foreign land with an army of Allied Forces fighting side by side against Germany's aggravated threat to the world. He had survived that war in one piece, although he was affected with what his father often referred to as "Soldier's Heart," a melancholy that lasted a few years after his return to Texas and took a toll on his family that still stood to this day. These days they called it "the thousand-yard stare" because of the unfocused gaze of men like him who'd come back whole in body but not in mind. It was an apt description. Better than shell shock, Sonny thought.

Martha had fought against his depression and lost quietly. Her sudden death was probably a relief to her, an escape from him that no legal document could guarantee. His son, Jesse, had been a teenager at the time of his return from the World War and was full of rage and distance—in some ways, the boy had not changed. They saw each other once or twice a year, at holidays, and sometimes at funerals. Brownsville was a world away from Wellington. The long miles that stood between them suited each of them just fine. The universe had conspired to separate them, and it was probably for the best.

He had mastered dressing with one arm, though buttoning a shirt had been a challenge in the beginning. He'd rigged up a dowel rod with a little hook on the end that he used to finagle a button through the hole. It was, he supposed, the shape of things to come, a hook as an appendage. He shuddered at the thought, recoiling from the vision of himself as a monster, a hooked pirate gone mad, slashing away at anything that got in his way, at anything that made him angry. A gentle moment quickly turned into a bloody accident. He would have to avoid touching anyone—even more so than he did now.

He'd found that boots were easier to get on than shoes that had be tied, but weren't as easy to get off. Mostly, he'd figured out how to survive, though weakly and slowly. It had taken him an hour to get dressed.

Before he was shot, dressing and shaving were acts that he gave little thought to. He'd just floated through the morning, doing one thing after the other. Now when he opened his eyes after a restless night of sleep, he dreaded putting his feet on the floor. He just wanted to stay asleep.

Sonny drew in a deep breath, the house around him silent but for the ticking of a dusty old grandfather clock, then squared his shoulders and walked out the front door. He had a doctor's appointment at ten o'clock.

CHAPTER 5

MAY 14, 1934

The nurse wheeled Sonny toward the door. "Is somebody waiting for you, Mr. Burton?" She was tall, blonde, and spooned into her white uniform that looked a little too tight and a little dull from one too many washes. At another time the woman, her voice husky and her perfume sweet, might have garnered a look of desire from Sonny—but not now. She was too young and he was too old. Desire of any kind had been stowed away long ago. It surprised Sonny that he even recognized such a thing at that moment.

"No," he said. It hadn't occurred to him to tell anyone about the surgery. "I drove myself here, and I can drive myself home."

The nurse stopped so suddenly and unexpectedly that Sonny nearly tumbled face-first out of the wheelchair. He reached out to steady himself with his right hand, but it wasn't there. The arm was gone. Hacked off in a sterile room while he had been anesthetized with some miracle drug that had taken him to the depths of sleep and to the edge of death, only to return him to the land of the living with a body he did not recognize—or want.

His brain had not adjusted to his new reality any more than his body had. His brain obviously still believed that his right arm was attached to his thin torso because the nerve endings under the incision burned like the nurse had doused the stub in gasoline and lit it on fire.

"You can't drive yourself home," the nurse said. She moved from behind the wheelchair and faced him, standing stiffly, like a drill sergeant, her glare hard as stone, her hands placed solidly on her hips.

"Well, I best start walking then."

The nurse flipped her gaze to the door, and took in the bright, hot day that awaited them both as soon they stepped outside the hospital doors. She shook her head.

Beyond being shapely, her fingers were bare of rings or jewelry of any kind. She looked to be in her early thirties, a slight pouch in her belly the only imperfection on her womanly body, a distraction from her obvious beauty, most likely caused by the recent experience of childbirth. Sonny had seen that shape before and was aware enough of his own loneliness, and status as a widower, to notice the effects of a recent pregnancy. It had to be that.

"There's no one to call?" the nurse demanded again.

Sonny shook his head. "My son lives in Brownsville. He's busy with a family of his own. I didn't want to bother him."

"That sounds like an unlikely story. You just had your arm amputated, Mr. Burton. What about church people?"

"I don't attend church, thank you very much."

"Another likely story."

"It's all I have to offer."

"I can't let you drive home alone. It's not safe."

"I drove here with one hand. The arm didn't work any better then than it does now. I live alone and once I'm gone from here, I'm on my own. What's the difference?"

"I know about it. That's the difference."

"I've learned how to do for myself with one arm. I'll be just fine. Push me to the door and leave me be. I'll manage. Beyond that, I'd rather you not push me into a rage and make me curse in front of you."

"You'll mind your manners, Mr. Burton, thank you very much. I am only interested in what's best for you. Doesn't matter how much you think you can do. I can't allow it. I'm sure Dr. Meyers wouldn't have released you if he'd known your circumstances."

Inwardly, Sonny smiled at the nurse's gumption and lack of tolerance at his crankiness. He liked her but didn't let it show, didn't think it mattered anyway.

A familiar voice rang out from behind the nurse. Neither of them had detected the presence of another human being. "I can drive him home, *señora*." It was Aldo, the middle-aged janitor who had visited with Sonny after he'd been shot. "If that is all right with *Señor* Burton and you? His house is on my way home."

Aldo looked at the ground sheepishly. His eyes were bloodshot, like he lacked sleep; most likely he had worked a double or triple shift. His brown skin looked even more unhealthy than it had the first time Sonny had met him, and the wrinkles on his long face looked deeper and harder, if that were possible. Worry had cut into the man quickly. He'd aged ten years in a matter of weeks.

The nurse stared at Sonny with questioning blue eyes that flickered with relief. He could see the ocean in her eyes. So much so, he had to look away. "I don't want to put anyone out," Sonny said.

"It would be my pleasure to drive you home, *Señor* Burton. You are a hero."

Sonny shook his head, but said nothing. Heroes walked away from the battlefield in one piece, whole like his father, who had survived more battles and wars than any one man should have and lived to tell about it.

"I think that would be a fine idea, Albert," the nurse said, reading the name tag embroidered on Aldo's work shirt.

"Aldo. His name is Aldo Hernandez," Sonny interjected tersely.

"It does not matter what she calls me, *señor*," Aldo said.

"Yes, it does."

"I'm sorry, I didn't mean any disrespect," the nurse said.

Sonny lowered his head when he realized that he didn't know the nurse's name. He'd perused her body, allowed himself a fleeting moment of attraction, and chastised her for treating Aldo differently because he was a Mexican, when, in reality, she probably wasn't. He was sensitive about prejudice. Maybe more so than he should have been. "What's your name?" he asked in a softer tone than he had yet used when speaking to her.

"Betty. Betty Maxwell," she snapped.

"I'm sorry, Mrs. Maxwell," Sonny said. "It's been a long day."

"Miss. It's Miss Maxwell, if it's all the same to you. But you can call me Nurse Betty. Everybody does."

Sonny continued staring at the floor. "I think it would be fine if Aldo drove me home. Just fine, Nurse Betty."

"That's good, Mr. Burton, because you certainly weren't going to drive yourself." Betty Maxwell turned to Aldo and, in impeccable Spanish, she said, "I am sorry to have offended you, Aldo. Could you please bring *Señor* Burton's car to the door?"

"He doesn't know which one it is," Sonny said, with a smile, his Spanish as perfect as hers.

The road was bumpy, and Sonny was surprised by the pain he felt shooting through the arm that wasn't there. Doc Meyers had said it might happen from time to time. Phantom pain, he'd called it. But Sonny hadn't listened too closely when the explanation had come. He didn't think such a thing was possible.

"Nurse Betty, she sure is something else," Aldo said, keeping his eyes straight ahead on the road. He drove the '31 Model A truck like it was a horse he'd ridden a hundred times.

There was no weather to contend with; it was just a cloudless day, the sun beating down with such force it made the ponds and creeks they passed look like mirrors instead of water.

"I'm sure she's a nice lady," Sonny said.

"She's had troubles."

Sonny nodded but said nothing for a long minute. He didn't want to think about Betty Maxwell's troubles. Everybody had troubles these days. "What about you?"

"Me, *señor*?"

"Yes, you."

"My troubles are my own. I would not want to bother you with such things."

"You're driving me home. How will you get to your house?"

"The same way I get home every day, *Señor* Burton. I walk."

Sonny stared out the window and could feel the hot sun beating in through the windshield onto his knees. It was only spring. The real heat of summer had yet to come to the Panhandle. He sat silently for a long while, aching not to return home but to tell Aldo to go into town, into Wellington instead. It would be a good day for a movie or a drink of cold beer in the tavern on the corner, across the street from the Methodist church. But neither was to be. Sonny had no desire to walk out into public, his shirt-sleeve pinned to his side, drawing stares, batting away whispers. He knew he would have to do that someday soon . . . but today was not that day.

"Do you have a family, Aldo?" Sonny finally asked.

The Mexican nodded. "Two sons, three grandsons, one grand-daughter, and one daughter—my youngest, *mi corazón*. My heart. She is my heart." His voice trailed off sadly when he said daughter. Sonny was sure he heard a quiver as the final *r* slipped away into silence.

"Is she all right?"

Aldo turned to Sonny quickly, taking his eyes off the road but keeping his grip tight on the steering wheel. "How do you know some-thing is the matter, *señor*?"

"I was a Ranger for a long time, Aldo. I've seen a lot of things in my life. I know heartache when I hear it."

"You do," Aldo said. He turned his attention back to the road just as it dipped. He hadn't been paying attention and was going a little too fast. The truck jostled and jumped a bit, causing them both to shift in their seats. Sonny banged against the door, but his bandaged wound didn't take a hit, because he had rolled down the window. "I'm sorry, are you all right?"

"I'm fine. What's the matter with your daughter?"

Aldo stared down the road. "She has disappeared."

"How old is she?"

"Old enough to know better but too young to be on her own. Away from me."

"Did she run off with a boy?"

"I fear for her safety," Aldo said.

"Why's that?"

"I fear that she will end up like that girl they found on the side of the road last year. Beaten and horrible things done to her, they say, before she died, left behind with no name and no one to claim her." Aldo paused. "It is best if you stay out of this, *señor*. I told you, my troubles are my own. I do not want any harm to come to anyone else."

Sonny was about to protest, but Aldo was slowing the truck and turning it into the long gravel drive that led up to his empty house. "I'd be glad to help, Aldo. I'm still capable. I remember hearing about that dead girl on the radio, but I know nothing more."

"It happened the same day you were shot. They found her outside of town, dumped in the middle of the road. Dumped just like a barrel of trash. No one knew who she was. They buried her in a *pobre's* grave. There are bad things out in the world, *señor*, not just Bonnie and Clyde."

"I have seen my fair share of bad things, Aldo."

"I'm sure you have. I appreciate your offer *Señor* Burton, I really do. I am sorry to have troubled you. You have enough to contend with on this day other than my sad stories. You did not deserve to be shot any more than that girl deserved to be killed. You know that. I just fear for my own. That's all." Aldo pulled the truck up as close to the house as he could and shut off the engine.

"You know where to find me if you change your mind," Sonny said softly.

"I do, *señor*, but trust me, there is nothing you can do. I fear my daughter is already dead."

A gang of blue jays mobbed the crow, darting in and out, pecking at it with their sharp beaks as they swooped around it. The jays wanted nothing more than for the crow to leave, to move out of their territory.

There were no nests to defend, no tasty young to feed on. They lived in fear of the crow, of the black-winged creatures who fed on the dead or anything else they could find.

There were tales of magic, even among the birds. Tales that gave the crows the power to see a soul safely to the heavens. But the crows knew that the tales were nothing more than that: just tales. They didn't mind. They kept to themselves. Crows depended only on crows.

But on this day, this crow was alone. Just like the girl standing at the bus stop.

In the cooling evening light, she looked just like the last one—maybe a little shorter, but her blonde hair was the same, just like the sadness and the innocence in her eyes. She was vulnerable, in need.

The killer downshifted and slowed down as soon as he saw her. His finger's tingled. It had been long enough. He was free to fly, to feed his own needs again. No one would notice. He saw the crow and felt a kinship to it. No one was mobbing him, though. He was unnoticed. The crow screamed out in alarm as a blue jay nipped its tail. The girl didn't hear it. She was waiting to be taken away and rescued, hungry for the attention she was about receive.

CHAPTER 6

The heavy, red velvet drape was pulled tight on the only window in the room. A musty smell permeated the inside, mixed with cigarette smoke and the potent scent of juniper berries and grain alcohol. It was almost too much for Carmen Hernandez to take, but she was used to the smells. Her father had made bathtub gin for years. It was his recipe that she had given to the Renaldo twins.

They were holed up in a motel off a farm-to-market road, in between Wellington and Memphis, Texas. Out of one county and into the next for Carmen.

Edberto and Eberto Renaldo were identical twins. Everybody called them the Clever, Clever boys because their names meant the same thing: clever, *inteligente*. It was true of Edberto, the oldest twin by three minutes, but not of Eberto. It was almost like Eberto had been shaken around and dropped on his head compared to his brother, who was perfectly smart and made all the girls swoon—including Carmen, who was his latest girlfriend. Eberto, Tió to his few friends and what family still lived in and around Memphis, followed after his brother like a puppy, always waiting to be told what to do next. He was slow, like all of the connections in his brain never matched up. But he could talk and wasn't entirely disabled. Tió was a genius when it came to motors or anything mechanical—which came in handy considering the business the Clever, Clever boys were in. It was when it came to dealing with other human beings that Tió showed himself less than normal. Strangers made him uncomfortable. But still, he had the face of an angel, just like his brother.

At that moment, Tió was standing in the corner eyeing his brother, whom he called Eddie, as did everybody else. Tió was still as a statue, a hardened scowl on his face.

He made Carmen nervous.

"What are you staring at, dummy?" Eddie said, standing up after filling the last large bottle that was sitting in the bathtub.

A wardrobe sat close to the tub, the door open, with room for one more bottle. It was where the gin sat and fermented. Contrary to its name, bathtub gin wasn't made in a bathtub, but the bottles it was made in were too big to fit in the sink and had to be filled in the tub or with a hose. Most people made the hooch inside, out of the way of prying eyes. It was the easiest drinking alcohol to make and had gotten popular since the onset of Prohibition. But the ban on alcohol had been repealed with the Twenty-First Amendment and the bootlegging and gin running business had changed, nearly dried up. Eddie Renaldo was none too happy with the prospect. He was going to have to find an honest job—or another way to make easy money—if things kept up the way they were going. He preferred easy money to work any day. Luckily, there was still a demand for Carmen's father's gin.

Tió didn't answer Eddie. He didn't flinch.

"Damn it, Tió, you're making Carmen uncomfortable."

She was balled up on the bed, her back up against the headboard, hugging her knees to her chest. "I'm all right. Leave him alone." She was nearly seventeen, but she looked like a little girl trying to stay out of the way.

"He pulls this shit all the time. It's not all right," Eddie said, slamming the wardrobe door closed. He jumped over the bed and was face-to-face with Tió.

If they had been dressed the same, it would have been like looking in the mirror. But they weren't. Eddie had his shirt off and just wore a white ribbed undershirt that was stained slightly brown on the armpit seams. He had on dark blue workpants and his boots looked a little cleaner than they should have. A gold St. Christopher's medal dangled from his neck.

Tió, on the other hand, was buttoned up with high-waist trousers, with round turned-up bottoms that were worn thin, a formal white shirt that looked like it hadn't seen a cap of bleach since it was new, and a waistcoat that matched his pants. The clothes came from St. Michael's, a donation to the less fortunate, which at the moment was about ninety percent of the county.

It was still easy for Carmen to get them confused sometimes. At least until Tió opened his mouth. They were both the same height, had the same flawless bronze skin and shiny black hair and facial features carved out of stone. They could have been conquistadors, ancient warriors, or movie stars, if Hollywood would let a Mexican do something other than sweep a floor. Eddie was so beautiful that he took Carmen's breath away.

The room was hot, and a gray metal oscillating fan was blowing the smells around in a constant flurry. Carmen thought she was going to throw up. She'd seen the two nearly come to blows before, but this time it looked certain to happen. Of the two, Tió seemed to be physically stronger. It probably came from the work he was able to do, lifting motor parts like they were feathers or carrying bottles of gin to the truck time after time with no complaints.

Eddie was the thinker, the talker. He was smooth, a romantic when they were alone, which was why she was there in the first place. That and she had nowhere else to go. She'd left home, knowing her father didn't approve of Eddie and he'd be really mad when he found out she'd given Eddie his recipe. The repeal had hit her father hard, too.

"Tell her you're sorry, Tió!" Eddie demanded.

Tió shook his head. "We don't need no *las niñas*."

"You mean *you* don't need no girls."

Tió didn't respond, he just glared at Eddie. "I'm not sorry, Eddie. I don't like her too much."

Eddie drew his head back. His jaw looked like it was going to explode. Carmen braced herself for the fight, for Eddie to throw the first punch. But he didn't. Instead, he pulled a small gun out from behind him. The .32-caliber pistol had been stuffed in the small of his back. He jammed the barrel to Tió's temple and cocked the hammer.

Tió stared into Eddie's eyes, unwavering.

"I should have done this a long time ago. Put you out of every-body's fucking misery."

The fan arched and turned, blowing a gust of wind directly on the boys. Any words, any screams that belonged to Carmen were stuck in her throat. A bead of sweat appeared on Eddie's forehead and ran down the side of his face. He didn't notice it or try to wipe it away. He pulled the trigger without hesitation.

The gun clicked. The chamber was empty of any cartridges. The click echoed inside the small room like a bomb had failed to explode. Relief washed over Carmen, and she let out an audible gasp when she realized what Eddie had done.

Tió said nothing, did not move. He'd just pissed his pants.

MAY 31, 1934

Sonny watched a car come up the road, leaving a trail of dust behind it a mile long. It was a clear, spring day, and he had been sitting on the front porch, relaxing, drinking a cup of coffee, and reading the newspaper. He'd laid the newspaper out carefully on the floor of the porch in front of him and anchored it down with baseball-sized rocks on each corner. He leaned down to read it, finding another one-armed solution to an everyday problem.

He stood up when he recognized the car. Surprised, since he wasn't expecting a visit.

The car, a year-old Plymouth sedan, was covered with dust and belonged to Sonny's only son, Jesse. The car came to a quick stop a few feet from the house.

"What're you doing up this way?" Sonny said, ambling down the steps, steadying himself the best he could. His balance was never going to be the same. He was still trying to find a way to compensate for that loss.

"Come to see how you're gettin' along, that's all, Pa," Jesse said. He was alone, dressed for work, wearing a white Stetson and the Texas Ranger Cinco badge. "Why didn't you call me? Us? Bethel and the kids would've come up and tended to you while you healed." There was an edge of anger in Jesse's voice, but that had always been there, so Sonny didn't see any reason to acknowledge it.

"I didn't want to bother you-all. It's a long drive and I can fend for myself."

"I can see that," Jesse said, looking past Sonny into the house through the open screen door. Unwashed dishes were piled up in the sink, newspapers scattered on the coffee table, and unopened mail was littered across the kitchen table. All the furniture was dusty, and a pile of dirty clothes was building just outside the bedroom door.

"I wasn't expecting any company," Sonny said.

"Well, it makes no difference now. I'm glad to see you up and about." Jesse stuck out his right hand for a shake, and Sonny stared at it, then offered his left hand, and shook it weakly.

"I've got some things to learn yet," he said.

"You heard about Bonnie and Clyde?" Jesse said, withdrawing his hand, as he headed to the chair next to the one Sonny had been sitting in.

Jesse favored his mother, was a little shorter and rounder than most of the Burtons, but there was no mistaking his heritage—his facial profile was the spitting image of Sonny and Sonny's father.

Sonny nodded. "I heard."

"Frank Hamer told me to send you his regards. He was sad to hear they had to take your arm."

"Were you there?" Sonny sat down, steadying himself as he did.

"No, I wish I had been."

"It was some shoot-out according to the newspapers."

"There were six of them that ambushed 'em," Jesse said. "Hamer put his manhunter skills to use, and since Clyde was such a creature of habit, always skirtin' the state line, it was an easy task in the end. They caught them unawares."

"There'll just be more."

"What?"

"Somebody else'll take their place. Bonnie and Clyde aren't the end of the line. Just the start. Somebody's going to come along and want to try and outdo them."

"What makes you say that?"

"Just the way it is. Just the way it's always been. When I was boy . . ."

". . . I know, I know, your daddy went after John Wesley Hardin and the likes of bad men like King Fisher. I've heard those stories a million times."

"So you wouldn't forget them."

Jesse stared at Sonny, started to say something, then restrained himself. Instead, he dug into his pants pocket and offered something to Sonny.

Sonny held out his hand, and Jesse dropped a shell casing into it.

"A souvenir," Jesse said.

"From the shooting?"

Jesse nodded. "Hamer thought you'd like to have it. He knows you would've liked to have been there, taken a shot or two yourself. He did it for you as much as the rest of the fellas those two killed."

Sonny handed the casing back to Jesse. "You take it. I've got enough to remember when it comes to Bonnie and Clyde."

"You sure?"

"Sure as it's daytime. Now, what are you really doing up here? I know you didn't drive all this way to bring me some present from Frank Hamer."

"No, I didn't," Jesse said. "I'll be around for a while. They transferred me up here for a little while. Remember that no-name girl they found on the farm-to-market road just outside of Wellington last year? There's been another girl found, just like the first. Another no-name, beaten, terrible things done to her, then dumped on the side of the road."

"Sounds like an animal's on the loose."

"Seems that way. County asked for help from us."

"I haven't heard anything about this one."

"They're trying to keep it quiet. Don't want to get everyone afraid."

"They should be afraid."

Jesse exhaled heavily and tapped his fingers on the arm of the chair. "I know the area better than anyone else they've got, so it was an easy choice for the captain to send me up here."

"You need a place to stay?"

Jesse shook his head and stood up. "I rented a room at the boarding house in town. I don't think I'll be around that long. Besides, I'll be driving back and forth to home every chance I get. I know you're not used to someone coming and going."

"There's room here."

"I don't think I can stay here, Pa, if it's all the same to you."

Sonny slumped his shoulders. "I'm not going to twist your arm."

"What's in the box?" Jesse said, pointing to a slim cardboard box about twice the length of a bread box and half again as narrow. He seemed to be looking for a way to change the subject.

Sonny glanced over at the box. The top had been slit open, cutting through the postage stamps. He was sure he could use it for something else. "My arm." He scooted the box closer with his right foot, reached inside, and pulled out a wooden arm with a metal hook attached to the end of it. "They call it a prehensor prosthetic. Sounds fancy doesn't it, like something special? The kids'll think I'm a monster."

"You gonna wear it?"

"Maybe. When hell freezes over."

CHAPTER 7

The only sound in the house was the radio. It was a faceless voice that rambled on night and day but never answered back when it was spoken to. The box still confounded Sonny. The little boy in him, the one who grew up under the tutelage of a Ranger legend, in a world without electricity or the thought of such a thing, still believed the radio was magic. Problem was, that little boy was buried too deep—even deeper these days—to have a say in things, especially about things such as magic.

Sonny stood at the front door, his eyes focused on his truck. There was no moisture to witness, no morning dew to offer sustenance to the dying grasses and clovers that blanketed the ground all the way to the road. Everything was brown, offering no sign of division in the ownership of the land. Fences blended in with the eye, or fell away completely on the flat ground, offering an infinite and democratic view of the struggle to stay alive, brought on by the summer sun. Everything was touched and tainted by the heat, the constant glare, the unrelenting oppressiveness of the long days. He should have been used to it by now, and maybe he was, but the loss of his arm had made him forget the most basic semblance of things. Like how to walk standing up straight, or wipe his ass, or fix his own goddamned breakfast. Lucky thing was Sonny didn't have to learn how to breathe all over again because, as things were, he might've just chosen not to take on such a task. It would've been easier. Less painful to just stop and give up the effort.

The blazing red sun arched upward into the clear sky like a torch intent on setting fire to any cloud that dared to materialize or to interfere with the coming heat. There wasn't even any birdsong to offer hope in the morning. If the early bird had been out for the worm, it had already hightailed it home in search of a patch of shade and a long nap.

Nothing living stirred within Sonny's view, and, if it weren't for the constant voice blaring over the radio, he might've had to consider that sometime during the night the world had come to an end and he'd woken up alone, the last man standing, stuck in the grips of a hell that looked pretty much like his own world.

"Lou Gehrig continued his continuous at-bat cycle," the sportscaster droned over the radio, breaking Sonny out of his miserable thoughts. "At this rate, the Iron Horse will surpass fifteen hundred consecutive appearances by September, certainly assuring him MVP status for the season. The Yankees pounded the Chicago White Sox eleven to two, with rookie pitcher Johnny Broaca on the mound. Broaca, a Yale graduate, fanned five times, setting an all-time Major League record. Stay tuned for the morning weather and other news of the day, after this brief message from Burma Shave."

Sonny turned his attention away from the truck then, from the outside world, certain that he wasn't alone in it, and made his way to the radio. He knew what the weather was going to be. He didn't need a damn weatherman to tell him what to expect for the rest of the day. Misery. Just more misery to add to the rest of the days ahead of him.

He turned off the radio with a quick twist and stood in the center of the kitchen, unsure of what to do next.

Baseball mattered little to him, and with Bonnie and Clyde dead and buried there was no need to know the news. The financial markets, the politics, the unrelenting heat, and the accusations and blame for the current state of economic affairs were of no interest to him. It was all just like the weather: misery heaped on misery. It was like a fiery cloud had blanketed every man, woman, and child with ashes of hopelessness. A Depression. No matter how sunny the sky was one day to the next, the oppressive gray mood of the nation wasn't going to go away any time soon.

Sweat beaded on Sonny's forehead. His dirty white T-shirt clung to his chest, damp from a night of tossing and turning. His scar had itched without relenting. Touching it only made the nightmare real; calling it a stump was almost unbearable. Looking at it in the mirror was worse. He didn't fear infection. Just the slow death brought on by it. He couldn't imagine lying in his own filth, the clock ticking away, the radio blabbering on, waiting for Jesse to happen by if he lost the ability to get to the telephone and call for help—or to his Colt .45 so he could put an end to his own suffering.

The telephone was another modern convenience that was just a reminder of his loneliness. The telephone sat on the wall, useless and silent, unable to offer anything but a way out. It never rang. No one had reason to talk to him. At least the radio brought music into the house from time to time.

Loneliness had never entered his mind; an empty bed was not a consideration of loss. He had grown accustomed to sleeping alone since Martha had died. He hadn't felt the need, or desire, to replace one woman with another. The thought of it was too much trouble. Love and physical need were best left to the young. He'd had his work as a Texas Ranger to occupy his mind and tire his body—at least until that fateful day when he saw Bonnie and Clyde walking out of the Ritz Theater like they owned the world.

Now, he had neither: no wife or job to wear him down. All he had was time. Silence and time.

Even awake, standing in wait of the day, Sonny just wished for sleep. Deep, restful sleep that wasn't filled with screams and visions of bloody, lifeless arms not attached to anything, just floating away from him. Out of reach.

Sonny had forgone breakfast, at least for the time being, and made his way to the water pump outside the house. The thought of a cold bath was the only thing that propelled him to step one foot in front of the other.

The muscles in his left arm were still not accustomed to carrying the entire load of his existence. The arm ached, and tightness came to it easily with every new task he introduced it to. There was no other choice of mobility—other than to wear the monstrous contraption that sat unpacked on the dining room table. That was not a solution as far as Sonny was concerned. How could it help him be whole? It was another impossible thought.

Pain shot up and down Sonny's left arm as he began to pump the water into the pail. Thankfully, it didn't take long until the water began to spew from the faucet.

In times of a hard drought, water was liquid gold. The difference between life and death. The well was deep and had never run dry. Of course, when times warranted, Sonny was frugal with the water. He knew the value of it. And just like all of the other modern miracles that had made his life easier, he knew that without them, at his age and in his condition, he would be lost.

He had not seen Jesse in a week, since he had first stopped by to tell him the news, to tell him that he was his local replacement in the Rangers. Sonny could tell it pained Jesse, irked him to no end to be called back home to take up where his father had left off.

The pail filled quickly, and with a deep breath Sonny heaved it up, and carried it in the house.

He decided to wash up in the sink instead of going to the trouble of filling the tub or heating the water. The idea of indoor plumbing, though he was more than able to afford such a luxury, was not a consideration. He had surrendered enough of his morals to the wonders of the present. The outhouse had been good enough for the first sixty-two years of his life. It'd do just fine for whatever time he had left.

It didn't take much effort to pull off his T-shirt, and that left him stripped down to his underwear, the same kind of button-down front shorts that he'd worn in the Great War. He left those on and went about washing himself with cold water.

The silence got to him, and he decided to turn the radio back on. "More of the same for today," the radio announcer said. "But a change is coming. The great predictors of the weather promise rain tomorrow. For how long and how much is anybody's guess, but more than a drop'll be welcome . . ."

Sonny smirked. Nothing had changed for weeks and nothing was going to, no matter what the radio said. He'd believe it when he saw it.

They had no choice but to bury the second no-name dead girl next to the first one. There was no grass on either grave. Just hard, dry, dirt that would turn to mud if it ever rained. Nothing grew there. It was like the ground was cursed, refusing to go unnoticed. No markers had been erected, just a plate in the ground at the head of each grave to mark it.

The first file had been found and put with the second one. They were almost identical. And no matter the set of eyes that looked upon them, Rangers or locals, they read the same way. They offered no clues to the killer.

But the crows knew everything. They had seen both murders from their hidden perches. They'd watched it all play out, and soon the killings were forgotten by them, too. All that really mattered to the crows was their own story, their own losses, and their own need to eat and kill. What one man did to another was none of their concern—unless it offered them an opportunity to do what crows did: just be crows.

CHAPTER 8

There was no food in the house. The larder was empty, vacant of even a tin of flour. The ants had deserted the small root-infested room in search of sustenance elsewhere. All that remained was the earthy, musty smell of slow rot and emptiness.

Upstairs, it smelled like something had already died—or was in the process of dying. Death had stuck its toes inside the front door and wedged it open; its foul breath hung under the ceiling like a thin fog, obscuring any clarity, offering a putrid announcement of things to come.

The roaches rejoiced, were emboldened by the turn of events. They darted about in the light, unafraid of death, instead exploring farther inside the house, into unexplored cracks and crevices. Making a living was easy. More eggs to lay, more legs to scurry about; nothing could stop them now. The flies, just as prolific and joyful, were not rivals to the roaches but peers, equals in their desire to survive and multiply in the decaying environment.

Martha would have thrown a fit, been ashamed of the state of the house. Her German lineage dictated that she be obsessively tidy and organized. A speck of dust was an enemy, rightfully discharged out the front door at the tip of a broom or mop. Roaches were crushed in the cruelest fashion—an extra twist of the shoe a demonstration to others who might be watching, offering a view of their own future if they didn't skedaddle away as quick as possible. "Tell the others," Martha would yell as she performed her over-exaggerated squish with wicked relish. There was a hint of an accent at the tip of her tongue. She had tried her best to hide it during the time of war, and even harder afterward. Sneers and whispers of "Kraut" followed her all of her life. She might as well have been a greaser, she'd once said to Sonny on the way home from church. Her prejudices and beliefs were different than his. He ignored them as best as he could, but it became harder as the years accumulated, as her anger and disappointment turned toward him.

He wondered sometimes, silently, of course, if he had ever killed any of Martha's kin in the old country. It had been a global Civil War, American mixed-bloods fighting their own unknown relatives across the water. He had stopped someone else's suffering, that's all he knew. It wasn't brother against brother, north versus south, but old Germany against the New World. That war was only a memory now, but there would be others. He was sure of it, just like his father had been. *Men will fight their own blood into eternity*, he had said.

Sonny had dreaded this day. Knew it was coming as the food stock grew thinner and thinner. The last bit of bread came sooner, faster, than he ever thought it would. He had tried to eat as little as possible. The dry mustard was gone now, too.

There was a decision to be made: To live. Which meant go out into the world, get some food, and get on with it—whatever "it" was. Or die. Go to the kitchen table, pick up the loaded .45 that sat waiting for action, put it to his temple, and pull the trigger. End of story. Lights out. No more phantom pains, no more reaching for something with a hand that wasn't there. No more sorrow. He could never be restored to his former self. It was impossible. No magic medicine existed to regrow arms, hands, or fingers.

The only way to avoid his current situation was to end it or accept it, simple as that. Except, it wasn't that simple. It was the hardest decision he would ever make. Either way, there was no going back. That was the real decision. Leaving regret behind. It would be easy to be dead. Harder to be alive.

It was time to decide.

He had no desire to starve to death. It was too slow, too passive a way to die. He was not totally broken, not totally incapable. He could still pull a trigger. He had played with the gun, held the cold barrel against his temple in the middle of the dark, cool night. Practice had always been a demand. Ticks of his own lineage. Martha was not any more unusual than he was. Just the opposite.

Sonny drew in a deep breath at the thought, held it in the pit of his lungs for as long as he could, then released it slowly.

It was time to decide.

He listened to the silence, half closed his eyes. The grandfather clock's long brass pendulum had stopped days ago. It gathered dust now, but time had not stopped along with it.

Outside, it was still morning. The sky was brilliant red with warning as the sun jumped up from the horizon and zoomed toward its apex. There was a promise of rain, of conflict in the sky—a brief storm or a long enduring downpour, Sonny didn't know for sure. He'd turned off the radio about the time the clock had stopped ticking. He had been into his last can of Van Camp's beans by then.

His stomach growled, forcing him to open his eyes fully.

Three roaches skittered out of the kitchen sink. Little brown fingerlings full of industry and bravery. He envied them for a moment. Their tiny brains could not dictate anything other than the drive for survival. Find food, have sex, tire out, and die. As far as he knew, there was no act of suicide in the roach world. *Did insects know guilt?* It was a question he'd never wondered about before.

Sonny glanced to the gun on the table. It sat next to the box that held the prosthetic. He took another breath, exhaled, and decided that he had the stomach for neither life nor death. Not today. He would have to do something with the regret. It would be easier if he could bury it like an old dog that had outlived its usefulness. But it wouldn't be that easy. He didn't know how he was going to rid himself of it. He just knew he had to.

Buying the truck had been like buying his last horse. At the time there had been no doubt in Sonny's mind that the machine would outlive him, that it would be the last set of wheels he'd ever buy. That had been before his encounter with Bonnie and Clyde, while he had still been working as a Ranger with nothing but the coming days of retirement on his mind. Retirement had been a fantasy, and his present reality was a nightmare that he could have never imagined. He had almost been proven right, but, obviously, he wasn't ready to die just yet.

He stood outside the truck's door staring inside the interior, wondering how in the hell he was going to drive the damn thing, much less get it started. It wouldn't have been so hard if the truck was a horse. He could easily control a good-natured mount with one arm and one hand.

Sonny settled into the truck and laid his .45 on the seat next to him. He would never have a chance at Bonnie and Clyde now, but the presence of the gun made him feel better, more whole, even though he had little confidence that he could fire it if he needed to. He'd put on a work shirt that matched his pants. Neither had seen a rub of suds in weeks, but it didn't matter to him. He was after food, and that was all. He hoped his stink would keep people away from him.

The steering wheel sat waiting. His first inclination was to reach over and pull the spark advance down like he normally would, except he couldn't, not right-handed. But he'd sworn to himself before stepping foot outside the house that he wasn't going to fight lost battles with every new step. Doing so over and over again would be another form of hell. Might as well have put the gun to his head and got it over with if he was going to live like that.

Instead, Sonny reached over and pulled the short lever down with his left hand. It was easier, anyway, since the spark advance was on the left side of the steering wheel. Then he reached across the steering wheel to the opposite side and pulled the hand throttle down. Next, he reached over the wheel and turned on the key. So far, so good. The easy part was next. He put his foot on the starter button on the floor, pulled the choke, and turned it. The four-cylinder engine chugged to life immediately, and a wave of relief washed over Sonny. There was no question that starting the truck was easier with his right hand when he had had one, but now he knew it was possible to start the truck with his left hand. That was encouraging.

He quickly adjusted the spark advance to smooth out the engine. All of the cylinders began to purr, waiting for his next command. Sonny was tempted to tap the dash and say, "Good, girl," but he didn't. Talking to a horse was one thing, talking to a machine was another. It didn't seem right. It was like you were talking to yourself.

With a satisfied breath, Sonny released the hand brake, pushed in the clutch, put the engine in gear a little clumsily but successfully, and headed down the short drive to the start of the road.

The first drop of rain hit the windshield, drawing his attention back to the stormy sky. It was gray all the way to the horizon, roiling slightly, like there was a little wind bound up inside the clouds—the red warning had been eaten up, vanished into the growing sheet of anger and precipitation. The sight brought a smile to Sonny's face. It had been a long time since it had rained. He rolled the window all the way down and breathed in the fresh air as it rushed inside the truck. It was the first time Sonny had felt alive since they'd taken his arm and he wondered, almost out loud, what he had been waiting on to get himself out of the house.

The crows hunkered down as soon as the first hint of wind kicked up and the urge of rain had become a certainty. They did not celebrate the change in weather like other creatures. Drought and struggle brought them a bounty of death to feed off. The taste of carrion did not deter them or offer them the thought that there were better days to come. A few crows longed for the opportunity to raid a nest of eggs, a sweet delicacy only to be found in the spring—and then they had to be shared with the brood, their own and the rest of the gang. With crows, it was one for all and all for one. A network of giving and surviving.

Lone crows died quickly. It puzzled them how humans managed by themselves so easily.

The storm's relief was a bath and a moment's rest for the flock in a tree just inside the town, outside a human-built structure; a house that offered protection from the weather, day and night. A permanent roost was a foreign concept to crows. Home was the accumulation of crows around them.

A shadow of a man appeared at one of the second-floor windows. The window was almost even with the branch that one of the crows sat on, standing as close to the trunk as it could. On a fine day, with the window open, a cat could have come and gone at its pleasure, out the window and down the tree easily. The crow would have never perched there, offered itself as prey. It was nearly invisible now and felt safe.

The bird was aware of the man, and the man was aware of the bird. But there was no threat to either. One just considered the other, wishing it had legs or wings—or others of its kind to hunt and kill with, instead of being alone.

Eddie rolled off of Carmen, spent and sweaty from making love. She still ached for him, wished that he wouldn't have finished when he did, but he'd seemed preoccupied, uninterested, in a hurry to get it over with. He sat up on the edge of the bed and lit a cigarette with his back to her. She liked how his vertebrae poked out, a perfect line down his back all the way to the crack of his ass.

"Are you okay, Eddie?" Carmen asked, rolling onto her side, resisting the urge to run her finger down his back.

"I'm fine."

"Tió won't be back for a while." She couldn't restrain herself, she reached out and touched the middle hump, but he pulled away, like he didn't want her to touch him. "We could go again." Sex was new to her. She had liked it from the start. Other girls complained that it was uncomfortable, hurt, was dirty, but she'd never felt that way at all. It just felt natural and fun, like everyone should do it. She pushed back the tremors of guilt fueled by the religion of her home, of her father's insistence on it. No amount of Hail Marys would make up for the things she'd done with her body. She'd run away from all of that. It was her life and she was going to live it. If there was a hell, she would see him there—her father, writhing in eternal damnation for the things he'd done, right along with her. He wasn't without sin. Running gin was against the law. He was no different that Eddie and Tió, even if he went to confession every week to absolve himself.

Eddie turned to her, his noble face hard as stone. His eyes glistened like black diamonds. "He's outside, listening. He's a creep. I should have shot him and been done with it."

Carmen shivered, pulled the sheet up to her neck, covering her small breasts.

The room was hot and all the oscillating fan did was disperse the already thick, humid air from one wall to the other. It didn't have far to go. The smell of gin permeated everything; juniper berries, lemon rotting in harsh grain alcohol. It was almost more than she could take. Gin seeped from the pores of Eddie's skin when he sweated, which was most of the time inside the small motel room.

"He's your brother," Carmen whispered. "You can't kill him."

Eddie turned to her, his face void of emotion. "He was born dead. Did I ever tell you that? The *comadrona* blew air into his mouth until he began to breathe on his own. He was purple, blue. That is why his brain don't work so good. She should have let him die."

"You don't mean that."

"I do. I will have to be the one to kill him. I am sure of it."

Before Eddie could say another word, a loud knock came at the door. *Rap, rap, rap.* Carmen nearly jumped out of her skin. She drew back into the corner of the bed. Tió had always scared her. Even more so now that she had shared a room with him, seen how he and Eddie really lived.

Eddie pulled his boxer shorts on and grabbed the .32 off the nightstand.

Rap, rap came two more knocks. "Open up, Renaldo, I know you're in there. Your idiot brother is standing next to me," a man's voice on the other side of the door said.

Carmen watched the tension drop from Eddie's shoulders, and she relaxed along with him, if only slightly.

"What do you want?" Eddie asked, speaking louder than normal so he could be heard through the door. He put the gun back where he had picked it up from, covered it up with a newspaper, then quickly tugged on his pants. A bead of sweat glistened at the nape of his neck.

"You need to pay up or get the hell out," the man said.

It was then that Carmen recognized the voice. It was the motel manager, Felix Massey. He was short, fat, always had a cigar sticking out of his mouth, and always wore white shirts with ugly brown stains under the arms. He looked at her like she was a piece of meat, like he wanted to eat her up all in one sitting. She didn't like him, but she was nice to him so he wouldn't rat out their gin-making location. Eddie paid him extra so he would keep his mouth shut.

Eddie's jaw tightened as he zipped up his pants. His muscles looked like stone. There was not one inch of his body that wasn't filled with anger. Not only did Tió make her nervous but Eddie's outbursts scared her.

Eddie hustled to the door and flung it open. A gust of wind pushed its way inside, announcing the arrival of some much-needed rain. "You'll have to wait, Massey. I ain't got the money right now."

"That's what you said yesterday." Felix Massey peered around Eddie, made eye-contact with Carmen. If she could have melted away in the sheets, she would have disappeared completely.

"Put your eyes back in your head, creep," Eddie said.

"We could make a deal," Felix replied.

Eddie stiffened and flexed his fingers at his side. It was almost like he was reaching for a gun that wasn't there. He stepped forward so he was within an inch of Massey's face. "Ain't gonna be no deal, you hear me? We done made our deals. I'll get you the money you need before you close up for the night."

"If you say so."

"I say so."

"Good. If you don't, I'm callin' the cops. They'll get you and your stink out of here."

Eddie reared back to take a punch at the man just as Tió appeared and rushed between the two men. "Ain't time for that, Eddie. Be bigger trouble'n we need right now."

Eddie stumbled back, his neck red as morning storm clouds with rage. Carmen couldn't see the look on his face, wasn't sure if Eddie would go after Massey, Tió, or give up. Eddie never gave up.

Tió followed his brother, so they were both inside the door. "We'll get your money," he said, as he slammed the door shut.

"I close the office at eight o'clock," Felix Massey yelled. "The cops'll be here a minute after, you understand, Renaldo. A minute after. You can count on it."

CHAPTER 9

Lancer's Market sat on the dry side of the county line. It was a long, narrow building that had been extended in length three or four times over the years. Sonny couldn't remember a time when the store hadn't been there. Mismatched clapboards gave away the extensions, faded and weathered, but apparent and unmistakable in their origin. They looked like yardstick marks on a doorjamb to note the age of a child, grown now and gone out into the world.

It had been a long time since the building had seen a coat of paint, probably since Haden Lancer had owned the market in the late teens. He'd sold it not long after the war had ended and he'd buried his one and only son, Louie, in the graveyard south of town, his coffin wrapped in a tear-stained American flag. There was no one to carry on the name, the tradition, the business, and Haden had just given up after that. Last anyone knew, he was working down in the Fort Worth stockyards, pushing cows into the slaughterhouse.

Sonny downshifted the truck and slowed to pull into the market's lot. He tried to push the thought of Louie Lancer away, but he couldn't. He never could get the boy's always-happy face out of his mind, which was why he almost always avoided shopping at this market in the first place. It held too many ghosts. Instead, he'd make his way into Wellington when it came to gathering up groceries and a stop at the butcher. If he had more time back then, he'd drive to Memphis. He liked the butcher better there. That was when an appetite, the taste and enjoyment of a meal, had meant something to him.

Louie Lancer had been killed in the spring of 1918, as the war wound to a close, in the Third Battle of the Aisne. It had been late spring, during a surprise attack by the Germans on the Allies, hoping to push into Paris. Poison gas had been dropped, and Louie Lancer, along with a lot of other soldiers, had suffered a slow, miserable death. Sonny never told Haden that he'd seen his son die, couldn't bring himself to. For the most part, Sonny wished to believe that his time across the ocean had been a nightmare, not real. Nightmares were best kept to one's self and not shared with the world.

He'd tried to avoid the reality of the war at all costs, but he felt he had no choice on this day. Lancer's Market was the closest store to the house. Sonny didn't want to push his luck and go too far, too fast. He didn't trust his skills with the truck, driving one-handed on wet, muddy roads.

A heavy, gray blanket covered the sky for as far as Sonny could see. The wind had stilled, and rain fell straight down in sheets, sometimes hard, unrelenting, blinding. It pounded on the metal roof like a thousand knuckles knocking, like something was trying to get inside the dry cab. And then, without warning, the toad-soaker would let up and fade into a sprinkle, revealing the road and what lay ahead. It was a wonder Sonny hadn't hit anything on the way to the market. But from the looks of the lot, he was the only fool out and about in such weather. It was empty.

Puddles had quickly pooled up, making for a tricky ride from the road to the front door. Ruts meant nothing when it was dry, and with the wind they'd mostly vanished in the drought, but the rain was coming down so fast the water didn't have time to seep into the earth and vanish, pooling up in any dimple it could find. The puddles amazed Sonny. He would've thought the ground was so thirsty that it would have sucked up all the rain in one big gulp. But that wasn't the case.

The steering wheel jumped out of Sonny's hand, lurching him to the right faster than he should have been going. Instinctively, he let off the gas, and the truck coughed and lurched forward, sliding sideways and coming to a stop about twenty feet from the front door. A cloud of steam rose from underneath the radiator, and the front of the truck tilted down. He hoped he wasn't stuck in the mud.

Anger and frustration quickly came back, and Sonny slapped the steering wheel with the palm of his hand. "Damn it," he said. "This is a big goddamn mess, just a mess. What the hell was I thinking?"

He glanced over at the .45. No matter where he went today, he couldn't get away from the war. The gun, a Colt .45 Government Model automatic pistol, was the sidearm he'd carried in France. He'd given up his standard-issue Ranger gun, a Smith & Wesson .38. One gun in the house with history was enough. Besides, he'd always preferred the .45. He'd carried it most days when he'd been on duty. It was the gun he'd faced Bonnie and Clyde with. The .38 had the kick of a kid's pony, even when it was loaded with regret.

Sonny reached over and grabbed up the .45. He wasn't going to use it, and he didn't think he would need it, but he felt uncertain and wanted all the confidence he could acquire. Walking out in the world with one arm made him wobbly from the toes up.

He leaned forward in the seat, reached around and pulled up his shirt, then stuffed the .45 down the small of his back. His belt was tight enough to hold the gun in place, and he could get to it pretty quickly if it came to that. The metal was cold against his skin, and he tried to ignore the discomfort of it the best he could. He'd hung up his holster for good. It was right-handed.

The rain finally let up, and Sonny decided to leave the truck parked where it sat. It wasn't like the market was teeming with customers. He opened the door, checked for a puddle, and swung out of the cab with as much of a jump as he could muster. He landed squarely on two feet and hurried to the overhang that jutted out over the front door.

There was little reason to give any attention to the row of build-ings that sat down the road a piece from Lancer's. Two roadhouses and another little market, which serviced mostly Mexicans, stood on the wet side of the county line, in about the same repair as the building Sonny was entering. As a Ranger, he'd made his fair share of visits to all three buildings over the years, but as a civilian he had no desire for the pleasures—and troubles—offered there. Things had changed since the end of Prohibition. People liked to gather in saloons and taverns, but Sonny never had. What went on in those places held no sugar for him.

Tom Turnell owned the market these days. It had changed hands more than once since Haden had first sold it, but the name Lancer's always stuck. Most folks would have probably objected if the name *had* changed, gone somewhere else, like Sonny wanted to, if that would've ever happened.

The screen door stood ajar, and the front door was open, like usual. Four empty chairs sat facing the lot, Tom's version of the liar's bench, most often found outside of such establishments, though these chairs sat empty on most days. Had since the Stock Market Crash.

Sonny pushed inside, wet from the rain and self-conscious of the empty sleeve pinned to his right side. He stopped just inside the threshold.

The store was dimly lit. A scattering of bare bulbs hung from the ceiling over the two aisles that reached to the back wall. The walnut wood floor was scuffed and scratched from the years of traffic and was nearly black in color. The shelves were thin, not heavily stocked but freshly dusted. Sonny was hoping for a week's worth of canned beans, but he'd make a pot to last if he had to boil some from a bag.

The market doubled as a post office, and an ice house sat on the north side of the building. Tom's nephew, Bertie Turnell usually ran the ice route, and Tom doubled as postmaster when Bertie was out making deliveries. Sonny didn't see the ice truck out in the lot, so he assumed that Bertie was gone. As it was, Tom stood behind the long counter at the front of the store alone, staring back at Sonny, his mouth slightly ajar, like he was surprised to see a living human being and didn't know what to say.

"How'd do, Tom," Sonny said, taking his hat off and shaking out the rain that had collected in the brim.

Tom Turnell was thin as a newel post and just as bald as the finial that normally sat atop it. His eyes were sunken, with dark half-moons of worry extending down to the top of his cheeks. Smiles were rare inside the market. Most folks had little money to spend and would most likely try and barter their next meal instead of paying for it, thus the sign that hung on the front of the counter: "All Transactions Require Money. No Exceptions. No Local Scrip Accepted."

Some towns had turned to printing their own currency since the banks and the treasury couldn't be trusted. Scrip was local money. Money for whatever the reason Tom had decided not to accept. That decision probably made business more difficult than it already was.

"Well, if it ain't Sonny Burton out on a day even ducks would declare too wet to swim in. What're you in need of that brings you here?"

"Got some empty space in the cupboard," Sonny answered. A puddle had collected at his feet from the hat. He broke eye contact with Tom and stepped toward the first aisle.

There was always an aroma in a grocery store that Sonny found comforting. Fresh vegetables, barrels of cornmeal and flour, along with talcum powders, Lux soap, and bag upon bag of potatoes, all mixing into a recognizable and expected smell of plenty. But on this day, all of those smells were distant, minimal, like they were just memories. There were no bags of potatoes to be seen, and all of the barrels had the lids pulled tight.

"Truck out of Dallas that brings me canned goods was hijacked three days ago," Tom said. "Ruffians emptied it, then set it on fire."

Sonny nodded. "Folks are getting desperate."

"You can say that again." Tom looked up at the metal roof, cocked his ear to listen to the rain pelt it, then watched a thin stream break across a rafter and find a place to fall to the floor. "I don't know how much longer any of us can hang on," he said, rushing to put a pail under the current leak. Three other pails sat scattered about in the aisles. "Most of us bought a bill of goods when we sent Garner to Washington to be Roosevelt's number-two man."

There was nothing Sonny could add to those sentiments, but he was in no mood to talk politics. Having a Texan as a vice-president had been a moment of hope that had fallen away as quickly as the shine of a new window. The victory had quickly become covered with the dust and grime of the Depression, just like everything else. "I suppose you don't have a week's worth of Van Camp's, do you?"

Tom shook his head. "Two cans is the best I can do for you. I got some cheese that I'll let go of for twenty cents a pound. Normally twenty-five, but you made an extra effort to come out. Besides, you took a rough bullet from them two outlaws. Be the least I can do for a man the likes of you."

"I'm in no need of charity, Tom. Thank you just the same."

The market-owner stared at Sonny, then moved from the pail to the counter where a pile of cheese rounds sat. "You don't want any cheese then?"

"Sure, I'll take a couple of pounds, but at the regular price, if it's all the same to you."

"If you say so."

"I do."

A look of disappointment crossed Tom Turnell's face, but he nodded with understanding and went about cutting off two pounds of cheese with a strand of wire knotted to two opposing wood handles.

Silence, with the exception of rain falling on the roof and the hum of the Coca-Cola box by the door, returned to the inside of the market. Sonny was glad for it as he realized the good fortune of bad weather. There would be no one to stare at him if his luck continued. He could get what he needed and get home without seeing anyone, or being seen by anyone, other than Tom.

His concern about his inaugural appearance to the outside world had been steeped in self-pity, conceit, and pride. Maria Perza, the Mexican woman, his *mommasita*, would have been disappointed in him. Pride was the biggest of all sins as far as she was concerned.

He picked up a basket woven of thin wood that looked like it had once served picnics instead of groceries, then set about navigating the aisles for his immediate needs. Long-term groceries would have to wait until another day—which didn't settle well.

First thing Sonny did was find the Van Camp's. He reached for them with his right hand, but realized, a half-second later, that it wasn't there. He let the basket slide to his elbow, hooked it there, then leaned forward to grab one can of the beans. Every act was going to require relearning. Even putting a can in a grocery basket.

It was awkward bending his wrist back and juggling the basket at the same time, but he managed on the first try with a little toss. The task would prove more difficult the fuller the basket got. Slowly, cautiously, Sonny made his way up and down the aisle, careful to put only what he needed in the basket. There was little on the shelves that offered reward, or pleasure. Sometimes a Baby Ruth candy bar would satisfy his craving for sweets, but it felt like a luxury he could ill afford. These days, most folks thought the chocolate was named for Babe Ruth, the Sultan of Swat himself, but Sonny knew better. Baby Ruth had been named for President Grover Cleveland's daughter.

Tom had the chunk of cheese waiting on the counter. Sonny hoisted the basket onto the counter next to it.

"Looks like that ought to keep you for a spell," Tom said.

Sonny nodded. "Probably best send Bertie out with some ice for the box first chance he gets."

"Won't be no call for that one of these days, I suppose. Frigidaires'll be in every house, if you can imagine such a thing. Bertie'll have to find something else to cart around. Ain't good for much else, but don't tell my brother I said that. He thinks the sun rises and falls on that boy. I suppose there are worse things."

Sonny ignored the comment. Any man in law enforcement was a keeper of secrets whether he wanted to be or not. He reached back and took his wallet out of his pocket, looked Tom Turnell in the eye, and forced as much of a smile as he could muster. "When I was a boy, I couldn't imagine driving a truck. Figured there'd always be horses and wagons. I would've never made it here on a horse on a day like today."

Tom Turnell smiled briefly. "Still are folks that just got a horse and a wagon, probably always will be, but I guess I see your point. Lord knows, you can't stop progress. Not even the government can do that." Tom began to punch in numbers on the cash register. After taking everything out, boxing it as he went, he totaled the machine, and said, "Well, Sonny, that'll be four dollars and seventy-eight cents."

Sonny counted out five ones and handed them to Tom. "If you get any more Van Camp's in, have Bertie run me out some."

"You got a phone?" Tom handed the change to Sonny, who laid it back on the counter.

Sonny nodded.

"You call me with an order and I'll save you a drive here. We quit doing delivering a while back because of the tone of things in the world, if you know what I mean. Same thing that happened to my delivery truck could happen to Bertie. Couldn't stand the thought of such a thing."

"Yes, I have a phone." The idea of getting groceries delivered heightened Sonny's mood. He almost smiled broadly for the first time in memory. "Can you add on one of those Baby Ruth bars?"

"Sure, I can. I sure can."

A pair of headlights swung into the parking lot, drawing Sonny's attention to the door. At first, he thought it was Bertie returning from an ice delivery, but it was a car, parked close to the overhang.

The rain had picked back up, and the distant horizon beyond the car—a make and model Sonny couldn't identify—was gray and murky, like a thick fog had settled in with the storm or a cloud had crashed to the ground.

It was hard to see anything clearly, but it looked like a woman, or a girl, was behind the steering wheel, which was the first thing that Sonny thought was unusual. Men drove most of the time, and women rode in the passenger seat.

Before Sonny could gather his thoughts or turn his attention back to Tom, two men rushed in the front door, their faces obscured by red handkerchiefs pulled over their noses, both waving shotguns like they knew how to use them.

"Hands up," one of them yelled. They looked like mirror images of each other: same hair, same height, and same skin color—Mexican. Only their eyes were different. One was confident, the other was fearful—a follower, that much was clear. "This here's a robbery. Do as I say, and nobody'll get hurt."

CHAPTER 10

Sonny hesitated, staring at the lead man, the one doing the talking. His mouth went dry, and a tremble started deep in his stomach. He allowed his left hand to dangle where it was, tried not to move, but the surprise of the robbery nearly knocked him off his feet. The last emotion he thought he would confront on this day was true fear. His previous tangle with two outlaws hadn't turned out so well.

Both men had stopped just inside the door. The quiet one, the fearful one, leveled his shotgun directly at Sonny's head. The other one, the talker, was focused on Tom. He was confident, strident, certain of the task at hand. Cockiness was a dangerous ingredient in a situation like this. Sonny knew that better than anyone.

"Didn't you hear what I said, old man?" The talker turned his attention to Sonny. Tom's hands had gone straight up in the air at the first command. For some reason, he didn't look surprised. Probably had been through a robbery before, or expected it to come through the door sooner or later. It was hard for Sonny to know for sure, since he didn't know Tom that well.

"I don't have *hands*," Sonny said. He was trying to figure out a way to help Tom, buy time, find an opportunity to turn things their way, and get to his gun without alerting the duo that he was armed.

"Hand. Then raise your damn hand." The talker brought his barrel level with his partner's so they were both focused on Sonny.

Tom stood still in the periphery, hands reaching to the ceiling. He looked like he was playacting a statue or a tree. There was no emotion on his face, and he barely blinked. It was like time had stopped, catching Tom Turnell unaware. But that wasn't the truth. The market owner was completely aware of every movement, every sound. Sonny was sure of it. Just as he was sure that somewhere close, under the counter or nearby, a weapon of some kind sat waiting. A man like Tom would be prepared for something like this, especially with the hooligan barns across the road. He just seemed too calm, too resigned, not to have some kind of plan.

"Go ahead now, old man, don't make me do somethin' I'll regret," the talker said, with a flip of the gun's barrel. There was an obvious, familiar accent at the end of his tongue. Sonny had already determined the two were Mexican, but he didn't recognize either of them. They'd covered their faces like old-time bandits, which wasn't a bad move on their part. Sonny probably wouldn't have known them anyway—they were young—but he could identify them later if he could get a good look at their faces.

"Your mother must be proud," Sonny said. He said it in Spanish as coldly as he could. *Su madre debe estar orgulloso.*

It surprised the talker that he could speak the language so clearly, so fluently. He glanced over to his partner. "Keep him covered," he said in Spanish as well.

The partner said nothing, just nodded as the talker lowered his weapon and walked over to Sonny, stopping inches from him. He was shorter than Sonny and had to look up to make eye contact. He smelled like juniper berries and sweat. The foulness spoke to Sonny. The talker'd been in a room with a batch of bathtub gin recently, but it was more than that. The kid—and that's all he was, a kid—was afraid, too. It was just harder to see at a distance. There was a twitch in his right eye. Sonny wondered if this was his first stickup.

"Don't try anything stupid, amigo," the talker continued in Spanish. "We just want money. No trouble, you understand? But I will hurt you if I have to. My brother might even kill you—just for the fun of it."

Careful, Sonny thought, *you're giving yourself away, amigo.* He said nothing, though, just nodded, looking at the talker's head, then over to the other one. Quiet ones could be even more dangerous than cocky ones.

Sonny didn't believe the fearful one had it in him to kill. That clearly wasn't their intent. But it could happen. Years as a Texas Ranger had forced him into the aftermath of a lot of human storms, some planned, most not—just circumstances that had spiraled out of control quicker than they were supposed to. An explosion of anger followed by fleeting regret. It was common. Rage, fear, often mixed with jealousy and alcohol, were more lethal than any gun sitting on a shelf or in a locked drawer.

"Now, amigo," the talker snarled, "I don't have much time to be nice, even to a cripple like you."

There it was. The loss of his arm had evoked a response. Maybe it would save his life—the irony wasn't lost on Sonny, and he offered no reaction to the word. He raised his hand straight to the air without any protest at all.

"That's more like it, amigo," the talker said in English. "You move a muscle and you will be shot. Do you understand?" He glanced over at Tom—who had not offered any evidence that he understood Spanish—making sure he understood. Sonny was betting that Tom understood every word that had been said. But it was hard to tell. Some folks refused to utter, or learn, a word of Mexican. It was un-American.

"Go about your business, *chico*," Sonny answered back in English. "And I'll go about mine."

Anger flashed in the talker's eyes, just as thunder crashed overhead. The steady rain had been pushed out of the way by a storm. A chorus of hammers thudded on the roof. Hail. A heavy downpour. The screen door slapped at the frame, and wind pushed inside, bringing water to the floor and a coldness that hadn't existed inside the store before.

Sonny could barely see the car parked just outside. The driver's window was rolled up, coated with condensation, steam from the heat of a human being sitting inside. She looked like a shadow, staring out into the grayness, fearing light, nervous for an escape.

The talker glanced up to the roof, then to his partner. With a nod and a redirect with the shotgun, refocusing on Tom, he moved to the counter, opposite the market owner. "Open it."

"I can't talk you out of it?" Tom asked. There was a quiver in his voice that hadn't been there before the two men had rushed into the store.

The talker shook his head. "Open it, or I'll shoot you and open it myself. That simple. We've been here too long the way it is."

"I've got a family," Tom said.

"I don't care," the talker replied. He stood sideways between Sonny and Tom. The three men were almost a perfect triangle. "Lower your hands real easy. One stupid move, and I pull the trigger."

"Isn't much here," Tom said, as he complied with the talker's demand.

Sonny stood still, his focus on the fearful one.

At the moment, Sonny was acting like a good soldier, doing everything the talker told him to. That didn't offer him much of a chance to do anything to help end the situation. If the storm hadn't been overhead, the only sound inside the store would be four heartbeats, all running at the same rhythms—fast, pumped up with nerves and adrenaline even though each man stood still.

Tom opened the cash drawer, gathered up the bills, then handed them to the talker. "You want the pennies, too?"

The talker took the money, looked at the thinness of the stack with disappointment, then stuffed it hastily into his front pocket. "Where's the rest of it?"

"I told you there wasn't much," Tom said. "Look at the shelves. I don't have much to sell—times are tough all over. Not just for you."

"You don't know anything about me," the talker yelled, lurching forward toward Tom, turning away from Sonny. The shotgun barrel was inches from Tom's mouth. "You have a safe in an office somewhere? Don't lie to me. Tell me, damn it. This isn't enough!"

Sonny remained standing still, his arm over his head. It was starting to ache, blood running out of it with the immediate threat of numbness. He'd never considered living life without two arms until that second. *Things could always be worse.* He didn't take his eyes off the fearful one—whose attention had been drawn to the talker by his outburst.

"Don't get mad, Eddie," the fearful one said nervously. "We don't need no more bad things. We just need rent and then we go, all right?"

Eddie turned to his partner, his eyes even more enraged. "Shut up, *me'jo*. Just shut up. Look what you went and did. Look what you went and did now, you fuckin' idiot." His back was to Tom.

It was the break the market owner had obviously been waiting for. In one quick scoop, Tom grabbed up the cheese wire, flipped it in the air so it wrapped around Eddie's neck, then grabbed the other handle as it swung toward him so he could put pressure on the boy's neck—which he did without missing a beat. It looked like a move he had practiced a million times. Choreographed it perfectly.

"You move one muscle, I'll pull this wire so hard it'll cut your head plum off. You understand me, *me'jo*?" Tom demanded. "Now drop the gun. You, too," he said to the other one. The quiver in Tom's voice was gone, replaced by anger-fueled strength. His eyes were black with unwavering certainty. He meant what he said.

When Eddie didn't immediately do as he was told, Tom pulled the wire a little tighter to prove he was serious. The shotgun clattered to the floor.

Sonny had watched the whole exercise casually, not surprised by Tom Turnell's ballet-like move. It was time for him to join in, while the fearful one's attention was focused entirely on the situation Eddie had got himself into. He dropped his hand, bypassing the temptation to shake some blood into it, pulled the .45 out from its hiding place, and pointed it directly at the fearful one—who had gone from quietly nervous and afraid to visibly shaking with fear.

"You heard what the man said. Drop the gun, like your brother," Sonny demanded, using his best authoritative Ranger-tone. He didn't have a badge or a right arm anymore, but that didn't mean he had abandoned everything that had carried him through his professional life over the last forty years—including the saying that followed every Ranger these days, "One riot, one Ranger." The saying was attributed to Captain W. J. Walker of Company B at the turn of the century. Sonny had known Walker personally and the man seemed to enjoy the attribution more than he did the admittance of his origin of it. These boys didn't know that he was an ex-Ranger, so the reputation that usually preceded itself in a tense situation and laid the ground work for an easy end wasn't evident to either of them. The saying meant nothing to them. But it did to Sonny.

"Don't," Eddie yelled to the other one. In just as swift a move, he rocketed his elbow upward, catching Tom just under the chin. The surprise hit propelled the man, breaking his hold on the cheese wire, sending it flying out of reach, allowing Eddie to lunge forward toward Sonny.

Tom crashed into the wall and fell to the floor, as Eddie pushed into Sonny, knocking him off balance, causing him to tumble into the shelf, sending cans and boxes crashing to the floor. But Sonny remained standing, the gun still in his hand, though pointed at the floor.

The fearful one stood frozen, his shotgun still pointed at the counter, even though Tom Turnell had fallen out of sight.

Eddie dove for his shotgun, but the barrel had spun around so it was closest to him, instead of the butt of the weapon. He picked it up by the barrel, anxious to reach the trigger, just as Sonny regained his balance and pointed his .45 at the Mexican.

Eddie swung the shotgun at Sonny like a club. The butt of it cracked against Sonny's wrist, sending the pistol flying into the air. It bounced off the top shelf and vanished into the other aisle with a skid, metal against wood, striking another mark in the floor.

Tom Turnell stood up, his nose bloodied by Eddie's elbow, and wavered, like he was dizzy, but stepped forward—toward the fearful one.

Thunder boomed overhead, rain continued to hammer against the roof, and a pair of headlights turned into the parking lot, offering a quick beacon of hope to Sonny. But both boys saw what he saw and whatever fear existed before was now elevated to a new, more desperate, level, like gas thrown on an already-raging fire.

Eddie's brother pulled one trigger of the shotgun. Tom was five feet from him and the shot hit him directly in the stomach, knocking him backward. But Tom remained standing, enraged, determined to put an end to the threat and the desecration of his store, once and for all. He gathered himself, pushed away the pain and surprise, and stepped forward again, his bare hands the only weapon he had.

It was a double-barrel shotgun; there was another trigger to pull. The second blast nearly cut Tom in half. He tumbled backward into the counter and collapsed into a pool of blood.

Eddie jumped past Sonny, grabbed his brother, and ran to the door. He stopped and looked back at Sonny, cold eyes considering whether he deserved to live or die, when the car horn sounded—an alarm, an urging, *let's go, we have to go.* The car that had pulled into the lot had stopped. Someone else was coming. Another witness. Another person to shoot. Hopefully it was Bertie—or the police. Eddie stood frozen, fingering the trigger on his own shotgun, offering no signals to the car what his intention was, just staring at Sonny, counting his odds. Finally, the horn beeped again, and Eddie disappeared out the door without saying a word or firing the gun.

Before Sonny could take another breath or consider himself lucky to be alive, the car and the trio inside it sped off into the tumultuous grayness, disappearing completely from sight. But there was no question that they had been there, that Eddie and his brother had started something that they might not have intended to.

The crows had gathered on the telephone line as soon as the rain had stopped. They didn't know what humans called them when they came together, nor did they know what a murder was; the killing of one's own kind by another. All they knew was that there was blood, that death had beckoned them with opportunity and potential. They would just have to wait. Patience was something they did understand. They could stand on the wire until the last bit of light drained from the sky. Stand until darkness came, making them invisible, silent, and ready for whatever came next, whatever had been left for them by the violence of another. It was as if it had all happened just for them, just so they could continue to exist, black wing against black sky.

CHAPTER 11

"**G**et out of the car," Eddie ordered Carmen. "Just get out." His clothes were splattered with blood, his face carved with anger so severe that it threatened to stay there permanently. His handsomeness had vanished.

Eddie had said little after he'd run out of Lancer's Market. "Go. Go back to the motel." Then he looked forward from the passenger seat, stared straight ahead tight-lipped, emotionlessly, as Carmen shifted through the gears, driving away from the market as fast as she could, but not so fast that she would draw attention to them. There were cars in the lot across the county line.

Tió had tried to apologize from the backseat. "I'm sorry, Eddie; he was hurting you."

"Shut up; just shut the fuck up, Tió." His voice was like lightning hitting the ground. Biting electricity spread throughout the interior of the car, followed by deafening thunder.

"I didn't mean to kill him, Eddie. He wouldn't stop . . ."

Now, in front of the motel, the engine running in neutral, the vacuum wipers slapping against the windshield, Eddie repeated himself. "Go. Get out of the car, Carmen. Wait. Just wait. I'll be back."

Carmen looked at Eddie, then back to Tió, who had shrunk into the gray upholstery like a fearful little boy on the verge of a spanking. Her gut told her not to argue with Eddie. Her gut told her to run from them both as fast as she could, as far away as she could get.

She pushed out of the driver's seat, her fingers numb from gripping the steering wheel so hard, and hurried to the door of their room as quickly as she could. There was no goodbye, no looking back.

For the first time since she had left home, Carmen longed for the comfort of her own bed, the smell of menudo simmering on the stove, her father sitting in his chair reading the newspaper after a long day's work at the hospital. Would he take her back? Forgive her if he knew what she had done? What about confession? Telling the priest? Something told her that there was no turning back, what was done couldn't be undone. She'd be marked for the rest of her life, all because she wanted to be with a boy, to strike out on her own. To be grown up.

A tear ran down her cheek, but she wouldn't let anyone see it. She could barely stand to wipe it away, acknowledge its sudden presence.

From the outside, the motel was as hopeless looking as it was on the inside. It was a long building with a sloping flat roof from front to back, like an old hog barn had been converted to house people on their way to slaughter instead of pigs. The motel sat outside of town, surrounded by fallow fields, along the main road out of Memphis that headed to all points north and south. Emptiness and squalid Indian reservations awaited in Oklahoma—a quiet kind of hell—while the draw of the city, Fort Worth, Dallas, and Austin, even farther south, piqued Carmen's curiosity with their size, opportunities, and places to disappear into. She needed to make a plan. She needed to decide what she was going to do next: Wait on Eddie—or go out on her own. "Wait," Eddie had said. It was an order, a command no different than her father's.

The overhang of the roof kept the weather from her as she pushed the key into the lock. What remained of the storm was weak, gentle, the aftermath not so threatening and severe as it had been. The wind had weakened into an intermittent breeze. The pelting rain was nothing more than a soft drizzle, almost a fog.

She could still see the lightning coming from inside Lancer's Market in her mind, the flash of a gunshot, followed by another, along with two defining booms.

No one was supposed to get hurt. Eddie had said he wouldn't shoot anyone. They just needed money for rent and gas to deliver the gin. Then everything would be golden. Just her and him on their own.

No more Tió. No more gin. A new life, a new kind of love away from the small town that she felt trapped in, suffocated by—they could be anybody they wanted to be, not Aldo Hernadez's daughter, or Eddie Renaldo's girl, just Carmen and Eddie, in love, the world theirs to be had. K. I. S. S. I. N. G. Eddie, behind a tree...

"I didn't mean to kill him" Tió had said. Kill him. Somebody was dead. The boys were in big trouble now. More trouble than Carmen ever thought was possible. All because of Tió. That didn't surprise her. She shivered, shook the key. The door fought her, wouldn't open.

Eddie had slid into the driver's seat, and the car had sped away. The road was too wet for the tires to squeal, but the immediate thrust of the motor echoed on the breeze, the accelerator pushed all the way to the floor, the desire to flee not isolated only in Carmen's mind or heart.

She was glad she hadn't seen the shooting, the dead man. The only memory she would have were the flashes in the rain and the smell of fear and blood when the boys had run back to the car, tossing their guns into the backseat, Eddie yelling, "Go, go..."

She glanced over her shoulder before pushing the door harder. It opened with a knee. Behind her, the car was gone. The road was empty. Only the lights in Felix Massey's office burned against the fog—a light she wished didn't exist.

Carmen slammed the door behind her, locked it, and stood staring at the mess in the room. The bed was unmade. Eddie's clothes, from the day before, were strung over the lone chair that sat cockeyed next to a cluttered desk. A makeshift sleeping pallet, a tangle of used blankets and sheets pilfered from the maid's cart, lay in front of the bathroom door. Tió's bed. The sight of it made her stomach queasy, made her feel like she was going to vomit. He was a killer now. She had smelled his breath. Touched his hand once, mistaking him for Eddie in the darkness.

There was no escaping the smell of aging gin in the small room. Rotting fruit and juniper berries coated her throat, attacked her hair, clung to her body like a magnet. A scream gurgled in the bottom of Carmen's stomach, or maybe it was bile; either way she forced it back, swallowed deeply, knowing full well that it was her pride that she was tasting. She refused to sob, to cry out loud any more than she already had.

Without any more hesitation, Carmen began to collect her clothes. She stuffed them in a pillowcase as quickly as she could. It didn't matter whether they were clean or dirty. She had to get out of there. Get out before Eddie came back. Something told her it would just be Eddie. He was going to ditch Tió—one way or another. She didn't want to know how, didn't want to see any more blood on his shirt, on his hands.

Eddie had promised her before they'd left for the robbery: "*No one'll get hurt, I promise. You just need to drive, Carmen. Can you do that?*" She'd nodded. Yes. She would do anything he wanted her to. But that was then. Now she was alone with her memories and fears, death on her heels.

Her brushes were on the desk. She had to step over the pallet on the floor. They were the last of her things. She had all she needed, all that mattered. Not that she'd ever had that much to begin with. She'd run off in the middle of the night, sliding down the tree outside her window under the light of the moon like a cat in heat, a molly in search of a tom to rub up against. She'd been lonely then. Lonely and trapped. Nothing had changed. Eddie's thumb was like her father's. Only now she was afraid. More afraid than she'd ever been in her life. She didn't want to end up like Bonnie Parker, ambushed on the side of some road with so many bullets in her body that her flesh was nothing but mush. She didn't want that. She was just a girl with her life ahead of her. Tears threatened again, but she pushed them back just like she had the bile.

Carmen scooped her brushes into the pillowcase and headed to the door.

But a loud thump stopped her. Somebody was knocking on the door. *Boom, boom.* Another knock.

"Open up, girl. I saw you go in."

Damn it, Carmen thought, but didn't say it out loud. She stood frozen, clung to the pillowcase like it was a Teddy Bear, and tried not to make any noise at all. Her heart beat so loudly she thought it was going to jump out of her chest.

It was Felix Massey come to collect the rent.

The bottom of the pillowcase teetered back and forth like the pendulum of a clock. Carmen eased her hand down and stopped it as quietly as she could. There was no other way out. A front window faced out, next to the door, curtains closed. The bathroom window was too small to climb through and only cranked halfway open. That was it.

She would just have to wait him out. Wait until Eddie got back. Everything changed so fast. Her head was spinning like a top, coming to stop in the same place: no options, no place to run.

Boom, *boom*, *boom*. Three more knocks so loud inside the small room that Carmen wanted to put her hands to her ears and pretend she didn't hear them.

Felix Massey said nothing. Quiet returned. The weather was faint, the storm so distant that it was almost like it had vanished, too. Maybe it all had just been a dream, a nightmare.

The knocks were replaced by the heartbeat of a girl so afraid that she thought she was going to pee herself, just like Tió had when Eddie had pulled the trigger of the empty gun.

A new sound quickly replaced her heartbeat. It was the sound of metal against metal. A key sliding slowly into the lock. Carmen dropped the pillowcase where she stood. There was no place to run. The bathroom door had no lock.

Felix Massey pushed in the door and stopped just inside of it. "I thought I smelled somethin' a little sour coming out of this room," he said, staring at Carmen.

She looked for a weapon, saw nothing until her eyes landed on a letter opener lying on the cluttered desk. "Eddie's not here. He'll bring you the money when he comes back." Her voice sounded like shattered glass tinkling to the floor.

Felix Massey closed the door behind him and locked it. "I got all the money I need." His eyes were glassy and cold. He was still dressed in the same work pants, same ugly stained white shirt, and muddy shoes. An unlit cigar dangled out of the corner of his mouth. He had just put it out. The smell of cheap tobacco touched Carmen's nose, causing her stomach to lurch again. She didn't have the will or the strength to stop it this time. She bent over and puked.

A look of disgusted surprise crossed Felix Massey's face. "That'll cost you. I'll have to have it cleaned up."

"I don't have money."

"Sure you do." Felix smiled. The cigar stayed put, like it was glued to his lip. He looked her up and down, from toes to breasts, stopping at her chest with a leer that was unmistakable.

Carmen felt naked, violated. She crossed her arms over her chest and backed up until she came to a stop against the bathroom door. She could taste her own vomit, and she spit it out at Felix as he stepped toward her.

The spit fell short, landed on the tip of his right shoe. It didn't stop him.

"I'll scream," Carmen said.

"Go ahead. There ain't no one to hear you for miles, or in the next room if that's what you're hopin'."

"Eddie'll kill you if you touch me."

"You think I'm scared of a gin-runnin' spic?"

"You should be." Eddie and Tió knew how to kill—she knew that now. But even in her state of fear, she knew better than to confess such a thing. She might've been afraid, but she wasn't stupid.

Felix Massey stopped inches from Carmen. "Don't make this hard girl. It ain't gonna hurt. Be better for both of us if it's fun."

Up close, Felix Massey was even more foul than he was at a distance. He probably weighed two hundred and fifty pounds and sweated like he had just run a sprint, smelled like he hadn't had a bath in a week. He was a whale come to swallow her up. His shadow took up half the wall.

Carmen opened her mouth to protest, to scream, but Felix pushed in quickly and covered her mouth with his skillet-sized hand. Her scream was corked. She was trapped with nowhere to go. His hardness pressed against her, announcing the seriousness of the threat.

He started to writhe, hump against her belly slowly. He was in no hurry, not afraid that Eddie would show back up any time soon. "Take it out," he whispered. "Touch it. We'll be even then. You won't owe me nothin'." He was breathing hard. Each word seemed difficult for him to say. His other hand pushed up under the hem of her simple cotton dress, rubbing her leg, fingers searching inward, toward her private place. "Come on," he insisted, "touch it. I promise, we'll be even."

It was a lie and Carmen knew it. He would want more. The only way out was to give in, or make him think she was giving in. It was all she knew to do, so she surrendered, relaxed, allowed the tension in her body to deflate. "I can't move," she mumbled through his hand.

A slow smile crossed Felix's face, and he pulled away two of his fingers, the ones pressing on her lips, like he was changing chords on a guitar.

"How can I touch it if I can't move?" Carmen asked.

Felix Massey drew in a deep breath and looked her in the eye for a long second, like he was trying to decide if he could trust her.

Carmen pouted, stared up at him innocently. Being a girl was the only weapon she had.

Felix relented and pulled back six inches, giving her just enough room to drop her arms, allowing her hands to relax across her chest and drop to her side. It also gave Carmen just enough room to raise a knee—which she did with as much power as she could, pushing Felix Massey backward at the same time.

He screamed out in agonizing pain as her knee slammed against her target, his ugly bulge. Bone beat flesh every time, no matter the level of excitement. Felix Massey wasn't the first man, or boy, she'd had to fend off in her life, and something told her he wouldn't be the last.

Felix toppled over like an egg rolling off a shelf, giving her just enough room to dart to the side and grab the letter opener off the desk.

He moaned, then hissed, "You'll regret that, you little whore."

Carmen gripped the letter opener like a knife and thrust it toward him, slicing at the air, coming nowhere near cutting his skin. "I'll cut your balls off you come for me again, you fat bastard. Then I'll send Eddie after you to finish you off."

Felix Massey struggled to stand up and Carmen knew she only had a second or two to make a run for it. In as graceful a move as she could mount, she hopped across the floor, dodged the puddle of puke, picked up the pillowcase and dashed for the door. She was a ballerina escaping a troll. Freedom lay beyond the castle. She wasn't so many years from believing in fairy tales. She felt like Rapunzel freed from the tower.

Carmen heard Felix try to stand as she fumbled with the lock. Felt him lunging after her as her fingers pulled the knob down. It clicked open and she glanced over her shoulder.

Two seconds, maybe three, then he'd reach her. She knew what he'd do to her once he wrestled her to the ground, and she couldn't bear the thought. At that very moment, she understood how easy it was to kill a man. The world would be a better place without a monster like Felix Massey. Still, something deep inside her wouldn't allow her to use the letter opener—she didn't want to cut him. Instead, she swung the door out, and slammed it into his head, clocking him hard, stunning him like a charging boar hit with a club.

Felix Massey groaned again, stumbled back, taking the hit without crashing to the floor. He was dazed, but he would recover quickly.

The stumble was all Carmen needed. She bolted out the door, unsure where she was going but running faster than she ever had before.

Felix yelled for her to stop, cussed, offered threats until she was out of earshot. She swore to herself that she wasn't going to stop running until she reached Dallas.

CHAPTER 12

The crows had begun to follow him like they did a wolf or a coyote. There would be blood left in his wake. Sooner or later he would kill again leaving them a bounty to feast on. The crows were sure of it. Just as they were sure that the moon would rise into the night sky offering them light in the darkness to see what was coming their way.

Sonny stood next to the screen door as Hugh Beaverwood, the local coroner and Wellington's only mortician, covered Tom Turnell's body with a sheet. Beaverwood was a droll man with a hound dog face; his jowls flapped thinly over his jaw, and he had a flat, turned-up nose that looked more suited to finding rabbits than inhaling embalming fluid. Sonny'd had more than his fair share of dealings with Beaverwood over the years, mostly on Ranger cases he'd been called in on and once for a personal matter, when it had come to burying Martha. He didn't have a strong feeling about the man either way. The coroner seemed cold and detached, distant, which probably went along with the territory of conducting business with death on a daily basis. He was all business, all the time. If Hugh Beaverwood was around it was not a celebration. That came after he left, if at all.

The Collingsworth County sheriff, Layton Jones, Jonesy to everyone in town, stood behind the counter, opposite the coroner, staring at the empty cash drawer. Bertie Turnell stood behind him, wedged in a corner, his face pale with shock—he had seen the robbers leave, had pulled in the parking lot just as the shots had gone off. Bertie was a shorter version of Tom with lighter hair, probably from his mother's side, a German-Dutch woman who Sonny had never properly met, but knew from a distance. No one else was inside the store. Even the mice had the good sense and enough respect to remain hidden and silent.

Outside, the day went on. Traffic bounded up and down the farm-to-market road out of Wellington, unaware of what was happening inside the store, pushing through puddles, offering an occasional splash. It was a rare sound.

The storm had pushed northeast, like most storms did, and the sun beamed brightly down from a pure blue, cloudless, sky. Fingers of steam filtered up from the hoods of cars in the muddy parking lot, and from the roofs of buildings across the road. Heat had already returned with a vengeance, and before long, everything that was wet would be dry again, faded brown instead of rich chocolate, and the days would fall back into the normal, desolate pattern that was nearly always the promise of summer.

But from where Sonny stood, nothing would be the same. He didn't feel lucky to be alive, to have survived the deadly armed robbery. All he could feel was regret. He could barely look at the sheet, at Tom Turnell bound for the mortuary, toes up, eyes closed, his body already cold.

Jonesy walked over to Sonny. He was a head shorter, a little soft in the middle, and had wiry white hair growing out of his ears. His head was bald, blotched with red spots that resembled islands on a map, and was usually covered with a hat. Sonny couldn't remember a time when a Jonesy hadn't been the county sheriff. It was their family business, just like the Texas Rangers was his.

Jonesy was getting to the end of his term, and rumor had it that his younger son, Bob—Bubba inside the family—was already angling for the position, campaigning on the sly to the men who it mattered to most in Wellington and farther reaches of the county.

"I'm gonna have to ask you to come down to the station and sign a formal report, Sonny," Jonesy said. His voice was scratchy, like sandpaper lined his throat. "I hate to ask you to do such a thing."

"I know the procedure," Sonny answered. He looked away from the body and stared down the aisle where his .45 lay, untouched where it had fallen—out of reach. "I'd like to take my gun home with me, Jonesy, if it's all the same to you."

"You didn't get a shot off?"

Sonny shook his head.

"Not to be indelicate, Sonny, but why in the hell did you have a gun with you in the first place?"

"You leave yours at home when you go out off-duty?"

It was Jonesy's turn to shake his head.

"Well, there you have it. Force of habit, and you're not being indelicate. My arm was amputated. This is the first time I've made it out of the house since I come home from the hospital. I might not have an arm, but I've always carried my gun. Didn't see a reason to change any more things. Be like bread without butter, now wouldn't it?"

"Well, I reckon I'd a done the same thing, if'n I was you," Jonesy said. "You say one of them called the other by the name of Eddie, and they was Mexican-skinned?"

"I'm certain of it."

"Sounds like the Clever, Clever boys to me, the Renaldo twins," Jonesy said with a sigh. "This is a big step for them, up from runnin' gin and pickin' fights in the school yard. A murder and all. They've been small time, until now. Sure never expected this from them. But there was a girl with them, you say?"

"Driving. I think. Behind the wheel."

"But you're not certain?"

"It was raining, hard to see. The windows in the car were fogged up. I couldn't make out any features. There were three of them. I'm sure of that, but it's all I'm sure of."

Jonesy stroked his chin. "That's interestin', to say the least. I don't know about no girl they've been palling around with. Maybe there's more to this than I think there is."

"What do you mean?"

"Just thinkin' out loud, I suppose. But I got two unsolved murders on my hands at the moment. First ones in a coon's age. Two Jane Does tossed to the side of the road, beaten and soiled in a foul way, if you know what I mean. No leads, no clues, a year apart, but pretty much the same MO from head to toe. The one Renaldo is pretty smart, while the other one, well, he's a little slow, unpredictable. I might have to look at them a little closer now that they've shown some meanness. I didn't think they had in them."

"You really think there's a link?" Sonny asked.

Jonesy shrugged. "Hard to say, but I figure it won't hurt to poke around. See what else those boys have been up to. If they can kill a man like Tom Turnell, they're liable to be able to do just about anything, the way I see it. Sure is a sad day."

"It was the quiet one that pulled the trigger. Tom had the talker subdued."

"With the cheese wire?"

"That's right."

A car turned into the parking lot and headed straight for the door, garnering both men's attention.

"Put the closed sign on the door, if you don't mind," Jonesy said to Sonny, his voice a little deeper with the order.

"It's Jesse," Sonny said.

"I wondered when the Rangers were gonna show up. Put the sign up anyway. Word's gonna get out. We don't need no carnival here. And I sure don't mean no offense, Sonny, but things sure ain't been the same since you hung up your Stetson." Jonesy glanced up at Sonny's bare head.

"Thanks, Jonesy. Jesse's still young. He's got a lot to learn."

"If you say so."

Hugh Beaverwood slid Tom Turnell's body into the back of the hearse. It was nothing more than a delivery truck, black in color, of course, that also served as an ambulance when the need arose. The coroner lowered his head solemnly, then closed the door of the hearse as gently as he could. "Be anything else, Sheriff?"

Jonesy, Sonny, and Jesse stood clumped together, just off the short porch that fronted Lancer's Market. Bertie had remained inside.

Jonesy shrugged. "No, not unless Ranger Burton needs anything more."

Both Sonny and Jesse shook their heads at the same time. It was a hard habit to break. Some days Sonny felt like Ranger was his first name instead of his vocation. Probably always would.

Jesse noticed Sonny's action and stepped forward. "I'd like to keep this as close to the vest as we can. If these boys are spooked, they could cause more of a ruckus than they already have, Mr. Beaverwood."

Hugh Beaverwood agreed with a nod, then looked over to the sheriff for real approval. Jonesy tilted his head forward subtly.

"All right," Beaverwood said, "if the newspaper comes snoopin' 'round, I'll send them your way."

"That would be good," Jesse said. "I'd appreciate it." He tipped the brim of his hat and smiled broadly. Anyone within a mile could see it was forced. Sonny knew Jesse had to work at being polite, but he'd never noticed it so much as he did just then. Probably because the sheriff had expressed some hesitation about Jesse's skills as a Ranger.

The coroner stood stiffly for a long moment, staring at the three men, then backed away and didn't turn around until he was just on the other side of the hearse.

Not one of them said a thing until the hearse started to pull away.

Jonesy shook his head, then looked at Sonny. "Man's got ice running through his veins."

"I've always tried to avoid him," Sonny said.

"You and everybody else," Jonesy answered.

Jesse stepped back so he was in line with both men. "He doesn't look like he's aged a day since I was a kid."

Jonesy sighed. "All the stories about him are the same, too, that he takes pictures of dead girls and does unspeakable things to their bodies.

But truth is they're just stories. I poked around early on to see if they were true or not. Turns out he's just a loner, a confirmed bachelor, a man that keeps himself busy with other folks' troubles. I guess he's like a buzzard, cleanin' up the mess that nature leaves behind. Somebody's gotta do it. This is bad enough," he said, letting his words trail off with a thrust of his head back to the store.

"You got anything else to tell me?" Jesse said to Sonny. It was an official voice, hard and to the point. Sonny knew the tone when he heard it. Had used it a million times himself. It sounded like an echo.

"I'm gonna check on Bertie before I go," Jonesy said, heading back inside the store.

Jesse waited until the sheriff was out of sight before he said anything else. "What the hell were you doing here in the first place?"

"What the hell do you think, Ranger Burton? I was hungry." Sonny stiffened, stood taller than he had all day. He didn't like what he heard in Jesse's voice.

"You could've called. I would've run you some food out, or Bertie could have delivered something."

"I thought it was best to get out of the house on my own," Sonny said. "Has to happen sooner or later. I didn't expect this. How could I have known? Besides, you made it clear that you preferred to stay in town."

"Because I'm not a boy anymore and no matter what you say, you'd treat me like one if I took up residence in my old room. You're doing it now."

"If you say so."

"I do. I got a job to do, Pa, and it's hard enough steppin' into your shoes. I don't need to be in your shadow, too."

"Well, then, pull down your damn hat," Sonny said, pointing to Jesse's white Stetson. "You look like you just got off the damn train."

Starting the truck the second time around was a lot easier than the first. The routine came back to Sonny pretty quickly, and navigating the exercise with one hand and one set of fingers was going to come easier to him than he originally thought it would. Either that or he was in a hurry to get away from Lancer's Market, which was more the truth. He thought little about the mechanics of his own existence once he stepped on the starter.

He wanted to be as far away from Jesse and the smell of death as he could. With about as much grace as he could muster, Bertie had carried a box of groceries out to Sonny's truck and refused payment for them. Sonny had insisted, but Bertie was forceful in his refusal. "*You did your best to save him, Sonny. Thank you. This is the least I can do.*"

There was nothing for him to do now but go back home. Close himself off from the world and try to figure what was next. The robbers were the sheriff's problem. Jesse's, too. But something told Sonny that Jonesy would be the one that brought the Clever, Clever boys to justice and not Jesse.

For a brief second, Sonny thought about turning around and going back, offering his help to Jesse. But the boy had made it clear that he was already struggling to fill his shoes. No need to rub his face in it.

The road was already dry, and the late afternoon sky was a perfect blue sheet that hung for as far as the eye could see. It met with the scorched vista, brown open land that looked to hold no life at all—a barren field that went on and on until Wellington rose out of it in the distance. No downpour could green things up instantly. It would take days of rain, a hurricane blowing up and weakening from the Gulf, to bring life back to the blades of grass now.

Sonny couldn't see the town yet, and his turn came long before any of the buildings would come into sight. But the openness of the way forward seemed even more lonely than it had earlier. The rain and clouds had closed everything in. Now there was nothing in between him and the emptiness of North Texas. He could already feel dread creeping back into the farthest reaches of his mind, but Sonny didn't mind being alone at all. Especially after everything that had happened.

He downshifted, and, as he turned south toward home, the box in the seat next to him slid forward, like it was going to topple over onto the floor. Out of instinct, he leaned over to stop the box from falling, but he did so with his invisible right arm. The groceries tumbled to the floorboard.

Sonny had taken his eyes off the road, and when he settled back up behind the wheel there was something standing in the middle of the road. A dog. He swerved to miss it. But he was too late. He hit the dog, sending it spiraling into the ditch with an eardrum-shattering yelp.

CHAPTER 13

Carmen Hernandez had never liked to run. Her knees were turned in slightly. She wasn't pigeon-toed exactly, pigeon-kneed maybe. It wasn't like she was a cripple, even though she'd been born early. Her mother'd had a hard labor, and she'd died three days after giving birth. Her father never forgave her for being the cause of her mother's death. The physical defect, if it could be called that, was barely noticeable when she walked, but her whole body arched to the right when she ran, and she was never very fast on the fly. She had never needed to be. Until now.

She ran away from the motel, from Felix Massey, as fast as she could. Tears blurred her vision, and she wished it was still raining so it would wash away the smell of the fat clerk pressing against her, grinding his hardness into her. She'd wished for a knife, too, but was glad it was out of reach. She already felt the guilt of blood on her hands. She didn't need any more.

But it wasn't raining. The clouds had pushed northeast. Only a dim gray line on the horizon remained, with an occasional flash of lightening, offering itself to Carmen as a reminder of the storm, of the gunshots inside the *mecado* and the lingering assault that came after Eddie had dropped her off at the motel.

Her lungs began to burn, sweat dripped down her throat, and, to make things worse, she had little idea of where she was. She knew how to get home, to get to Memphis and Wellington and back, but not what stood in between, off the side roads, down the farmer's lanes. Out in the middle of a field she was lost. She could barely tell north from south, east from west, but the sun saved her. She could tell where she was running based on its place in the sky.

The motel stood like a decaying monument alongside the road, surrounded by vast, open fields. At one time the building had been a stagecoach stop on the route north. Rooms for let had been added on over the years, but it wasn't until the advent of cars, of lots of cars, that the rooms had been converted, in haste and greed, as an offer of rest to travelers again. It had been a perfect place for Eddie to hole up and mix his gin.

Carmen looked behind her every few seconds to make sure she wasn't being followed. So far, she was alone. Felix hadn't appeared on foot or in a car. There was no sign of anyone.

She had to watch closely where she stepped. Rabbit holes became snake dens, and during the heat of the day rattlers slept on the lip of the entrance, soaking up sun to keep warm, so they would stay alive during the cool nights. The last thing she needed was to get snake bit or break an ankle. She could fall and disappear into the scrub, lie there and die. She wondered if Eddie would come looking for her—or be done with her now that she had disappeared, ran out on her own? There was no way to know the answer. Carmen didn't know what Eddie would do when he came back and found the room empty of her and her things.

The ground rose up in the distance, giving her sight of a long berm. It was a railroad track running north and south, parallel to the road, though it sat about a half mile from it. The tracks gave her a place to run to, a place to follow. Farther to the north, a line of trees poked up along the tracks. Telephone lines edged along the berm both ways. Some of the poles tilted one way or the other. They looked like giant cactus, offering no sustenance, only a place for the crows to roost.

She picked up her pace and didn't stop to catch her breath until she was on the far side of the railroad tracks. It wasn't a perfect place to hide, to rest, but it would have to do. She sat down and tucked her head between her legs so she was out of sight, at least from the road, and tried to settle herself down.

Carmen's heart raced, nearly outrunning her mind, as she allowed all of the day's events to play out behind her closed eyes. She began to sob, cry from the depths of her belly. She trembled and shook, then vomited again, just like she had inside the motel room. Only now it was just bile, offering a sad, familiar taste in her mouth. Salty tears crossed her lips just after, adding to the discomfort and desperation of her situation.

She wiped her mouth with the back of her hand and realized that she was thirsty and hungry. The thought only made her cry harder.

She wanted to go home, but she knew she couldn't.

Sonny slammed on the brakes and brought the truck to a stop. The engine coughed and protested but kept running. He looked in the rearview mirror just in time to see the dog try to stand up in the ditch, then fall back down into the mud.

He exhaled deeply, muttered, "Goddamn it," then reached over, picked up the .45, and pushed his way out of the truck.

A warm breeze greeted Sonny, wrapping around him, offering up the smell of the recent rain and of mud and decay. He was in the middle of a crossroads, and the nearest house sat a mile up the road. It had been empty since the middle of last winter, when the Crunhalls, all eight of them, had loaded up into a flatbed truck, along with the belongings they could fit into it and hadn't used as firewood, and headed west to the promised land of California.

The dog could've come from anywhere. It could have been dumped off by somebody without the means to feed it. Or it could have run off from a nearby farm, simple as that. There were still a few farmers trying to hang on. Whatever the animal's story was, Sonny didn't much care. He was just unhappy that they'd crossed paths in such an untimely way.

He made his way to the side of the ditch with heavy steps, then stopped and looked down. His trigger finger edged its way across the slim piece of metal, finding its proper place with ease. The weight of the .45 on his left side made his shoulder droop like the scales of justice. He was off balance, sinking in mud.

The dog stared up at Sonny and whimpered. It looked underweight, ribs showing just under loose fur, like it had been doing a poor job of scavenging food, just like every other creature left to fend on its own this side of Wall Street.

Sonny would have been surprised if the dog weighed twenty-five pounds soaking wet. But it wasn't a pup. There was some gray showing on its upper lip, contrasting starkly against its black coat—what part he could see that wasn't tainted with mud.

To his surprise, the dog didn't act aggressive at all. Most animals this side of wild would try to skitter away with a growl and barred teeth if they were hurt. But not this one. It stared into Sonny's eyes, whimpered again when he didn't respond, and held up its front paw.

"You're gonna make this hard on me, aren't you?" He looked quickly under its belly, and added, "Boy."

The dog just stared at Sonny. It was more than he could take. He looked away again and took in the gathering loneliness of the situation. He knew the best thing he could do was to raise the gun and pull the trigger without any further ado. Be done with it. Get it over with and get on down the road. *Put it out of its misery and go home.*

Sonny lowered his head. He couldn't do it. He'd seen enough death and killing for one day. The image of Tom Turnell taking a shotgun blast in the stomach flashed through his mind. He couldn't find it in himself to shoot the poor dog, pull the trigger, or kill any living thing.

The dog was a hound dog of some kind. A mutt. Short haired, mostly all black from what Sonny could see, with a white patch on its chest and on the tip of its tail. He shrugged at the realization, walked back to the truck, and deposited the .45 under the driver's seat, then made his way back to the dog. He eased down into the ditch until he was about three feet in front of the dog. It hadn't moved an inch.

"Can you walk?" Sonny asked, then said, "That was a stupid question wasn't it? Like you can understand a word I'm saying." He crouched and offered his hand to the dog, balling his fingers into a fist, protecting them from a sudden attack. He didn't know this dog, still didn't trust it.

Sonny'd had dogs come in and out of his life since he was a boy. Working dogs mostly, ones that had a job around the house and weren't there to be a pet. Ones that kept the coyotes and foxes out of the chicken house, when there had been one, or to bark an alert when there was a need. Mostly, a dog was an extra mouth to feed, a luxury if there was no task for it to keep up with—one that saved money. Scraps were tossed into the yard to feed it . These days, most folks didn't have many scraps to offer an animal.

Dogs that offered comfort or just plain old friendship were a thing of childhood. Jesse'd had a few dogs, but they would disappear or come up dead, until the point came when Martha said no more would be allowed around the house. Sonny was always working, and she was the one that would end up burying them.

The dog leaned in and licked Sonny's knuckles. Sonny smiled, then slowly opened his hand and gave the dog a gentle rub on the side of the head. The dog leaned into him and whimpered softly again.

The cry was more than Sonny could take. He stood up, leaned down, scooped up the dog and stuffed it under his good arm.

It occurred to Sonny that the bed of the truck might be too hard on the dog, so he walked over to the passenger-side door and eased the dog onto the seat. It was then that he saw the bone protruding from the right front leg. The movement caused blood to flow outward, and Sonny quickly settled the dog into the seat, pulled out his handkerchief, and wrapped it on the leg, the best he could, using it as a tourniquet to slow the flow of blood. One more time, his battlefield experience had come home with him. The dog stayed quiet and didn't seem to mind the handkerchief. It settled down into the seat and didn't move another inch.

Pete Jorgenson lived three miles south of Wellington on a sprawling piece of land that had been in his family since the white man had settled in the county. Pete was tall, blonde, a hulking man of obvious Swedish descent who wouldn't hesitate to reach in and pull a calf out of a cow if he had to or bind a sparrow's wing and see it to flight again, even if he thought the bird would die before it healed. He was a gentle soul and the only animal doctor within fifty miles. It was the only place Sonny knew to take the dog.

Like the rest of the houses along the county road, Pete's house looked like it had fallen into disrepair. The two-story clapboard house was in serious need of a whitewash. The boards were gray and weathered, and a few of the shutters hung cockeyed, one way or the other. Most folks didn't have the money to pay Pete for his services, though he kept up with the calls for them the best he could. They'd barter food if they had it or services if they could provide them. Currency had come in a lot of different forms, including relief from the government, if a man could bring himself to take it. Sonny doubted Pete did.

By the time Sonny stopped the truck and had his hand on the door handle, Pete was already coming out the front door, followed closely by his wife, Lidde, a short, round woman, as tall as Pete's shoulder and jolly as an elf was expected to be. Her cheeks were always poised to break into a smile. But there was no happiness on her face at the moment, only concern.

"Didn't expect to see you on this day, Ranger Burton," Pete said, looking up from Sonny's missing right arm and into his eyes as quick as he could.

"Sonny," he said. "I've quit being a Ranger, Pete. I figured you'd heard that."

"I heard that, but I didn't believe such a thing was possible. World don't seem right without a Ranger Burton in it."

"There still is. My son, Jesse, took my place."

"Um, I heard that, too, yah." The tone in Pete's voice changed. There was a hint of disapproval in it. "What brings you here?" he asked, changing the subject as quick as he could.

The reaction stunted Sonny's response for a second. It concerned him that folks thought less of Jesse than they did him, but he knew it was a simple thing: these people didn't like any kind of change. They'd had their fair share. Jesse was going to have to prove himself. It would just take time. Simple as that. At least Sonny hoped that was what it was.

"Well, I hit a dog," Sonny said. "He's over here in the front seat." Sonny walked around to the other side of the truck. "Broke his leg. I put a tourniquet on it and I was hoping you could fix him up, then find out where he belongs."

"I'll see what I can do," Pete said.

Lidde stayed on the porch, watching over them, drying her hands on a freshly bleached apron. "I'll clean off the table and get the things ready," she said, turning and disappearing inside the house.

"I *can* pay you, Pete," Sonny said, as he opened the passenger door.

"Oh, I'm not worried about that."

"He seems friendly. He let me pick him up," Sonny said.

"Well, that's a start, yah?" Pete let the dog smell him, then reached in, pulled him out of the seat and headed toward the house. The dog didn't offer a peep and Sonny followed after Pete dutifully, prepared to wait and see about the dog's outcome. It was the least he could do.

A gang of blue jays appeared out of nowhere and began to mob the crows. They had been sitting on the telephone lines watching for anything that moved, anything that would offer them an opportunity to feed after the storm. If nothing appeared, they'd make their way to a cache of food stored away for just that reason. Times were tough, grain was hard to come by, as was anything else on the desolate land.

The nuisance that was the jays was not welcome. They came out of nowhere and were intent on chasing the crows off for no reason. It was long past nesting season, so there were no eggs to protect. Most likely, it was for fun, entertainment, or to get the attention of a nearby hawk. Flying off with an annoyed chorus of caws, it was then that the crows saw the girl and the man stalking her, and their hopes for a meal of flesh and blood were raised.

CHAPTER 14

"Well," Pete Jorgenson said, "I think he's going to be all right."

Sonny was sitting in a small parlor just outside Pete's office. It was empty with the exception of another chair, worn and soiled with the faint smell of an old animal, and a dusty bookshelf that held two books, the King James Version of the Bible and *Moby Dick*. Sonny hadn't felt compelled to crack open either book while he waited.

He stood up. "That's good to hear. You have any idea where it might belong?"

There was a speck of blood on Pete's sleeve that hadn't been there before. His hands were clean and his eyes tired. "Can't rightly say that I do. Looks like he's been on his own for a while and doin' a poor job of it at that. Vern Maxwell used to raise hunting hounds that kind of resemble this one, but they were a little more mottled. Blue like him though. Clean him up and set 'im out in the sun and this one will look like the dark evening sky. Boy, ole Vern had a bitch that could tree a coon like nothing I ever did see. Those were good days, out hunting with Vern. He loved them dogs. Was real stingy with the studs and even stingier with them bitches, wanted to keep the line pure. Most times, he'd have the pups fixed before he sold them off. And sell 'em he did. Probably made a decent sum every spring and fall. Kept records of the mutts, too. I never seen nothin' like it, really. Well, there's folks back east that do such things, but they got them fancy dogs. We don't see that much here."

Sonny sighed. Pete was a talker, but he was a good man and he still carried a hint of a Swedish accent, and that made him interesting to listen to. But Sonny was past the point of tired. It had been a long day, after all, and he wanted to go home. "Vern Maxwell died about three years ago, if I recall."

"Sounds about right, but seems longer, yah," Pete said. There was no sign of the dog or Lidde. The house was quiet, other than the tick of a cuckoo clock hanging on the wall in the foyer. "Vern took ill about a year and a half after the Crash. He was seein' it tough before then, though."

Sonny nodded. "So this dog probably doesn't belong there."

"I doubt it; it's just his daughter and her boy in the old place now. She's got no interest in dogs like her father. Last time I was out there, she was down to one, and that bitch, the dog mind you, was past the point of havin' more pups. Cow had colic. Poor thing got into a patch of beans. I had to do a rumenotomy right then and there."

Sonny stared at Pete blankly.

Pete read Sonny's lack of understanding right away. "Cow had gas it couldn't pass. I had to puncture the first chamber of the gut with a cannula and leave it there for a few days so's all of the gas would escape. Kind of like a needle with a valve on it. Anyway, the cow survived and Betty had a source of milk again, so everything turned out dandy." He smiled broadly for a second, then let it fade.

Something clicked in Sonny's brain, a connection that he hadn't made until then. Not that it mattered. "She's a nurse?"

"That's right. Betty Maxwell. Most folks just call her Nurse Betty." Pete's tone changed when he said her name, just like it had when he'd shown slight disapproval for Jesse.

Sonny eyed him carefully, thought about pressing it, but decided not to. It didn't matter anyway—even though Nurse Betty had been kind to him, which as it was, was most likely nothing more than her doing her job. He felt bad that he hadn't offered her a condolence for the loss of her father. "So the dog's most likely a stray?"

"Most likely, yah," Pete said. "Could of come from Vern's line, though, sure could be a Maxwell hound by the looks of him. He starts bayin' after a coon you'll know for sure."

"Well," Sonny said, "I doubt I'll notice."

"I can't keep him, Ranger Burton." Pete's voice was certain as steel, and his eyes drew hard, staring straight at Sonny. "I got more mouths to feed now than I can afford."

Sonny drew back. There were no barking dogs about. Just a chicken in the yard. The rabbit hutches looked empty, and Pete and Lidde never had children of their own but were known to take in a "troubled" girl on occasion and see her through difficult times. Most times, those girls would move on with their lives once their troubles were past.

Sonny decided not to pry, but the comment struck him odd. He could reason it out, though. Folks who had a little more these days felt charitable to those that had less—which was the majority of folks in the county. It was hard telling who Pete and Lidde were feeding. He ignored the Ranger comment, too. No use correcting the man since it was obvious he was opposed to the change.

Pete ran his hands through his thick blonde hair. "I thought you meant for me to fix him, not to keep him. I was able to set the bone and splint it. With food, water, and a place to rest, he ought to be back to normal in a few weeks. Might have a limp to show for his troubles, but he'll have all four legs. I was afraid I was gonna have to cut it off at first. But since it just happened, we were lucky. There was no infection. He would have surely . . ." The clock seemed to tick louder, and Pete Jorgenson stopped talking midsentence, sucked in a breath, and dropped his head. His face turned pale as soon as realized what he'd said.

"How much do I owe you?" Sonny asked, irritated.

"Whatever you can pay."

Sonny looked Pete in the eye when he raised his head back up. "I can't keep a dog."

"Well, you should have shot him before you brought him here then."

"I thought about it."

"I know you did. I would have thought about it myself. The world's a hard place for a dog like him. Even harder now, no offense, with a bad limb. Who's gonna wanna dog that's broke?"

Sonny didn't say the words that formed in his head and made their way to the back of his tongue. *The world's a hard place for us all*. He just stared past Pete and took in the silence of the house for a long minute.

Lidde must have been out feeding the one chicken Sonny'd seen pecking at the dirt, out the back door, when he'd driven up. The dog hadn't made a peep since entering the office. It was probably sleeping. He knew the silence, the loneliness of an empty house, and, truth be told, past the uneasiness he felt, he was not looking forward to going back home.

Madness waited inside those four walls. He had only the voice in his head and the voices that came from the radio. At least there was that, at least he had a radio. Problem was the radio brought bad news into the house, brought in the meanness and ugliness people did to each other. But as he thought about it, he had just witnessed the madness of the world firsthand—again. Home didn't seem so bad. At least it was safe. And he could turn the radio off when it got to be too much.

"Well, I suppose I don't have a choice but to look after him till he gets better," Sonny said. "I did run over him."

"I don't think he'll be much trouble," Pete answered. He smiled, relaxed like a burden had been lifted from him. "Those Maxwell hounds were good around the house. Offered a bit of talent as a watchdog, if I recall. I always swore that favorite bitch of Vern's slept with one eye open."

"You'll keep an ear out, then, just in case he belongs to someone? If they come looking for him? Or you hear tell of a lost dog?"

"Oh, you betcha, I will." Pete turned away with a successful smile and hurried back toward the office. "I'll get him for you."

"I suppose you wouldn't know its name, do you?" Sonny called out. His stomach was suddenly nervous.

Pete stopped at the door, and turned back to Sonny. "Well, the thing is, I don't. If you're gonna keep him, then that's up to you, isn't it?"

"I didn't say I was keeping him, just looking after him till he's well," Sonny said. "Maybe I'll run him out to the Maxwell place and see if he belongs there, if I get the chance."

Pete shrugged, and the smile on his face disappeared. "Let me go get him for you."

A cawing crow startled Carmen. She looked up just in time to see a crow lift off the top of a telephone pole about a hundred and fifty yards to her left. A group of other birds were screaming at the big black crow, diving and pecking at it to drive it away from something. Carmen didn't know what kind of birds they were, and she didn't care. The suddenness and volume of the caws alarmed her.

She looked down the track and saw nothing unusual for as far as she could see. Just shadows from the telephone poles and lines and the occasional stretch of scrub brush or trees. Her breath had regulated, and a certain level of calmness had returned to her.

I didn't do anything wrong, she'd told herself. Nothing at all. Tió pulled the trigger. Eddie robbed the store. I just drove. Eddie made me. I had no choice.

The crow cawed again, rushing away in the opposite direction so it was nothing more than a black dot in the clear blue sky followed by a swarm of smaller birds. Something moved on the ground, catching her eye. A shadow crossed the track, then stopped.

Carmen exhaled, trying to push the fear away again. When she looked again there was nothing there. It was probably her imagination. The crow's shadow. A deer moving along the trees, looking for something to eat. Nothing. It was probably nothing.

Or Felix Massey coming after her. The thought was loud and clear, and it propelled Carmen straight to her feet.

Fear or no fear, it was stupid to stay there. She had to run again. With as much swiftness as she could muster, Carmen tapped the letter opener in the front pocket of her dress, then picked up the pillowcase and looked down the tracks. Nothing, not even a crow. It had flown out of sight.

She had no idea where she was or where she was going, but she damn sure wasn't going to sit there and wait to be found. There'd be worse things in store for her than stepping in a snake hole and breaking an ankle if she did.

For a brief second, the air was thick with humidity, and then, the next second, a dry blast of wind swept across the open field. The sun had burned away all of the moisture left behind by the rain in a short time. It was almost like the storm had never existed. Puddles were gone, and drops left on the brown grass had evaporated in the blink of an eye rather than soaked in. The grass was as brittle as it had been before the rain even came.

Carmen ran as fast as she could toward the first building she'd come to, a small white church that at any other time she would have ignored, fled from. It was a Sisters of Mercy church, an old white stucco single-level mission-style church—bell, *companario*, and all. It must have been over a hundred years old or older.

She was certain that she was being followed. Three coveys of doves, fifty feet apart, had exploded into the air behind her sequentially, and she was sure that she had heard footsteps behind her. But every time she looked over her shoulder there was nothing there. It was like she was being stalked by a ghost.

The pillowcase was not heavy, but it was awkward. Carmen shifted it from one hand to the other and back every so often. The letter opener made her run even more stiffly than she normally would. Her knees hurt. She had thought about putting it in the bag, but then it would've been hard to get to. She wasn't so scared that she couldn't think things through. If the opportunity to cut Felix Massey's balls off came again, she was going to take it. It would be a favor to the world and every girl in Collingsworth County.

She dodged a dip in the ground and made her way to the double-front doors of the church. With a hope and a prayer, she yanked on the right door and found it to be locked. Her heart sank. She looked over her shoulder again. Nothing. No one. But the birds were silent. There was not a sound in the world. Just her heartbeat. *Boom. Boom. Boom.* It rattled her ears, and her chest heaved with each breath. She couldn't remember a time when she'd run so fast, so far.

Luckily, the left door was unlocked. She pulled it open the best she could with one hand. The door was heavy, thick, made of oak, and the handle was cast in bronze, a winding chainlike design that allowed her fingers to fit like they belonged there.

Carmen stepped inside the church, closed the door behind her, and, out of habit and immediate need, genuflected, then made her way to the font, and dipped her fingers into the stoup. She splashed cold holy water across her face, allowing some to touch her thirsty lips, genuflected again toward the altar. Christ stared at the ground, crucified on a cross, his head cocked to the right, his head bleeding from the crown of thorns. It was a lifelike statue. The blood looked real.

The church was empty. A table of vigil lights sat off to Carmen's right. About half of the small votive candles were lit, flickering in the dim nave. Memorials for the dead and hope for the dying.

Shadows danced on the walls and ceiling, offering little comfort, but Carmen wasn't afraid now. No one would hurt her in a church. She was certain of it.

She made her way to the back pew, tossed the pillowcase onto it, and sat down. It took about five minutes for her to catch her breath, to settle down. All she could do was stare at the altar, at the lifelike Christ. She ignored the confessionals. Two stood empty on both sides. It wasn't time.

Just as Carmen was beginning to fully relax and try to figure out what to do next, where to go, the door opened behind her. She froze and forced herself not to turn around.

She began to pray silently. *May the hand of God protect me, the way of God lie before me, the shield of God defend me . . .* She repeated it over and over again as her fingers moved to her pocket, and she slipped the letter opener out of it as discretely as she could.

The door closed heavily, and someone stepped inside. They were not afraid of being seeing or heard.

There was no place to run.

She was trapped.

If she was going to die, she could think of no better place. The angels would find her here.

Carmen turned around slowly. She stopped when an image came into view, just in her periphery. It was not who she was expecting to see. It was not Felix Massey come to rape her. She took a deep breath and lowered her head. It was Eddie. He had come to rescue her. He was her shield and protector after all.

Carmen stood up and faced the boy, a happy, relieved look on her face—that disappeared as soon as she realized her mistake. It wasn't Eddie. It was Tió, and he was carrying the shotgun that he had used to kill the man at the market.

"I've been lookin' for you, Carmen," Tió said. "And now I've found you."

CHAPTER 15

"*If you name it, you own it,*" Sonny remembered his father saying. The elder Ranger Burton had been tall as a tree, and when Sonny was a boy and he looked up to him, he had sworn the man's open-crease Stetson rubbed against the bottom of the sun. No matter where he went, his father wore the white hat. It had been a permanent fixture on his head, even in death.

Sonny had worn a similar hat his entire career, but he'd put down the hat, and his Ranger revolver, for that matter, when he'd left the service. He knew his father would have been disappointed in him.

The truth was, his father's tallness was just perspective, a mirage of childhood memories. So was everything else Sonny remembered now, as a man of sixty-two looking back—except, of course, the disappointment in him held by his father. He was certain that it was real. Still, he strained to hear the Texas in his father's distant voice. It sounded more like his own than a dead man's. But the wisdom that echoed through the years was certain as it whispered in his ear. "If you name it, you own it," Sonny said out loud, just to see if he was right.

He wasn't sure, but Pete Jorgenson had told him just as much, and Sonny knew the minute he'd put the dog in the truck that it belonged to him—as long as no one came along with a claim to him.

It was a quiet, uneventful drive back to the house. Sonny was glad of that. He'd had enough excitement for one day, if it could be called that.

Hours before, the house had felt like a prison. Now it was a haven, a utopia that teemed with roaches, filth, and the comfort of familiar shadows and noises. When he drove up the clay road, his whole body felt lighter, almost like he was flying, relieved of the tragedies that he had witnessed, been kin to. But no matter how hard he tried, he couldn't get the smell of blood out of his nose.

The dog had been a good passenger. It sat staring out the window, unconcerned about the movement of the truck, about being held captive inside a rolling metal box. It looked content, though troubled by the wrap on its leg, but that came in worried looks instead of chews, thankfully.

The groceries Bertie Turnell had put in the truck sat securely on the floorboard. As Sonny brought the truck to a stop, he wondered if there was anything in it fit for a dog to eat. Hunger was obvious in his own belly, and he assumed the mutt had struggled for a meal in the past few days just like he had. Its coat looked like a ratty black sheet thrown over a small, abandoned carcass.

Sonny eased out of the truck and walked to the other side of it, glancing to the house out of habit, making sure everything was in its place. It stood hollow and unattended, just like he had left it.

"Well, come on," he said, as he opened the truck door, holding it with his left hand, staring down at the dog—unsure of what to call it, how to command it to do what he wanted it to.

It had been a long time since he'd been in charge of an animal of any kind. His horse, a big paint gelding, had lived to be a ripe old age of thirty-three. Snag had laid down in the pasture out back one day when enough was enough and never got back up. There had been no need to call Pete out. Sonny knew what was happening. No animal doctor in the world could've saved Snag from the inevitable. Martha had made the arrangements to dispose of the horse the next day. A short time later, two men showed up and winched Snag into a trailer that was hitched to a beat up panel truck that looked like it had done service in the previous war. Sonny hadn't stayed around to see them leave. He went into the office and shuffled paper for the rest of the day, wondering if he licked the glue of an envelope at some point in the future, if he would be tasting the remains of Snag.

Sonny never bought another horse. Snag was the last animal on the place, save a few chickens that came and went to the pot or to a coyote's litter. Never seemed appropriate, or necessary, to name one of the dumb birds.

The dog sat in the passenger seat, looking as unsure of what to do as Sonny did with the command.

"Well, I don't suppose it would feel too good if you jumped down, now would it?" Sonny asked the dog.

The dog cocked its head and stared at Sonny down its long hound nose. Its eyes were a dark brown with sunflower corneas; a curious contrast to the coat that Pete had said was blue, not black. The dog looked black to Sonny.

He took a deep breath and slid his arm under the dog slowly. He didn't assume any trust had been achieved between the two of them, and he was right. It was too soon for that. When he started to lift up on the dog, it growled slightly. It wasn't a warning, though, it was the voice of discomfort, which Sonny fully understood. He could barely stand to be touched when his right arm had been bandaged, before it had been amputated. A wrong move by a less than studious nurse had sent pain shooting down to his toes, and a look of rage shot out of his eyes, even if she had been one of the kindest nurses who'd tended to him.

Sonny stood back for a moment to consider another way to get the dog out of the truck.

Impatience took over for the dog and it angled itself down from the seat slowly, side-stepping the groceries until both of its front legs were secure on the floorboard.

A half-smile lit across Sonny's face, and he reached down to help it, but he was too slow. By the time he got to the dog, it jumped out of the truck, letting out a slight yelp as its bandaged paw hit the ground.

Sonny stood back and watched as the dog hobbled to the front of the truck and stopped, surveying the house in front of it, like it was trying to get its bearings, figure out where it was. At least that's what Sonny thought. In reality, he corrected himself, the dog was probably looking for a place to take a piss. He half expected it to hoist its leg to the front of the truck and let loose—but it didn't.

The sun had settled behind them both, hovering just above the horizon, casting a perfect golden light on everything that lay west, in its path. There was no breeze, and the air was hot. The humidity had wrung out of the air almost as soon as the storm had passed, leaving it dry, normal for this time of the year. From where Sonny stood, all the world looked right, like it was supposed to. He might not have known that if he would have stayed at the house, never gone to the market in the first place, or if he'd put the .45 to his temple. If that had been the case, he'd be dead. The world black as the dog's coat, and it would still be out foraging on four good legs.

"I'll be darned," Sonny said to the dog, "You really are blue."

The light soaked into the dog's dirty, mangy coat, and at its root, at the depth of the fur, it glowed blue from the inside out in the golden light. Not a sky blue but a dark blue, like the call of evening just settling over the trees at the end of a perfect day.

The dog looked back at Sonny but didn't move.

"Well, I think that settles it. I'll call you Blue, if you don't mind?"

The dog turned back and stared at the house.

Sonny assumed the dog didn't care one way or the other after that. It would take some time to see if the name stuck, if the dog came when he called it out.

Satisfied, he reached into the truck, grabbed his .45, stuffed it in his back waistband again, then looked at the grocery box.

The first thing he went after was a can of the Van Camp's. He tucked the beans under his arm and looked again. Somehow, Bertie had managed to wrap up a slab of bacon and had sent it on home with him. Must have been from a private keep, since the market didn't offer fresh-cut meat. Sonny grabbed the bacon and made his way to the house. He'd have to divide up the rest. The days of lugging in boxes were over for him.

"Come on, Blue, let's go," he said, as he passed by the dog.

The dog had typical hound dog ears that flopped to the side, but the tops of them perked up when Sonny said, "Let's go."

Blue limped after Sunny, then swerved off to the right, stopped about ten feet from the root cellar door, and peed on the biggest rock he could find.

Martha would have never tolerated a dog in the house, but Sonny didn't think much of her concerns these days. Martha was dead, and, left to his own devices, Blue couldn't have fended off a coyote if he'd wanted to, not in the shape he was in. It would have worried Sonny to no end to tie Blue up and leave him unattended for the night. He knew himself well enough to know that rest would come to him hard, and he'd be up looking out the window every five minutes, checking on the dog's welfare. One night inside wasn't going to hurt a thing.

Once inside the house, Sonny piled up some blankets on the floor at the end of the counter, just under the water pump. "There you go, boy," Sonny said, pointing at the impromptu bed.

Blue just looked at Sonny and stood as still as a statue.

"All right, suit yourself," Sonny said. He pumped some water into a small pan, set it on the floor for the dog, and went out to the truck to retrieve more of the groceries. A bag of rice, more Van Camp's, and a loaf of bread.

When he returned to the kitchen, the water pan was empty, and Blue was standing in front of it, water dripping from his flues to the floor, with an expectant look in his eyes.

"I guess you might be thirsty and hungry after the day you've had." Sonny filled up the pan again, then set about making himself—and the dog—a meal.

He fried a few thick strips of bacon for himself and heated up a can of the beans, then cooked a bit of rice for the dog. Sonny topped the rice with a cracked egg, shell and all, drizzled it with half the bacon grease, saving some in the crock that sat next to the stove, and crumbled up some bacon on the mess of food. He'd seen a fox rob a rattlesnake nest once, and the fox had eaten the eggs shell and all. Sonny figured it would be good for the dog's bones.

When Sonny put the plate on the floor, Blue wagged his tail for the first time since he and Sonny had met.

Sonny stood back and allowed Blue to get to the food. He felt guilty feeding decent food to a dog, especially when there were so many people in the world struggling from one meal to the next, but Sonny felt responsible, sad for the dog. It needed some strength to help it heal. It was the best reason he could come to, and it would have to do. Besides, he wasn't going to go around telling folks how well he'd fed a stray dog. They'd think he'd lost his mind right along with his arm.

They both went after their meals like the starving animals they were, though Sonny stopped and looked up from his food from time to time, taking a moment of enjoyment, and watching the dog eat.

Blue wasn't a slob. Nothing hit the floor, and by the time he was done eating, there wasn't a scrap of egg, bacon, or rice left. The plate was licked clean.

After he finished his own meal, Sonny put Blue out to relieve himself, then let him come back inside. Dusk had settled, and darkness would come soon.

"You can sleep in here tonight, you understand? But don't go getting used to it. Once you're healed, I'll find a place for you out back." At that moment, Sonny realized that he was, for all intents and purposes, talking aloud to himself. He didn't care. The dog had to know his voice. "Don't go taking advantage of my kindness, you understand?" he added.

Blue offered no clue as to whether he understood or not. He just remained standing, watching every move Sonny made.

Sonny made his way to the chair next to the radio in the parlor and sat down. Blue limped after him, keeping a decent distance.

The dog didn't seem bothered by much of anything, wasn't timid or skittish about going into other rooms or different places, and that encouraged Sonny about their future together. He wasn't sure he could keep a dog that was scared of everything that moved or was uncertain about his surroundings. Not that he planned on keeping Blue forever. Once he recovered from the day, he figured he'd run out to Vern Maxwell's place and see if Blue belonged there or if they knew where he did belong. It was the only clue to ownership he had. As it was, Sonny was just glad the dog seemed to be comfortable and wasn't making a nuisance of himself.

The radio remained off. Sonny thought about turning it on, but he was tired, had had enough bad news for one day the way it was. Just as he settled into the chair and got comfortable, just before he dozed off into the nether land of sleep, he felt Blue ease up next to his leg and lay down at his feet.

A loud knock woke Sonny up. At first he thought he was dreaming, lost somewhere in a land where he was whole. It was wishful thinking. The knock came again, louder, more insistent, forcing his eyes open.

Blue was still at Sonny's feet, a quiet sentry standing stiff, staring straight into the kitchen. The dog did not bark. Sonny wasn't sure what to make of that. Pete had said the Maxwell dogs were supposed to be good watchdogs. Maybe he was wrong about it being a Maxwell.

"*Señor* Burton, are you home?" a man's voice called out from beyond the door.

It sounded familiar.

"It is me, Aldo Hernandez. Are you all right?"

Sonny pushed himself up with his left hand and turned on the floor lamp that sat next to the chair. Light flooded into the room, hurting his eyes, causing him to squint.

It was dark outside, late into the night. The mantle clock said it was near midnight.

"I'll be right there," Sonny called out. Even though he recognized the voice, he grabbed up the .45, stuffed it into his back waistband so it would be out of sight, then made his way to the door, flipping on lights as he went. Blue followed at his heels, the limp noticeable as his nails skipped across the hardwood floors.

Sonny turned on the outside light and peered out the curtains that covered the window in the door. Martha had sewn them just before she died. They were starting to fade and get dry rot. "It's awful late," he said through the door.

"I'm sorry, *señor*, it is important that I speak to you. I fear my daughter is in serious trouble. I am certain that it was her that was driving the car for the Clever, Clever boys when they robbed the market today."

Sonny exhaled, dropped his head, unlocked the door, and opened it—but he didn't open it wide, just a crack, so he could talk to the man face to face. "You should go to the police, Aldo, there's nothing I can do to help you, especially if it was your daughter driving the car today."

The night air had cooled, and the sky was clear of clouds. A thumbnail moon hung midway in the sky, and silver pinpricks peppered the blackness for as far as the eye could see, offering a bit of diffused light behind Aldo. The porch light burned brightly in front of him, casting a hard light across his face. The porch light attracted flying insects almost immediately.

Aldo looked older than Sonny remembered him being when he had driven him home from the hospital, more hunched over, worry lines folded deeper into his face, like a flood of emotion had eroded his skin, cutting deep crevices on every inch of flesh it could find.

"I have been to the *alguacil*," Aldo said in Spanish. "He is of no help. If Carmen is with those *criminales*, then she is a villain, too. That is what he said. It is not true, *Señor* Burton. Carmen is a lot of things, but she is not a bad girl. She has a good heart. If she did anything wrong, they made her do it. I am sure of it. Just as I am sure that the sun rises in the east and sets in the west. Carmen is not a bad girl. She has just made bad choices. That is my fault and I know it. I will set things straight if I see her. I have to see her again."

"The sheriff is a good man," Sonny replied, speaking English. Blue stood behind him quietly, almost as if he wasn't there. "I can't get involved in this. Have you spoken to my son?"

Aldo shook his head. "I would rather have your help."

"I have no position, no authority. You must know that."

A large moth swooped toward the light and flitted across the front of Aldo's face. He swatted it away. "Please, *señor*. There is nowhere else for me to turn. I am afraid of what might happen to her if they go on a hunt. I beg of you, please. I do not want to bury my daughter." Aldo continued to speak in Spanish.

Sonny sighed. "All right, come in. But I don't think there's anything I can do to help you. I'm useless these days, if you haven't noticed."

"You know Frank Hamer, the Ranger who helped find Bonnie and Clyde. Maybe if you ask him, he will know where to look?"

Sonny opened the door to let Aldo inside. "I'm not a Ranger any more, Aldo. I don't know if that'll mean anything to Frank. He's a busy man these days, from what I hear."

"You will always be a Texas Ranger, *Señor* Burton. Everybody knows that but you," Aldo said, stepping inside the house, taking off his hat as he crossed the threshold. "They did not cut your courage out when they took your arm. There are still plenty of things you can do. You are still a man. You are still everything that you were before. Maybe more."

CHAPTER 16

The inside of the small church was warm, like someone had lit a coal furnace and opened the flue wide. It smelled like a library of books had gotten wet—musty, old, uninhabited. And the light was dimmer, like the sun had gotten eaten by a cloud outside.

Carmen gripped the letter opener tighter. She never thought she would die in a church. She hadn't really ever thought much about dying, until today. "I'll use this if I have to," she said. Her voice cracked, and she wasn't convinced of the threat herself.

"Put it down, Carmen," Tió said. He was standing at the lip of the font, holding the shotgun tightly but keeping the aim away from her. One of the double doors stood open behind him.

Where's a priest when you need one? Carmen thought. *It must be time for confession.* She drew in a deep breath and shook her head. Tió was scaring her. His left eye was swollen and bruised, there was a jagged scratch on the opposite side of his face, and he had a fresh tear in his shirt. It looked like he had run through a wall of thickets. "Where's Eddie, Tió?"

"Out lookin' for you. Same as me."

"You're lying, I can tell."

"You don't know anything."

"You killed that man."

"I don't know if he's dead or not."

"You shot him. You said he was dead."

"He was hurtin' Eddie. You would've shot him, too."

"Maybe." Carmen's arm was getting tired. The vigil candles flickered from the breeze pushing in the open door, the light glinting off the

115

letter opener. It still smelled inside the church, even with new air. She didn't know how to escape. There had to be another way out, behind Jesus. The nave was small and there was no attached rectory like the bigger churches in town.

"Put it down," Tió said again.

In the shadows it was almost impossible to tell Tió from Eddie—until he talked, then there was no question it *was* Tió, that it was the damaged twin standing before her.

The only thing she had other than the letter opener was being a girl, just like with that *cerdo* at the motel. She could close her eyes and pretend Tió was Eddie, let him touch her. But not here. She had to get out of the church.

Carmen lowered the weapon, let her arm fall gently to her side. "Okay," she said, softening the edges of her tone. She looked Tió in the eyes and held his gaze. His eyes were different than Eddie's. Hard, impenetrable, a dark fortress with secrets buried in the dungeon. It was hard to tell what he was thinking, whether it would be possible to distract him with the offer she was about to make him. All she wanted to do was stay alive. Dying scared her.

She let go of the letter opener. It bounced on the terra cotta tile floor, metal against hard-fired red clay. The sound echoed into the rafters. A pigeon fluttered, announcing its existence, alerting Carmen that there were other creatures like her, seeking refuge in the Sisters of Mercy church.

The bird drew Tió's attention away from Carmen for a brief second. If she had planned on stabbing him and running out, this was her chance. But it passed as quickly as it came. He looked back at her with his black swollen eye.

"Did Eddie hurt you?" Carmen asked, summoning what bravery she had left by stepping forward.

Tió responded by stepping backward. He had never shown any interest in her touch; he just watched her every move from a distance. Carmen assumed that he was like all the other boys, but now she was not so sure.

"Don't matter. Eddie's lookin' for you, too."

Carmen walked slowly toward Tió. She could see all of him, even in the dull, flickering light. It was his eyes and his fingers, specifically his fingers on the gun, that interested her. "I won't hurt you, Tió. I promise."

He backed up against the wall. It was sweating as much as he was. "You have to go," Tió said.

His male smell rushed up inside Carmen's nose. Tió smelled sweeter. Even though he was a threat, up close his features were softer than Eddie's. His nose was gentler, not so much a conquistador's but a servant boy's from some fable; lost in the woods outrunning an army of trolls. His eyes, too, now that she could see them clearly, were not so vacant. Tió was afraid.

"I won't hurt you," she said softly, without any intention of arousing him. He looked like an injured bird in need of tending to. It was questionable whether he would fly again, or . . . if he had ever known the pleasure of it in the first place.

Tió turned his head away. "I don't like you."

"I know," Carmen said. It was a hush, a whisper. She raised her hand to the side of his face, reached toward his bruise with her index finger.

Tió drew back slowly as his eyes grew wide. If his head could have melted into the hard adobe wall, it would have.

His skin was warm and without thinking about anything any further, Carmen allowed her instincts to take over. She angled her face upward and brushed her lips across Tió's cheek. He swallowed hard.

"That's enough."

The voice came from behind them, and it startled Carmen. She stepped back and turned around quickly. She knew the voice. It was Eddie.

Like normal, Tió sat in the backseat and Carmen sat in the passenger seat, pushed up against the door. The Ford had a bench seat in the front and there was plenty of room for Eddie and Carmen to be comfortable. It was a different car, a newer one, but she didn't ask any questions. If it was stolen, she didn't want to know.

Eddie usually liked for her to sit as close to him as she could, his hand on her leg. Sometimes, he would slide his hand under her dress and rub her in her private place, causing her to breathe hard, get wet, and be embarrassed because of Tió sitting in the backseat, usually looking out the window—or acting like he was. Eddie always flashed a grin to his brother in the rearview mirror. But not today. Eddie and Carmen sat as far from each other as they could.

"We have to get out of here," Eddie said.

Carmen stared out the passenger window, into the darkness. Night had fallen, and there were very few houses that sat on the road they traveled. Distant lights flickered like lightning bugs. She could never catch them when she was a girl and had chased after them. "I want to go home," she said.

Eddie shook his head. His face was illuminated by the soft glow of the dashboard lights. "You can't. If anybody knows you were with us, they'll come looking for you there."

"How would they know?" Carmen asked.

Tió rustled in the seat behind her.

"He used my name," Eddie said. "It won't take them long to figure out it was us."

Carmen flinched but continued to stare out the window. She had always thought she could go home if she really wanted to. "Where are you going?"

"Oklahoma. At least to the other side of the state line. We'll have to lay low for a little while. But we have to make a stop first."

They were way past Wellington and Memphis. Carmen knew they were heading north, but she had no clue where they were. "I don't want to go."

Eddie turned to her. "We're not going back. I can't risk it. Not for a minute. You're with us, Carmen; that's just the way it is. I'm not letting you out of my sight. Not ever again. Do you understand?"

Tears started to well up in her eyes, but she fought them back. They would just make Eddie madder than he already was. She tried to swallow the fear and the sadness, make it go away anyway she could. She started counting the stars in the sky.

Eddie pressed on the accelerator and the engine roared, almost like it had been sleeping the whole time and had just come to life. They sped down the vacant road, and Carmen restrained herself from looking over at the speedometer. If they crashed, she hoped she would die fast. Get it over with. *Por favor, Dios, que sera rapidó.* Please, God, make it fast.

Up ahead, there were lights on the horizon, and, in a few blinks of the eye, they were upon a row of buildings. Another county line that offered roadhouses and a place for gas. Eddie slowed the car and turned into the first parking lot he came to.

He stopped the car in the shadow of the building, dug into his back pocket, and tossed a handkerchief at Carmen. "Put it on."

Carmen let the piece of red cloth fall into her lap. "Why?"

Eddie ignored the question and looked over the seat at Tió. "You stay here," he ordered, then turned back to Carmen. "We're gonna need some money, Carmen. I had to leave all that gin behind because of you. Now, you're gonna be my Bonnie Parker."

Carmen felt like she was trapped in a deep well. Her fingers were gripped tight on the door handle, but she knew she wouldn't get far if she made a run for it. It was hard telling what Eddie would do to her if he caught her.

"Give her your gun, Tió," Eddie said, tying the bandana across his face. "And honk the horn if you see somebody coming."

JUNE 28, 1934

The crows were accustomed to road traffic, were glad of it actually. They could perch on a telephone line for hours staring down at it, waiting for a mouse, raccoon, possum, or any other slow-footed animal to meet its fate darting from one side of the hard surface to the other. The crows would caw and flutter about, celebrating the ease of the hunt. It took no energy, just a leisurely amount of patience. Skill was needed in timing after the kill had been made—a crow would have to fly away from its feast frequently, depending on the traffic, or risk meeting the same fate as its meal had.

The larger the kill, the more of them joined in on the feast, brought in by an unmistakable, echoing announcement that could be heard for miles around. Flocks were usually greeted with explosions from humans, who would appear out of nowhere, pointing long guns at them, with flashes of fire and death erupting from the ends of them.

Guns made no sense to crows, but they understood the concept of tools. In difficult times, they would drop a nut or a turtle in the right place on the road and wait until one of the machines crunched it open. Then rush in to feed. The humans didn't know they were being used by crows, and that suited the birds just fine.

On this day, a lone crow sat at the top of a gangly and spiraling live oak, keeping watch over the road. The recent storm had slowed his feeding. He was in the middle of the town, among the buildings, but the perch was perfect to see everything that was going on below and to call from, when there was reason.

One building took up the whole block, sat right in the center of it, like it was an important nest. Other smaller buildings sat around it, with people coming and going throughout the day. At night, it was quiet, and starlings huddled in the few trees surrounding the big building, playing their safety in a numbers game. Coyotes and foxes trailed through the streets after the moon vanished, and raccoons raided trash cans, dining on the food left out for them by the humans, or so thought the coons.

This crow was accustomed to the ways and sounds of the town during the day. But it was surprised when a long bus lurched around the corner. Usually the machine appeared at the same time that it had the day before, and the day before that, just when the sun started to drop shadows on the red brick street from left to right. But it was early. The sun hung high in the sky, lighting the world, warding off any more rain or storms for the foreseeable future.

The crow liked the bus. People would straggle out of the big machine, never the same number, never a crowd either. Sometimes, they would drop shiny things, and the crow was just as interested in those as it was in food. Crows loved shiny things.

The machine stopped across the road, and a big puff of black smoke belched out the rear end of it. No one seemed to notice or care, but the crow jumped. It sounded like a big gun had gone off.

After it calmed down and reclaimed its spot, the crow waited and watched intently as people exited the machine. They reminded him of ants, only they were bigger, with fewer legs but far more dangerous. He was hoping one of the smaller of them would drop a cookie, a sweet. It liked sweets almost as much as it did shiny things.

One of the humans caught the crow's attention, drew it away from the possibility of food. It was a female, not that old, looking very unsure of herself, unsure of where she was. She looked lost, and she looked like she was carrying a child inside her; at the very start of showing a brood, yet to lay her eggs. Eggs for humans were different than they were for crows. The crow knew that much but cared very little beyond the thought.

The other people pushed past the girl as she stood and stared up and down the road. It concerned the crow that the girl was alone. If she were a crow, there would be wings everywhere, fussing over her and her coming brood. But humans were more solitary than the crows.

The machine pulled away, coughing out more black smoke, and all of the other humans had disappeared. All but the girl.

Finally, after pacing up and down in front of the spot where she had exited the bus, she sat down on a bench. Comfort did not ease her nervousness. The crow couldn't take his eyes off her, even though there was nothing shiny on her or about her.

It wasn't long until another machine, a smaller one, pulled up in front of the girl. The driver leaned over and rolled down the window. "You look lost," he said.

The crow had seen him before, followed him. Saw what he did. People trusted him right away, even though they shouldn't have. It was the one thing that perplexed the crow. Hawks were hawks and sparrows were sparrows. There was no question about what they were and how they hunted. But humans could be anything they wanted. At least, that's how it seemed to the crow.

"I'm waiting on someone," the girl said. She had a box with her, like a lot of the other humans. Sometimes trinkets fell from them. But the box was locked tight, and the crow had very little interest in it.

"Pete Jorgenson, I suspect," the male human said.

"Yes, how'd you know?" The girl relaxed, allowed a smile to flitter across her face. A bead of sweat ran down from her forehead to her chin. She wiped it unconsciously.

"I can take you out to his place."

"Oh, I wouldn't want to be any trouble. He'll be along shortly, I'm sure of it."

"The bus was early, and Pete might have his hands full."

"You know him?"

"Everybody in town knows Pete." The man pushed the door open and motioned for her to get inside.

"I don't want to be any trouble," the girl repeated.

"Oh, don't worry, you won't be any trouble at all. No trouble at all." He patted the seat next to him.

The girl nodded, stood, and leaned down to pick up the box—but by that time the man had jumped from his machine and was at her side.

"I'll get that," he said. "You go on, make yourself comfortable."

The girl smiled. She seemed to like the man, just like the other girls had. "I've always heard there wasn't anything like Texas hospitality, and I guess it's true."

"All true, all true," the man said, with a broad smile on his face as he put the box in a compartment in the back of the machine and slammed the door closed.

The girl slid inside the car, smiling back at him, though she still looked like she was nervous. The man closed the door for her and almost skipped around to the other side of the machine.

The crow could take no more. It cawed out in a panic, like it was being mobbed by a gang of blue jays—but there wasn't a jay to be seen.

The alarm didn't stop the vehicle or alert the girl. It was too late. She was going to be dinner. She just didn't know it—yet. Just like she didn't know she was riding with a hawk, even though she thought he was a dove.

CHAPTER 17

The house was empty, with the exception of Blue, who had slept at the foot of the bed. Aldo had left in the darkness of night after convincing Sonny to help him. It was almost like the Mexican was a wraith, a memory buried in a dream. Not quite a nightmare. But not rooted in reality, either. The visit was nothing but faded images after Sonny woke to the new day. Images flickering in black and white like a newsreel, voices distant and hard to understand. But there'd been no question of what had happened. Sonny was going to talk to Frank Hamer, poke around and see if he could help bring Aldo's wayward daughter home.

He thought it was a fool's errand, that there was no chance of success, but he'd given the man his word. Besides, if it helped bring those Clever, Clever boys to justice, all the better. His word was his word. That much he remembered, as he rambled through the house in his boxer shorts and undershirt. He liked wearing undershirts. There was no empty sleeve left to bang at his side, reminding him of what was not there. He had the phantom pains for that. The doctor told him it would happen and it had. Shooting pains down his arm would wake him in the middle of the night. Or an itch came and went. Sonny ignored them as best as he could, other times he screamed out in frustration. There had been no one there to hear him until now.

Blue padded after him wherever he went, his bum leg stiff, tapping on the floor like a constant snare drum. It was a new sound in the house, one that brought comfort instead of concern. The bandage and splint had held through the night, and Sonny was glad of that.

Sonny made his way to the kitchen and turned too quickly after filling the coffee pot with water, readying it to boil. He nearly stepped on Blue. He wasn't accustomed to having something underfoot, on his heels, no matter where he went.

Blue didn't yelp, just skittered out of the way the best he could. Then looked up with his hound dog face expectantly. "I'm sorry," was all Sonny could offer.

There was no morning routine that involved the dog. Sonny supposed he'd have to figure that out. But not on this morning. He felt like he had a hangover from the day before. It was worse than an all-day drunk. Not that he would know what that felt like. It was just a thought. He'd never liked liquor all that much. The end of Prohibition hadn't affected him at all. But the events of yesterday had left him feeling more unbalanced than he'd felt in a long time.

"I suppose you don't like coffee?" Sonny said to Blue, when the dog didn't change its expression.

Sonny shook his head, then went about fixing his coffee. Once the dinged-up steel pot was on the stove, he turned on the radio. It was habit, part of *his* routine, more than anything. He welcomed outside voices in the house most mornings. It was one of the ways he knew he was still in the world.

The familiar announcer's voice droned on automatically, like the conversation had never ended. "The Brooklyn Dodgers fell to the Chicago Cubs yesterday, five to two in regulation play, at Wrigley field. It was another win for Lou Warnke, putting him at ten and five for the season. That wraps up sports for yesterday, June 26. Coming up in the news, FDR signed the Federal Credit Union Act in an effort to promote savings and the offer of credit. But first, a message from our sponsor, Sudsy, a P and G product that stays so fresh . . ."

A quick-paced song began just as the water began to boil. Sonny was tempted to turn the radio off. He quit listening as soon as the sports ended and the topic of politics came up. Baseball was a respectable distraction. Just once he'd have liked to have gone to a professional game at a big field like Wrigley, but he figured that wasn't going to happen now. Such things were for big city folks anyway—Brooklyn, Chicago, Boston, all places that held little draw for him, and little imagination, as far as that went. Sonny liked the openness of North Texas, of the Panhandle. Most of the time, you could see things coming long before they arrived. A fella could be ready for a storm long before it hit and get things put up out of harm's way. Most times. He didn't see the storm coming yesterday. Didn't see it at all.

He sighed and stared out the window over the sink. The day was going to be just like most days in the summer, the sun a bright blow-torch hanging in the sky, scorching everything in sight. The world was brown, dull, and flat, and it was most likely going to stay that way for a good while to come.

Sonny turned back to the mess in the kitchen and thought about what the radio announcer had said before the commercials started to air. The president wanted people to save money and borrow money. It made no sense to him, but he had little interest in the workings of Washington these days—or tried not to. Folks had to have money to save and money to buy on credit, and there weren't many that could do either. They were lucky if they could pay cash for groceries they needed to get through the day. The Depression was a conspiracy between man and nature as far as Sonny was concerned, dust storms caused by bad farming techniques, weather patterns, government policy, and the age-old greed of man. There was not one person to blame, but there were days when the need was there to lash out at someone for the mess. It would be helpful to be angry at one person—but the world's problems were more than that. All the blame in the world wouldn't change things, fill the bellies that went to bed hungry at night. Sonny knew that to be true, but it didn't help.

He lowered his head at the thought. He was one of the fortunate ones. But the sadness that suddenly flowed through him was more about the memory of yesterday, about the murder of Tom Turnell, than it was about those suffering without a bank account, a roof over their head, or a chicken in their pot. Tom was dead after doing his best to defend the store, and Sonny, as far as that went, and there was no kind of legislation that could change what had happened.

All Sonny could do now was try and help Aldo find Carmen. If she was with the boys that had killed Tom, then he would have his chance to redeem himself, pay back something to Tom by putting Frank Hamer on their tail. It was the first thought he'd had when he'd opened his eyes this morning. In an odd way, Sonny was grateful to Aldo for coming to him. It had given him a way to get even with the world, a reason to put two feet on the floor.

He poured himself a steaming cup of coffee and walked out of the kitchen. Blue followed, and the radio played on, but Sonny wasn't paying attention to the words, to the music, to the advertisements. He had everything he needed to get through the day. Everything but his right arm.

He stared down at the table in the dining room, at the closed box that held the prosthetic, wondering if he had worn the prehensor, the hook, if things the day before would have turned out differently for Tom Turnell.

Sonny set his cup of coffee down next to the box, then opened it.

The prehensor was all leather straps, buckles, and polished metal rods, all connected to a shiny hook at the end. He stared at the thing for a moment. It was the longest he had ever looked at the man-made contraption that was supposed to take the place of his arm. *Impossible*, was the first word that ran through his mind. It was an impossible, ugly-looking thing, and there seemed no way to him that it could be useful, now, tomorrow, or yesterday. Until he touched the point of the hook, and then he realized that it could have been a weapon. Not as accurate as an index finger on a trigger, but a weapon nonetheless. The point of the hook was sharp and could be sharper.

The radio saved Sonny from traveling any farther down a path of regret. The announcer came back on, promising local news, an update on the County Line Murder. That's what they were they calling it. He left the prehensor in the box and made his way back to the kitchen.

"Tom Turnell, aged forty-nine, was killed at point-blank range," the announcer read on emotionlessly. "A lone customer was in the store and was unhurt. The police have two suspects in the heinous murder, Edberto and Eberto Renaldo, also known as Eddie Renaldo and Tió Renaldo. Both are about five feet, eight inches tall, with medium brown skin, brown eyes, and black hair. They are reported to be identical twins. The same in every feature. There are also reports of a female companion, who may have been driving the car they fled in. A second robbery was reported late last night at Drummond Station, just north of Shamrock, at the intersection of Route 66. No one was injured in this robbery, but it is believed to be the same trio, even though the perpetrators were a man and a woman. The description for the man is the same, and the woman was a head shorter, young in movements, but brown in skin and eyes. Her hair was black, and her face was obscured by a red bandana. If you see the described people, do not approach them. They are to be considered armed and dangerous. Call the police or Texas Rangers immediately."

The announcer started to say more, but Sonny turned off the radio. He'd heard all he needed to.

Aldo had never told Sonny where he lived. It wouldn't have been hard to figure out or find. Sonny spoke the language, had the confidence, even now, to go where most Anglos wouldn't dare. He wasn't afraid of Mexicans or repulsed by them. He had been raised by one. Maria Perza was the first woman he had ever loved. She might have been the only one that he'd truly loved. But now was not the time to consider such a thing. He needed to find Aldo, even though his gut told him that it was already too late to save Carmen.

It took Sonny an hour to bathe, shave, and dress. He was getting better at aiming the dowel rod, fashioned with a small curtain hook, and buttoning up his shirt. The fly on his pants was a little more difficult, but he could manage. Zippered pants would be easier, but there was nothing the matter with the pants he had except it took a little longer to get them on and off. He couldn't just throw out all of his pants and go buy new ones. Times weren't that easy. Luckily, he hadn't had any emergencies that required quickness of hand—yet.

Blue hobbled along after Sonny at every turn, and it wasn't until Sonny was halfway through his morning routine that he thought about putting the dog out to do its business and feeding him. Once outside, Blue rushed back to the door the best he could and waited on the stoop until Sonny let him back inside.

The last thing Sonny did before leaving was grab up the .45. If the events of yesterday had shown anything, it was that his decision to leave the house armed had been a good idea—even though his gun hadn't saved Tom Turnell's life.

"What am I going to do with you?" he asked Blue, as he stopped at the door. The dog looked up at him and wagged its tail slowly. Not happily, just a couple of twitches to respond back to Sonny in the only way it could.

"Well, I guess it wouldn't hurt if you came along." Sonny opened the door and walked out. Blue didn't need to be asked. He followed dutifully, limping past Sonny as he closed the door. The dog got halfway to the truck and stopped to look at Sonny, like it wasn't sure where to go next.

"Go on," Sonny said, pointing to the truck. "I'll lift you in." Blue didn't move. He waited for Sonny, then followed him to the driver's side door.

Sonny pulled up in front of the hospital and stopped the truck. Heat rushed in the open windows at the first opportunity, as soon as the breeze of motion had stopped. A matter of seconds turned the interior into an oven. It wasn't yet noon, but the sun blared so brightly that the clear sky held barely any color at all; it was white, baked, almost ready to burn completely away. But the discomfort—if it could be called that, since the heat was always present—didn't spur Sonny to jump out of the truck. He sat staring at the hospital, summoning up the courage to face the place again.

It was like walking across an old battlefield. No matter how high the grasses had grown, and how long it had been, there were memories to deal with, ghosts to face down, weaknesses to run away from, memories to dodge. He was certain his arm had been burned up in the hospital's furnace, a part of him cremated, ashes carried on the wind and deposited on the ground—perhaps right in front of him. Sonny wondered how he would feel if he walked on a part of his former self. The attachment had been severed. Nerves were dead and gone. Just like soldiers killed on the battlefield.

Blue had taken to the passenger's seat like his name was on it. The dog seemed comfortable in the moving vehicle and liked to stick his head out the window, allowing his ears to flap in the wind like streamers on a parade float. Now that they were stopped, Blue stared at Sonny, waiting to see what was next.

Sonny didn't pay attention to the dog. He was fixed on the hospital.

It was nothing more than a big old house, Victorian style, with a broad porch wrapped across the front and the north side. A few ceiling fans whirled overhead on the porch, and there was a line of chairs, for the recuperating and visitors alike, mostly empty, facing out to the street. Two old men sat in rocking chairs, staring out at Sonny. Patients passing time, escaping the antiseptic smells and gloom inside.

Rumor had it that the house was slated to be torn down and a new, more modern hospital erected in its place in the next year or two. But that's all it was, a rumor. The Depression had stopped progress in its tracks. At the rate folks were fleeing from North Texas and Oklahoma, there wouldn't be anyone left to build a big hospital, more less populate it with their illnesses.

Finally, the heat got to be too much. "You best stay here, Blue. I don't think Doc Meyers would take too kindly to a dog being in his midst. I hope you know what stay means, but I guess if you don't, you won't limp off too far, will you?"

Blue cocked his head as Sonny got out of the truck. He then leaned back in and said, "Stay. I kind of like having you around." Then he walked up to the porch, shifting the .45 back in place, hoping it wasn't too visible, but not caring too much if it was.

He nodded to the two old men on the porch, then stepped inside the hospital.

A nurse in a pure white uniform, wearing a matching white cap, sat at a desk just inside the foyer. What was once the parlor was a waiting room. It was full of empty chairs. The nurse looked up as a bell attached to the closure jingled.

It was Betty Maxwell. Nurse Betty. Sonny stopped just short of the desk, not surprised to see her. Glad of it, actually.

"Well, look here. It's Sonny Burton," she said, with a smile.

"Miss Maxwell," Sonny said, taking off his hat, a gray felt Stetson. Old habits died hard, though his days of wearing a white Stetson were over.

"Nurse Betty'll do. Told you that once already."

She looked a little different than the last time he had seen her, slimmer, her face thinner. And he noticed a stray gray hair sticking out of the side of her otherwise blonde hair.

"It's good to see you, ma'am," Sonny said, looking away from her gaze.

She looked down at the open book that sat in front of her. "You don't have an appointment today, Mr. Burton. What can I help you with?"

"I was hoping that Aldo Hernandez was here. I need to speak with him."

Nurse Betty shook her head. "No, he's not here. Word came in he had some family problems to tend to."

Sonny tried to stay focused on Nurse Betty. The door to the left of her led into the room where the doc operated, where they'd taken him to amputate his arm. "Well, I'm sorry to hear that. You wouldn't happen to know where he lives do you? I think I might be able to help him some."

Betty Maxwell looked Sonny up and down, from head to toe. "I see you're not wearing the prosthetic. Is there a problem with it?"

The question nearly knocked the wind out of Sonny's chest. "I was just hoping to speak with Aldo, ma'am, if it's all the same to you."

"If it doesn't fit, we can send it back and get another one."

Sonny shifted his weight and said nothing. Murmurs came from behind the operating room door. A ceiling fan whirled overhead, pushing around the bleach smell that permanently resided inside the hospital. Traffic went up and down the street outside, and Sonny's palms began to sweat.

"I'm sure it's difficult to adjust to," Nurse Betty continued. "Hard to get on and off. But you'll get used to it. Everybody does."

The last comment touched an angry nerve, and Sonny balled his first, almost unconsciously. "I haven't had it out of the box," he snapped. "I'm sorry to have wasted your time." He turned then and started for the door.

Betty Maxwell stood up quickly, like she'd sat on a tack and was propelled upward by a sudden explosion of discomfort and pain. "Wait, I'm sorry," she said. "That was thoughtless of me."

Sonny exhaled, released his grip on the doorknob, and stopped. He looked over his shoulder at her. "I can help Aldo."

"And I can help you." It was almost a whisper.

"Thank you, but I'm getting along just fine."

"Sure you are." She made her way around the desk and stopped in front of Sonny.

He didn't take his eyes off her. She was shapely, had legs cut of marble. A fair assessment, if a man was to do such things, was that Betty Maxwell was a fine looking woman. She was in her mid-to-late thirties, and, to his surprise, Sonny glanced down to see if she was wearing a wedding ring. She wasn't.

Without asking permission, Nurse Betty reached up and unbuttoned the top button of Sonny's shirt. It wasn't until that moment that he realized that he'd missed a button midway down. His shirt was buttoned lopsided. He flushed with embarrassment and frustration but said nothing as Betty unbuttoned his shirt down his chest, then gently and purposefully buttoned each one, without saying anything either.

Betty Maxwell smelled like all the good things of spring—wildflowers, a gentle breeze, and a partly cloudy sky offering the hope of rain for miles around. Sonny couldn't remember the last time he'd been this close to a woman. Past the embarrassment and frustration, he suddenly felt lonely and was surprised by it.

"There," Nurse Betty said, buttoning the last button, tapping it slightly.

Sonny stepped back. "Thank you."

"There's three houses right off 1847, the farm-to-market that goes north and south."

"I know it."

"Aldo lives in the last one before the curve. Most likely a couple of goats grazing out front."

"I appreciate it," Sonny said. He grabbed the doorknob again.

"I meant it," Betty Maxwell said. "I can help you with that prosthetic."

"I'll think about it."

"Well, I guess that's progress."

Sonny nodded and looked Nurse Betty in the eye. She'd meant what she said. He was sure of it. "You're Vern Maxwell's girl, aren't you?"

Betty returned the nod, as a curious look fell across her face. "I am."

"You haven't lost a dog lately have you?"

She shook her head. "Only dog we've got these days is Old Max, and he's too blind to wander off and be lost."

"I hit a dog the other day and Pete Jorgenson said he might be one from Vern's line."

"Well, I suppose there are still some of them around, at least with that blood in them. Is it all right? The dog you hit?"

"He's out in the truck, waiting on me." Sonny glanced out the side glass of the door, to see if Blue was still there. He was. Hadn't moved an inch. "I named him Blue. Pete said he wasn't as mottled as most of Vern's. He's almost blue in the light of day. That's what I named him, Blue. Seems smart. Always underfoot. Likes to be with me wherever I go."

"Well, that sure sounds like one of daddy's dogs. They were loyal as the Royal Guard. At least that's what daddy always said. I hope he'll be all right. I assume it's a he?"

"It is. A he, I mean. Pete seems to think he'll be all right. Might end up with a limp, but he should be able to do most things like he always did."

"Well, it sounds like you like him."

"I do."

"I'm glad of it. A man like you could use a dog like Blue."

CHAPTER 18

They were parked behind an abandoned barn. The front of the stolen car faced north, hidden behind a pile of rusted barrels, farm tools, and old mule harnesses. The car was a big Buick, long as a keel boat, as fast as a top-dollar race horse, and as pretty as a movie star. It was maroon, the color of blood on a dark night.

Eddie couldn't resist stealing the Buick as they fled Shamrock after the robbery. It had been sitting in front of a house that was bigger than a movie theater and just as fancy. Probably belonged to one of the owners of the gas wells outside of town. Eddie liked the hood ornament, a chrome likeness of Mercury with wings and a fine hat, leaning forward, into the wind, into the future; a fast runner going somewhere, getting there before anyone else—getting away.

Tió had told him it was Mercury as they sped away in the darkness. "It's a Roman god, Eddie."

"How do you know this stuff?" Eddie asked.

Tió shrugged and looked away. The mechanics of his mind were a mystery to everyone. Even him.

They'd driven out into the flat, treeless, nondescript wonder that was the Panhandle of Texas with the headlights off, navigating a country lane by the sliver of a moon that hung overhead. Carmen had sat in the passenger seat, quiet, too, as far away from Eddie as she could get. The smell of her own sweat disgusted her.

"Mercury is the patron god of luck, Eddie. And of travelers, trickery, and thieves. He will look out for us. You'll see," Tió said.

"I'll keep it, then," Eddie had answered, meaning Mercury and not the car. Once they'd found the barn, a place to hunker down for the night, Eddie had sent Tió out looking for another car to steal. One that wasn't so noticeable.

Eddie had climbed into the back once he was sure they were safe. He nearly had to beg Carmen to join him, but she relented, gave in without much of a fight.

Where else was she going to go?

The backseat was like a big soft couch that had been bolted into a red velvet cavern. The fabric looked like it had never been touched by human hands, and it had a fragrance of newness that was foreign to Carmen's nose. She had never seen anything so plush and expensive. It made her nervous to touch it, like she'd get in trouble if she scarred it in any way, left a mark on something, even by accident. She didn't like being a thief.

"Relax," Eddie said. There was no hint of gentleness in his voice. The word was a hard command, and there was no way Carmen was going to relax. Something in Eddie had changed since the shooting at Lancer's Market. He leaned in and tried to kiss her, pushed his hand up under her soiled dress like he had a right to. "I need you," he whispered. "I need you to be with me."

Carmen withdrew, pushed away his hand, and tried to melt into the velvet. "No."

Eddie recoiled like he'd been slapped. "No? What do you mean, no?"

"Not here. Tió will be back any second."

"He just left."

"I don't want to, Eddie. I want a bath and a place I feel safe. I don't want to sleep in this car, and I don't want to—make sex with you in this car."

"You can't go home. Not now. If that's what you're thinking."

"I know."

The windows were down. and the night air drifted in and out, the breeze steadier and cooler than it had been in the day but still tinged with warmth and the oppression of summer. There were sleeping cows close by, but they were mostly quiet. A gentle moo here and there drifted upward in the distance. Cows didn't smell as bad as pigs would have—at least there was luck in that. Only the insects buzzed about outside the Buick. They were a distant chorus of low-pitched notes, rising and falling like a high-pitched snore, hundreds of bows wafting over tight violin strings. The urgency of spring was over. They didn't want to make sex, either. It was too late in the season.

Eddie pushed up next to Carmen and pulled her in as close as he could. "I won't make you do anything else you don't want to." His voice had changed. It was the sweet Eddie, the one that she had followed out of her house and into the life she now had. He had charmed her before by flashing his little-boy eyes at her, allowing her to see that he wasn't always tough, always *machismo*. Sometimes when he touched her it was as if he were the softest, sweetest boy in the world. Those times bewitched her. His spell was solid, making her wonder if he were a male *bruja*.

A train cried out in the distance, its whistle echoing across the flat land like a sad moan. The cargo was mostly broken men, hobos, going to nowhere in particular, leaving behind the lives they knew, because they no longer existed. Newsreels showed cops crabbing into the railcars with clubs, cracking kneecaps, banging heads. Some men just stood there and took it.

"Promise?" Carmen looked into Eddie's face. His eyes were half open, dreamy brown orbs offering an invitation to believe every word he said was the pure truth, believe that every breath he took was just for her. She could've crawled right inside of him, then, fallen deep in love with him all over again, but she looked away just as he edged closer for a kiss.

Eddie pulled back. "You're still mad."

"I just want to go to sleep, Eddie."

"Fine. Have it your way," he said, pushing away from her. He opened the door, jumped out, and slammed it behind him. The red velvet vibrated under her thighs for a brief second, a tremor, a warning of things to come if she continued to push him away.

Carmen listened to him stalk away into the weeds, strike a match on something, and light a cigarette. She listened until she couldn't hear him anymore.

She hoped he would keep walking until he fell off the edge of the earth, but she knew that wouldn't happen. He wouldn't go that far. She could still feel his eyes on her, his angry face all aglow in the orange light of the cigarette. And she was certain that he would come back for her. Just as certain that the Roman god on the front of the car was no more real than the God in the church was. He hadn't protected her, rescued her, saved her from anything. Things were worse now than they were before.

A tear streamed down her cheek, and the darkness and aloneness that she felt left her feeling more lost than she'd ever been.

Tió came back in the middle of the night with a plain black Model A Ford that was more than a couple of years old. "It's all I could find, Eddie." The four-door sedan was missing a right front fender, and the paint was scratched up, like it had been run through a barbed wire fence day after day for the last year.

"It's a turtle, you idiot," Eddie said, with a slap to the side of Tió's head. The crack of the slap echoed on the cool night breeze like a gunshot.

"Ouch." Tió stepped back, rubbing his temple. "I did what you asked, Eddie. Why'd you hit me?"

"Why do you think?"

Carmen was half awake, laying in the backseat of the Buick, trying to ignore the conversation, trying to pretend it was part of a bad dream, even though she knew it wasn't. She could see the two of them standing opposite each other, silhouettes that looked like mirrors made of ash. Even in the daylight, it was hard to tell the two of them apart. Until they opened their mouths or you looked into their eyes.

"It's got a 201 CID 3.3 liter engine, and the 4 I4 transmission is a three-speed sliding gear manual. It goes real fast, Eddie. Drive it, you'll see."

"I don't know what the hell you just said, but it's not gonna be fast enough. Not up against those new Fords the coppers are driving these days. They'll run us down in a flat second if we come up against any of 'em."

"I can boost up the acceleration, tinker with the carburetor." Tió quit rubbing the side of his head and stared at the car he'd brought back like it was the worst piece of junk he'd ever seen.

"I don't know why you can't do one goddamn thing right."

"It's all I could find, Eddie. I didn't want to lead no one back here." Tió lowered his head. "I'm sorry, Eddie. I'll go get another one."

"No," Eddie said. "This one'll have to do for now."

It grew silent then. Even the insects slept, tried to sleep, or waited for another outburst. But none came. The silence remained. Eddie walked around the Model A silently, like he was about to buy a new horse.

A few minutes later, Eddie slid into the backseat of the Buick, eased behind Carmen, and pulled her to him. She stirred and faked a whimpering snore. Surprisingly, it was enough to ward Eddie off, enough to keep his pants buttoned.

They slipped away from the barn in the Model A just before the horizon started to turn gray with new light. A lone robin called out in a hoarse morning voice, announcing the coming day, hoping for a response. None came, at least that Carmen heard.

The clatter of the Model A's engine took over everything within earshot once Eddie punched down the accelerator, propelling them down the road, away from the barn, at a quick rate of speed. Tió was right; the Ford was fast, but not as fast as the Buick had been. That car floated down the road so fast that all the air jumped out of its way and made a happy wind from its tail.

A cloud of dust roiled behind them, and Mercury, the hood ornament from the Buick, tumbled to its side and fell into Carmen's lap.

She picked it and put it on the floor. It was heavier than she thought it would be.

"Be careful with that. It's our good luck charm."

Carmen was in the passenger seat next to the door, opposite Eddie. There was miles of room between them, and the attitude was cold, even though the windows were all rolled down, pushing around hot air. Tió sat in the back, like usual. He always acted like he wasn't listening, which meant that he was.

It didn't take long for morning light to eat away at the darkness of the night. Clear blue sky pushed up in front of them for as far as the eye could see, offering a typical day, if that were possible, and a clear view of the road ahead.

Sleep had been fitful for Carmen, and she was hungry and in need of a bath. They all were. "Can we stop and get some breakfast?" Carmen asked Eddie.

He shook his head. "Not until we're out of Texas. I don't want to chance it. There's a little greasy spoon in Madge, just the other side of the state line. We'll stop there." They were heading east on State Road 203. Madge was a few miles inside of Oklahoma.

The sun peaked over the horizon. The top curve of it looked big and red. Carmen had to look away. She knew why Eddie wanted out of Texas—it would be harder for the cops to arrest them—but she didn't want to leave all she knew behind.

"I don't like that place," Tió said. "They always cheat us, and their gravy's always runny."

"Nobody's gonna cheat us now, Tió. We got money and we got guns. Get somethin' else if you don't like the gravy."

"I just want breakfast," Carmen said. "I don't want anybody to get hurt."

Eddie cast Carmen a hard side glance, then looked up at the rear-view mirror. "Nobody's gonna get hurt. I promise." He pushed the accelerator to the floor. The Model A lurched forward with a cough, then roared ahead.

Carmen looked over her shoulder to see what had got Eddie's

attention. A black car was speeding toward them, catching up from behind, leaving a plume of dust that looked like it could have come from an explosion. Her heart began to race when she turned back to Eddie, who had a worried look on his face.

There were no flashing lights on the car, but most police cars in the Panhandle didn't have the new bubbles that some of the big-city police cars had. Some Texas Rangers still drove their own cars, so it was difficult to tell if the black car was a police car, a Ranger, or just someone in a big hurry.

"I don't want to go to jail, Eddie," Carmen said.

"Nobody's gonna go to jail." Eddie looked up at the rearview again, only this time he wasn't interested in the car. He looked at Tió. "Get the shotgun and be ready, all right?"

"They're getting closer, Eddie, and there's two cars, not one," Tió said. His voice was jittery.

In the blink of an eye, the first car was nearly on their bumper. A loud, hand-cranked siren suddenly whined loudly, joining the rushing wind inside the car. The sound made Carmen's eardrums hurt.

"Push 'em back, Tió." Eddie's eyes were glued to the road ahead. He was driving directly into the glare of the rising sun, into the promised land of Oklahoma.

The temptation to pray was strong for Carmen, a habit when things got bad. Only now the habit made her mad and sad at the same time.

"I don't want to kill no cop, Eddie," Tió pleaded. "They hang you for that."

"Shoot the fuckin' tire out, Tió." It was a scream matched by the siren and the wind.

Carmen pulled her knees up on the seat, hugged them, and looked out the back window. She could see the driver of the car waving wildly, ordering them to pull over. He wore a brown felt campaign hat. The kind the county police wore.

Tió grabbed up the shotgun, leaned the barrel out the window, aimed it downward, and pulled both triggers. In a move that belied his experience and knowledge of guns, he pulled the gun inside, popped the shells out, and pushed two more inside with such ease that the whole exercise looked like it only took a second, two at the most.

The pursuing car slowed, pulled back, as the second car caught up with it. They were driving bumper to bumper. One man was giving the other an order. Tió hadn't hit the tire—he'd hit the radiator. The first car was spewing steam, losing power, falling back into a brown and white cloud of nothingness.

"We're almost there," Eddie said.

The klaxon siren had died away. All Carmen could hear was her heart beating, matching the constant bang of the cylinders in the engine.

Eddie looked over at Carmen, pulled a pistol out of nowhere, and held the butt of it out to her. "Take it."

She shook her head. "I've never shot a gun, Eddie."

"All you have to do is pull the trigger."

"I don't want to."

"You have to. Just shoot it at the same time Tió shoots his. You don't have to hit anything. They need to know we're serious."

"I don't want to. You promised you wouldn't make me do anything I don't want to."

Eddie dropped the gun on the seat between them, then grabbed Carmen by the collar of her dress. "You want to die? Do you want to go to prison?"

Tears streamed down Carmen's cheeks. "I want to go home."

Tió held the shotgun in his lap. He'd quit paying attention to the road, and the car behind them. He was focused on Carmen. "I told you we didn't need no girls, Eddie."

Nobody had time to respond. The second car had caught up to them. It rammed them from behind. The collision broke Eddie's grasp on Carmen, and she nearly fell off the bench seat.

The Model A veered wildly to the right, and Eddie had to fight with all of his strength and skill to keep the car from spinning out. "Shoot, Carmen, shoot."

Tears and sweat rolled down her face as she watched Tió ready himself. He popped the barrel of his shotgun out the window, but didn't have time to pull the trigger.

The driver of the car pulled his trigger first. The eruption was deafening, as was the scream that came from Tió as he tumbled back into the seat. Glass shattered inside the Model A as the window exploded.

Carmen screamed and knew she had to react; it was the only way she was going to survive. She stuck the pistol out her window, closed her eyes, and pulled the trigger.

The explosion of gunpowder burned inside her nose and made her cough. When Carmen blinked open her eyes, she saw the windshield of the car behind them had shattered, and she watched in horror as the car spun out of control and slammed hard into a lone fence pole.

Eddie slapped the steering wheel and began to honk the horn. "Hello, Oklahoma. We're free! We're free!"

The fence post had been a state-line marker. Texas cops couldn't follow them into Oklahoma. They had no jurisdiction there. Clyde Barrow had made everyone aware of that.

"You all right back there, Tió?" Eddie asked as he continued to celebrate.

Carmen waited with baited breath for an answer to come from the backseat—but none did.

Somewhere in all of the mechanical madness, a rabbit had tried to dart across the road and got caught up in the melee. A wheel crushed its head and split open the animal's soft, warm belly.

Two crows had watched the whole thing from atop a power pole. They cawed in unison and descended down to the road to inspect the kill.

The first one pecked at the rabbit's eyes, while the second, the larger of the two, drove its black bill straight inside the furry creature, not stopping until it reached the kidneys. They were still warm and soft, easily pulled out of the body with a tug.

The larger crow lifted off into the air, holding its bounty as tight as it could. Others would come and try and take the meal away. The crow was sure of it. Just as sure as it was that there was more blood to follow. Today was going to be an easy day to make a living.

CHAPTER 19

Sonny turned left onto the farm-to-market road, just like Betty Maxwell had told him to. The first house was abandoned and looked like it had been that way for a while. Shredded curtains fluttered through open windows. The barren yard was littered with glass shards, shining in the sun like ice that would never melt, and not much else. Even weeds refused to grow there.

He looked past the first house to the second. It wasn't in much better shape than the first, except that there was glass in the windows and all of the curtains were drawn tight. It was a single story house in serious need of paint and maintenance, but that cost money and didn't look to be in the plans anytime soon. An old Model T truck sat behind the house, rusting away slowly. All of the good parts had been filched, probably traded, sold, or stolen. It was a metal skeleton, sinking into the ground one wheel at a time. There was no one to be seen, man or animal, around the house, and Sonny had to wonder whether it was occupied or not. It was hard to tell these days.

There was no question that the third house was occupied. Sonny slowed the truck, turned, and came to an easy stop. "This should be it," he said to Blue. The dog's ears perked up. He had sat next to the passenger door the whole trip, head out the window, licking at the wind, enjoying the ride.

Aldo's house sat off the road farther than the other two houses. It was two stories and had probably been built late in the last century, around the time Sonny had been born, by an optimistic farmer or land owner. An old barn sat out back, and what had once been a pasture was still fenced in. There were long brown blades of buffalo grass waving in the wind, long dead, but not brittle enough to break off. The pasture was empty, mostly hard dirt that couldn't feed anything, and the barn's roof was starting to collapse. A few relaxed pigeons bobbed about near a boulder-sized hole at the peak.

A tall oak tree stood next to the house. It was so close a squirrel could have skipped over to the roof and hidden an acorn under a shingle—if the tree was healthy enough to bear fruit—without any effort at all. The leaves were sparse, and the tree looked like a palsied fairy tale giant standing guard over a decaying fortress.

"Stay here," Sonny commanded Blue as he angled out of the truck. The dog didn't move. Nor did it take its eyes off Sonny. "I'm glad you're an old dog so I don't have to teach you everything." Of course, there was little worry that Blue would dart out of the truck. It was difficult for the dog to walk with the splinted leg, more less break into a run. Regardless, the mutt seemed content to just stay and wait.

Sonny headed down the narrow lane that led to the house, eyeing three goats carefully. They looked to be tied to long iron stakes driven deep into the ground, bound by a collar of the same metal. The collars looked uncomfortable, but goats had a mind of their own and liked to wander. A big buck stood guard atop a pile of rusted barrels, while the two does lay on the bare ground in the shadows. The goats noted Sonny's presence, but they weren't guard dogs and did nothing to announce his arrival. Still, he gave them a wide swath. He'd seen the power and cleverness of a goat before.

Along with the goats, there were two white chickens pecking about the dirt in front of the house's porch. There was surely a coop around somewhere, but Sonny didn't see one.

Instinctively, he looked up to the sky in search of a soaring chicken hawk, but didn't see one. The sky was as clear as a crystal blue lake that went on for miles and miles. Yesterday's rain was just a memory for Sonny and the dirt.

Aldo appeared as Sonny walked up to the house. The Mexican eased out the front door, dressed in his janitor's uniform, like he had been every other time Sonny had seen him, and stood in wait at the top of the rickety porch stairs.

"I went up to the hospital. Figured you'd be there," Sonny said, as he came to a stop at the freshly swept stoop.

Aldo's house was in no better repair than the one next to it, but it was tidier upon closer inspection.

"*Hola, Señor* Burton." Aldo spoke in Spanish, and there was a sparkle in his eyes, even though he looked tense in the shoulders.

"*Hola,*" Sonny replied, a little flustered.

A brief smiled flashed across Aldo's weathered face. "One of the *cabras* chewed its rope and wandered off. They are too valuable to not chase after."

"Those are some fine looking goats," Sonny said. He looked over his shoulder. It must have been a special goat to have had a rope lead when all of the others were bound with a metal chain. It was just a thought, and he decided it didn't matter. Just curious that one of them could have gotten away. Of course, an errant goat could explain the need for metal over rope.

"Tasty, too." Aldo smiled, flashing a mouth full of uneven teeth.

Sonny nodded. He'd had *birria*, a traditional goat dish served in tortillas more times than he could count when he had been a boy.

The air was already thick and hot, even under the sparse shade of the oak tree. Sonny looked over his shoulder again, this time to check on Blue. The dog was sitting in the truck where he'd been left.

Two old hitching posts stood off to the left of the porch steps, and the sight of them darkened Sonny's mood almost immediately. His days on horseback were most likely over, and that was a loss he had yet to accept. He was not sure he ever would.

The smell of something cooking caught Sonny's nose, and he suddenly felt like he was intruding. "I'm sorry. I guess I could have asked Nurse Betty for your phone number and called to warn you I was coming by. I just thought after your visit last night, you'd be interested in what I had to say." Sonny started to back up, intending to leave.

"No, no, stop, *por favor*. I have no phone, *señor*, so it would have done you no good. It is fine that you are here. I was hoping to see you today. Have you had *desayuno*?"

Sonny shrugged. "I had a bit of breakfast before I left the house. I was thinking maybe we could go into town to the Rangers' office and see if we can't get ahold of Frank Hamer, one way or another. It's the least I can do."

"I appreciate that, though I believe my fears have come true. I am certain Carmen is with the Clever, Clever boys, and they are on a fierce ride."

"You've heard about the robbery in Drummond Station, then?"

Aldo nodded. The weight of sadness and defeat forced his neck to bend forward, so he was staring directly at the ground. "I have failed her."

Sonny shifted his weight. "Do you really think she's with them on her own accord?"

Aldo didn't answer straight away. When he finally looked up, his eyes were glazed with tears yet to fall, and he nodded. "I do, *señor*. I do. And I am certain that it is my own fault. I have spoken some harsh words to Carmen that I wish I could take back, but that is impossible. She is angry with me and now that anger has put her in the company of men who do not wish her goodwill. They will destroy her. She was such a sweet, inno-cent *chica* when she was small." He shook his head in disappointment.

"I'm sorry, Aldo. We all say things to our children that we come to regret."

Aldo looked up, took a deep breath, and said, "I fear Carmen, she is already dead. You listen to the news. You saw firsthand the power of the newspapers, making Bonnie and Clyde heroes so all of the boys and girls want to be like them. You saw how that turned out. She will be dead or in prison for a long time. Either way, my dreams for her are gone now. Poof. Like that, she is *mala* forever."

"I can help," Sonny said. A goat bleated behind him, but he paid it no mind. "You can't give up hope. Maybe we can find a way to save her. I've been face-to-face with those boys, and I don't think they're so clever. If I'd been better prepared, if I had both of my . . ." He stopped before he said arms, gathered himself, then continued speaking. "If I'd had my wits about me, I could have taken them both. Maybe Tom would still be alive and your girl would be home where she belongs."

"One Ranger . . ."

"Something like that." He wanted to get even with the Clever, Clever boys one way or another. Justice needed to be served for the murder of Tom Turnell, even if he had no power to serve it.

Aldo exhaled and looked over his shoulder. "Would you like a cup of *café* before we go?"

"Yes, sure, I would like that."

It had been a long time since Sonny had been in a Mexican kitchen. The floor was covered with red terra cotta tiles, and the walls were painted yellow. At one time, the walls had been bright yellow, but they had faded over the years. Two windows let in a good amount of light, warming the room. A simple pan sat on the two-burner stove, with remnants of uneaten porridge in the bottom of it.

"Sit, *señor*, I'll be happy to get you a hot cup of *café*," Aldo said.

Sonny sat down at a long wood table, cut from an oak tree, with seats for eight. The chairs were all in various states of repair but functional. From what Sonny could see and hear, Aldo was the only person in the house. It was quiet beyond the kitchen, and there was no sign anyone else had been at the table.

There were smells and utensils in the kitchen that Sonny hadn't been exposed to in a long time. Once he'd married Martha, his diet had consisted mostly of German-influenced food—potatoes, boiled meat, cabbage in a variety of forms but mostly fermented into sauerkraut. It had taken him a long time to adjust to the digestion of such food. Of late, before the loss of his arm, Sonny had been trying to recall more of Maria Perza's recipes. Bad thing was, he'd never spent much time at her apron as she had gone about her duties of the day, cooking and providing for him and his father. He wished he'd paid closer attention now to what she had been doing and how she had been doing it.

Aldo set out to make coffee, and Sonny sat back and tried to relax.

The stub of his arm itched even though he had washed it roughly and covered it with a half a sock to keep the tender skin from rubbing on the inside of his shirt. Doc Meyers had told him it would take a couple of years to toughen up, sooner if he wore the prosthetic.

He noticed a clay *comal*, a flat plate for making tortillas, roasting and charring chilies, and toasting other vegetables and spices, sitting off to the side of the stove. Maria had used one nearly every day. It had come from Mexico with her *abuela*. It was a treasure. Aldo's looked nearly as old.

Other utensils jarred Sonny's memories, things he had forgotten about over the years, as he'd moved farther and farther away from the Spanish way of living and eating. A *molcajete*, a gray mortar and pestle made of basalt volcanic rock, sat on the counter, just under a strand of *poblano* chilies that dangled from the ceiling. The *molcajete* was used for grinding corn, garlic, rice, or whatever else was called for in a recipe.

But the thing that really caught Sonny's attention and warmed him the most was the *molinillo*. It was a short wood whisk with a bulb at the end, marked by several deep indentations. It was used to make the froth for hot chocolate. Just the thought of the warm drink made by Maria Perza's thick, knowledgeable, brown hands, brought a smile to Sonny's face. The happy feeling, though, was quickly followed by a flash of sadness. He had not mourned the woman properly. He knew that now.

"Is something the matter?" Aldo asked, as he began to grind coffee in the *molcajete*.

"I was admiring the *molinillo*."

Aldo cast a glance at the whisk. "Carmen always enjoyed a good cup of hot chocolate."

"With cinnamon and ground almonds?"

"*Si*, of course. I will make some for you one day, if you like?"

"I would enjoy that," Sonny said, as he settled back in the chair. He felt more comfortable than he had in a long time, and the memories that Aldo's kitchen had brought him were a welcome surprise.

Aldo chose to ride in the bed of the truck, leaving Blue in his spot next to the passenger door. The gesture disappointed Sonny and made him happy at the same time. He enjoyed talking with Aldo, but he appreciated the fact that the Mexican realized that Blue could cause himself more harm in the bed of the truck with all of the stops and starts between Aldo's house and downtown Wellington. Concern about the dog's welfare made Sonny forget about his itchy stub—some of the time, briefly, but enough to be a respite from his own pains and suffering. He probably should have brought a dog into his life long before he did.

The sun had burned all of the color out of the sky, and the way forward was unhindered by any weather at all. As Sonny drove into town, his thoughts wandered in and out about Frank Hamer, hoping the ex-Ranger could help them. Hamer was famous now that he'd put an end to Bonnie and Clyde, and he hoped the man would have some time to help them find Carmen, or at least put them on a trail that would eventually lead to the girl's safe return home. Sonny knew saving Carmen was a long shot. It might not be possible. Especially if the police got to her before they did. And there was nothing to say that Carmen was not culpable for her actions. She might very well deserve to be handed over to the police. He knew he would have to prepare Aldo for that possibility before it came.

The road was dry and left a plume of dust behind the truck. Sonny had adjusted to the mechanics of driving with one hand, but on occasion, he still missed a shift and ground the gears. Which is what happened as Sonny came to a crossroads, stopped, and started again. Blue looked at Sonny oddly, and Aldo yelled from the back, "Are you all right, *señor?*"

Sonny nodded, frustrated, looked down, shifted again, and made a smooth transition the second time around. "I'm all right," he yelled back and caught sight of Aldo settling back down into the bed.

When Sonny looked back up, he saw a car ahead of him, pulled off to the side of the road. There was no mistaking that it was the sheriff's car, Jonesy's new-model Ford. He pulled his foot off the accelerator and slowed as he approached the car.

Jonesy was standing out in a field, about thirty feet from the berm. He was looking down at something like he was puzzled. The engine drew his attention, and he looked away from whatever it was he was looking at and made his way back toward the road.

Sonny eased up alongside the Ford and stopped, leaving the engine running.

Jonesy was standing at the edge of the fender. A piece of short grass dangled out of the corner of his mouth. "I thought that was you, Sonny."

Sonny nodded, hung his left arm out the window, and looked out into the field but didn't see anything of note. "Something the matter, Jonesy? You look a little pale."

It was true. The sheriff's face was white as a fresh-bleached sheet.

Jonesy shook his head. "Hard to believe." He sighed heavily.

Aldo had edged from the middle of the bed to the driver's side and nodded at Jonesy, but the sheriff ignored him. He stared straight at Sonny and said, "There's another girl out there, Sonny. Murdered and dumped like she was trash. Dead as a doornail, but still fresh enough to bleed out like a stuck pig."

CHAPTER 20

Sonny stepped out of the truck with a heavy sense of dread racing up the back of his neck. It wasn't like he'd never seen a murder victim before. Hardly—not after nearly forty years as a Texas Ranger—but he'd been prepared for that when he was on duty. Not so much these days. If there was one thing he hadn't missed about being hale, hearty, and on the road with a badge on, it was being a witness to the unexplainably violent things human beings did to one another.

"You stay here, Blue," Sonny said, as he closed the door. The dog had limped across the seat and stood on all fours next to the steering wheel, wagging its tail, wanting to follow along. Sonny ignored the dog the best he could. "You best stay here, too, Aldo," he said.

The Mexican nodded, then looked at the floor of the truck bed without saying a word.

Sonny made his way to Jonesy, who still looked pale and haggard from the find. The sheriff said nothing once Sonny caught up to him, and they walked on, matching steps easily, toward the spot he'd been originally standing in.

The girl was apparent now that Sonny knew what he was looking at. A lump of earth-tone clothes that, in the right light, melded into the solitary landscape. Only her skin stood out, alabaster white, like broken bits of porcelain obscured by drought-hewn weeds and out-of-place fabrics.

"How'd you see her?" Sonny asked. He stopped before arriving at the destination of the death. He wasn't ready to see the details of it all just yet. Instead, he looked past the body like it was an old log and scanned the horizon.

An abandoned house sat off in the distance but not much else. Just fields as flat as the bottom of an iron. The brown ground met the blue sky with a few withering trees in between. Only the crossroad brought the promise of movement, of life, and even then the traffic was nonexistent. Not one car or truck had passed by since Sonny had stopped.

"Saw a glint in the sun," Jonesy said. He'd stopped short of Sonny without voicing any opposition. He didn't seem to be in any hurry to see the girl again, either. "She's still wearing a pendant on her neck. My eyes have been trained by the other finds. Always on the lookout, I suppose." There was a sadness in his voice that was unmistakable. It was a hard job being a sheriff, being a law man. Moments like this never made the newspaper in election years.

"Gold?" Sonny asked.

Jonesy shrugged. "Not sure. I felt her wrist for a pulse even though I knew there wasn't gonna be one. That's all I did. Then you pulled up."

Sonny changed his focus from the far surroundings to the ground in front of him. "Any footprints you could see?"

"Nope. But I haven't looked real close. Kind of seems like she just fell out of the sky."

"Or somebody carried her out here."

"Most likely." Jonesy spit out the soggy piece of grass he'd been chewing on. "I think it's the same person who done it," he said, staring straight at the girl now.

Sonny followed suit. The girl's body was about twenty feet ahead of them, but she was close enough for him to see the color of her hair. It looked like straw in late summer; not quite brown, and not quite yellow, still healthy. From a distance, her hair might have looked like a thick bush, dead from the beating of the sun's rays. But that wasn't the case.

"Why would you think that?" Sonny asked.

"Everything's pretty much the same, at first glance, anyways. Face pummeled, nearly beat to a pulp, and I ain't never seen her before. Looks like another Jane Doe to me. I bet there ain't a stitch of ID on her, just like there weren't on the others."

"The necklace might help."

"Might. But you know how that goes. Takes time to track stuff like that down. Time enough for a killer to get away."

"Or kill again."

"Exactly."

Sonny nodded. "I don't know much about what's going on with the other two. I haven't been paying close attention."

Jonesy looked up at Sonny and studied his face. The man's gaze made Sonny uncomfortable. "They started just after you got tangled up with Bonnie and Clyde. Strangers coming up dead every once in a while. Two of them found on the side of the road just like this one. We held some things back from the newspaper so folks wouldn't know everything. Only me and Hugh Beaverwood knows all the details."

"And you trust him?"

"I do. Said so earlier at Tom Turnell's store and I'll say it again. Hugh Beaverwood is soft. Man ain't got an ounce of meanness in him."

"You know him better than I do." Sonny drew in a breath, listened to the silence around him. The insects were holding their breaths, like they were afraid of being discovered or waiting for a curtain to fall, and there were no birds about to sing. It was like the earth was dead, too. When it came to murder, Sonny didn't trust anyone, not even the local coroner.

He felt eyes on him and looked up at the road. Blue and Aldo were staring at him with unwavering curiosity from the truck. "There's fair reason for unknown girls to come to this county from points beyond, Jonesy," he finally said.

Jonesy looked away from him, back to the girl. "I've been out to talk to Pete Jorgenson a couple of times if that's what you're sayin'."

"It is."

"He didn't know any of the girls. Claimed he'd never seen them before. Of course, all we had was a picture of them that Hugh took at the morgue, and I dare say they probably didn't look anything like they did when they was alive."

"You believed him? That he didn't know these girls?"

Jonesy nodded. "I do. I've knowed Pete Jorgenson all my life. His mother was the same, soft-hearted, you know. She took in wayward girls, too, and Pete's just carryin' on the family tradition. He says girls just show up out of nowhere at all times of the day and night. Hobos mark you on the curb so's they can find a soft touch, get a handout out at the back door. I suppose easy girls got the same kind of ways of telling one another where there's a place to go to solve their troubles. They stay 'til they're past their problems. Lidde does the midwifery and there's been a slew of babies taken to the county orphanage out of that house. There's a docket kept, a list of girls that've come through that house. Pete showed me. So, I've poked around plenty and haven't come up on anything that makes me distrust what Pete's tellin' me. But I sure do agree with you, Sonny; it's an odd coincidence that these girls appear out of nowhere. Pete's the most obvious link, but I'll be damned if I can't come up with a connection that turns on any of the lights except for the obvious." Jonesy bit his lip and looked back at the girl.

Sonny followed the sheriff's gaze and found himself at a loss for words. It was as if the two of them were trying to will away the body, make it disappear, or travel back in time, so they could see what had truly happened to the girl. Sonny wasn't sure he really wanted to know. He eased forward in silence and walked softly toward her, like he was on hallowed ground. Jonesy followed, sniffling like he was trying to ward off the onset of an allergy attack.

There might as well have been cotton stuffed in Sonny's ears. He couldn't hear a thing in the outside world once he got close enough to really see the girl.

Her face had lost its shape. Her cheek bones were shattered, caved in like they had been ramrodded with a club, making her eyes bulge out. Blood trailed out of the corner of each eye, bright red, fresh, still gooey if someone were to touch it. Sonny had no intention of doing that. The blood reminded Sonny of a statue he'd seen once of Mary, the Mother of God. It was in an old Mexican mission church, a long time ago. She'd stood under the crucifix staring up at her dying son with tears of blood. If he had been a religious man, then and now, he would've crossed himself, genuflected. But that was not the case. Instead, he kneeled and very gently took the girl's cold hand into his. "She's still limp," he said to Jonesy. "Rigor hasn't had time to stiffen her up."

"Fresh. I told you."

Sonny breathed in deep, exhaled, then laid the girl's hand back down as gently as he'd picked it up. He gazed up and down her body, coming to a stop at the big red pool that had seeped out from underneath the low part of the girl's midsection. A shiver ran through him, and he looked away immediately, not stopping until he found Blue in the distance, staring back at him. "The others, they were like that?" he asked, breaking eye contact with the dog and finding the sheriff's eyes.

"We kept that out of the papers for a lot of reasons."

"They were all pregnant?"

Jonesy nodded. "If Pete was somehow involved in this, we didn't want him to run off. And if he wasn't, we didn't want folks paintin' a black hex on his mailbox and throwin' rocks through his windows. You know how things like that go. He's got more than a few folks that don't take kindly to the work he does anyways, and they've been pretty vocal about it. Says it reflects poorly on the town."

"And you agree?"

Jonesy shrugged. "None of my business, now is it, if there ain't no laws broke in the process?"

"I suppose you're right," Sonny said. "But he seems like the most obvious suspect."

"He does, but that don't make him a heartless, cold-blooded killer, now does it?"

"Innocent until proven guilty. I know the process."

"Pete don't seem nervous at all. Lidde, neither. She still drives into town and does her shoppin' like there's not a care in the world. I don't think that woman could fake her way out of a brown paper bag. Pete, neither, as far as that goes. I've had him down to the station more times than I can count, and he always claims innocence and has an alibi for his whereabouts. I can't arrest a man on a hunch. Simple as that."

"But the killer knows you're holding back information."

"Sure, but that don't seem to be stoppin' him, does it?"

Sonny exhaled and stood up. He wanted to run as far away from the girl as he could, but he knew he would never be able to forget her. "You said they were all pregnant. What happened to the unborn babies?"

Jonesy shrugged. "Beats me. No sign of anything. Just like this one. A pooch in the belly and cuts with a sharp knife in places cuts ain't supposed to be."

Sonny felt woozy, pale at the thought. "You don't suppose these girls wanted to get rid of the babies and something went wrong?"

"I asked Hugh the same question. He said he'd seen that before—a coat hanger, you know—but this was something different. There's intent, anger, no care at all for the girl. He claims he don't know of any places nearby that might do such a thing, and I think Pete would know that, too—and tell me. Seems to be against everything he stands for."

"It's a sad way to die," Sonny said.

"I'd say."

Silence settled between the two men again, and nature's sounds started to return around them. The leg saw of a cricket. A distant caw of a single crow. The breeze picked up, changing direction from the west to the southwest. It wouldn't be long before it was a full-out wind. There was a sound to that, too. Air sweeping across the flat land, rippling the cotton sleeves on Sonny's shirt, especially the one that was pinned to his side. It was starting to flap against him like a flag bound up on a pole.

Jonesy kicked the ground with the toe of his right boot. "You wouldn't mind running up to the closest house and giving Hugh a call for me, would you? I hate to leave her out here alone. We need to get on with the business of moving her and tryin' to find out what really happened. If that's possible."

Sonny nodded. "Sure," he said, then looked around.

"I think the nearest phone is over at the Maxwell place, about a half mile yonder. You know where it's at?"

"I do," Sonny said, "but I 'spect Betty is still at the hospital. I saw her there a little while ago, before I picked up Aldo."

"Her boy, Leo, ought to be there. You tell him the call's for me. He'll let you in."

Sonny had driven past the Maxwell place a thousand times in his life, but he'd never had a reason to stop there. He wasn't sure he wanted to now, but Jonesy really hadn't given him much of a choice. There was no other way of getting Hugh Beaverwood out to him, other than driving into town and tracking him down. That would take too long.

There was talk of the possibility of radio communication between police cars and base, that it was on the cusp of possibility and affordability, but as it was, such technology hadn't found its way to Collingsworth County. That technology would change everything when it came to law enforcement, at least as far as Sonny was concerned. It would give the police an advantage over the criminals of the world. And, after what he'd just seen, the police needed all of the advantages they could get their hands on.

The Maxwell place was simple, a single-story house, well-kept, set back off the road, with a wraparound porch and a single dormer window facing the road. That window was cranked open, but everything else looked buttoned up, like there was no one home. The front door was closed. As was the door on the barn behind the house. There was no livestock about, and Sonny had expected to see a dog or two, but there weren't any. Just a few empty cages to the east of the barn.

He parked the truck next to the house and looked over at Blue. "I hope somebody's home. You stay." He climbed out of the truck and stopped at the bed. "This should only take a minute, Aldo."

The Mexican nodded. They hadn't spoken since they'd left the spot where the body had been found. "Perhaps this is not a day to ask questions, *señor*; the *policía* seem to have their hands full."

Sonny studied Aldo's face for a long second. "You want me to take you home?"

"*Sí*, I think that would be a good idea. Maybe another day, and then we can find a way to speak with *Señor* Hamer."

"Carmen may not have another day."

"It is out of my hands, *señor*. I will have to live with whatever happens."

"You don't know anything about this, do you, Aldo?"

Aldo looked at Sonny curiously. "About the *niña*?"

"The girls? The murders?"

Aldo shook his head emphatically. "Absolutely not. I have seen many terrible things working in the hospital, but none so bad as what has happened to these *niñas*."

"All right, but if you hear of anything, you'll come to me or Sheriff Jones?"

"*Sí, absolutamente.*"

Sonny turned away from Aldo then and found himself looking at a boy who was staring at him. The boy was standing on the porch, on the top step, his arms crossed in front of his chest and his jaw set tight.

"You must be Leo?" Sonny said.

"Who the hell are you?" the boy answered, with a nod. He was more a young man than a boy, approaching sixteen or just past it, tall as a cornstalk, with a thin face void of whiskers. It didn't look as if any had ever grown there or that any would begin to sprout any time soon.

"Sonny Burton. Sheriff Jones sent me up to use your phone."

"Who says we got a phone?"

"The sheriff. Is your mother home, boy?"

"She's at work."

"What about your father?"

Leo scowled deeper, then squinted at Sonny. "He's not around."

"I beg your pardon, then."

"Ain't no skin off my back. What happened to your arm?"

Sonny glanced at the empty sleeve unconsciously, then looked back at Leo. "Had it amputated so the gangrene wouldn't spread and kill me."

"You're that Ranger that run up against Bonnie and Clyde, ain't you?"

"I am."

Leo stared at Sonny for a moment. He was wearing a thin white shirt that looked like it had come just out of a barrel of lye and brown canvas pants that were a little too short, the hem coming to a stop just above the ankles. He'd obviously had a growth spurt since they'd been bought or made. The wind blew his hair, blonde and thick like his mother's, and he had to wipe a long drape of bangs out of the way of his right eye to see clearly. It had been a long time since Sonny had come face-to-face with a teenager. It felt familiar. Jesse had been an angry boy, too.

"I suppose you can use the phone. Who you gonna call?" Leo asked.

"That's police business, son."

"If you say so."

"I do." Sonny stepped forward and climbed up the steps, but he had to stop. Leo was still blocking the way. Arms still crossed, feet planted apart solidly, like he was expecting a toll.

"That Mexican needs to stay in the truck," Leo said.

Sonny looked over his shoulder, then back at Leo. "He's not going anywhere."

"His kind ain't welcome here. Anything comes up missin', I'll be looking to him first."

"I'll only be a minute," Sonny said. There was a hard tone in his voice that was meant to urge Leo out of the way. It didn't work.

"That your dog?" Leo asked, with a push of his chin. He stared at the dog, breaking eye contact with Sonny.

Sonny shrugged. "I'm taking care of him, at the moment. You know him?"

"Kind of looks like one of my granddad's dogs."

"Pete Jorgenson said as much. Do you know him?"

"Jorgenson? No way. I stay away from that place."

"Why's that?"

"Hell, man, I'd rather associate with that Mexican than people like that."

Words bubbled up on Sonny's tongue, but he clamped his lips together as hard as he could until they passed by, unspoken. But he couldn't help himself. "Why's that?"

Leo glared at Sonny. "Phone's hanging on the wall, just inside the kitchen, mister. I wouldn't want you tellin' my mother I was inhospitable."

"What do you have against the Jorgensons?" Sonny insisted. He could smell the boy's sweat, and it wasn't pleasant. Even the wind couldn't carry away the smell of anger and discomfort.

"I said the phone's on the wall. Are you deaf?"

"All right, then. You don't know the dog, then?"

"Nope, ain't never seen it before in my life," Leo said, stepping aside, letting Sonny pass by. "We've been out of the dog business for a long time."

Sonny pushed by Leo, hesitated at the front door, then pulled it open and headed straight for the phone without looking back.

CHAPTER 21

Carmen crawled over the front seat as cautiously as she could. There were shards of glass everywhere. The shooting had stopped as soon as they had crossed into Oklahoma and the car that was chasing them had spun out in a cloud of dust and disappeared from sight. She had no idea what had happened to the car, or the driver, and at the moment she didn't care. Now was not the time to confront the possibility that she might have killed a man, become more than a thief.

"Are you okay?" she asked Tió. Her voice shook like a bird's wing flapping against the wind. She had no sense of anything around her. It felt like she had fallen into a deep hole.

Tió was crumpled on the floorboard, stuck between the front seat and the back, on his knees, facing down. His right shoulder was red with blood. The stain on his shirt grew like a thunderhead on a clear summer day. Carmen had never seen so much blood.

She repeated herself as she settled onto the seat, avoiding the glass the best she could. "Are you okay?" She restrained herself from touching him. He had never shown her anything but distaste. There had been no mistaking that her presence was not welcome—and she had felt the same way about him. More than once, Carmen had wished that Tió would disappear. But she didn't want him to die.

Tió didn't answer, but Carmen could see the rise and fall of his chest through his shirt. His breathing was slow, almost like a tremble.

"Tió! Don't you fuckin' die on me," Eddie yelled out from the driver's seat. He looked over his shoulder at Carmen questioningly.

She nodded, and mouthed, "He's breathing."

The Model A was shimmying, threatening to come apart at the

welds, as Eddie pushed it to the upper limit of its speed. Gravel bounced up underneath the car, banging the chassis like popcorn—or the shots from the famed Tommy gun.

"I lost the gun," Tió said weakly. His forehead was still glued to the floorboard. The words were muffled, overtaken by the sounds of the speeding car. "I lost the gun," he repeated, louder this time. He began to beat the floor with his fist. The cloud of blood on his shirt grew with each thrust of his arm.

Carmen reached out to touch the back of Tió's neck, cautious to not move any of the glass and cut herself—or him. He flinched at her touch but didn't pull away. If anything, he arched into it, happily surprised, desperate for comfort. "It'll be all right," Carmen said.

Wind pushed in through the shattered window. Tió looked up at Carmen. He had tears in his eyes, slobber coming out of the corner of his mouth. "How come I can never do nothin' right?"

At that moment, more than any other, she saw the little boy in him, the one who was always in the shadow of the braver, stronger, more handsome brother, trying to keep up, never able to prove himself. Tió was not weak, but tender. Her fear of him evaporated. Even though he'd just tried to kill a cop.

"Are you all right, *me'jo*?" Eddie demanded. He looked over the back of the seat again, and scowled at Carmen.

She recoiled from Tió and swallowed the words of tenderness that were on the tip of her tongue. There would be no time for comfort.

Tió nodded, then pulled himself up carefully from the floor. He looked at the wound on his shoulder. "I think it's a graze. Or went in and out. It really hurts, Eddie."

"You dropped the gun, you idiot." Eddie swung a closed fist wildly at Tió as he steered the Model A with his left hand. The car swerved, and the tires tried to grab the gravel.

The swing missed. Tió ducked, like he had anticipated Eddie's reaction and burrowed as far back into the corner of the seat as he could.

Eddie turned his attention back to the road. "It was the only shotgun we had."

"I'll get another one," Tió said. He pushed glass off the seat and onto the floor.

Carmen watched Eddie and remained silent. He was scanning the road ahead of him, then looking behind them. She followed suit. The road was empty. There was nobody following them. That was a relief.

"We need to get as far away from the state line as we can," Eddie said.

Tió glanced down at the blood on his sleeve. "I'm hungry," he said. His face was pale, and his eyes looked weak.

"We're not stopping in Madge. It's too close. You can forget that," Eddie replied.

Carmen leaned over to Tió. "Let me see. Can you take off your shirt?"

Tió stared at her, then nodded. He pulled his left arm out of the shirt first. He grimaced and groaned in pain as he did.

"Don't be a sissy-boy, Tió," Eddie said.

"Don't be mean, Eddie," Carmen snapped. She glared at him with daggers. She was losing her fear of him, too. "It's all right, Tió. Go ahead."

Tió had a sleeveless undershirt on underneath the work shirt that he'd been wearing since they'd first joined up. The right side of it was heavy with blood. The wound was worse than he'd let on.

"He needs a doctor, Eddie, or taken to a hospital," Carmen said, upon seeing the wound with the shirt off. It was gaped open like a filleted loin of meat, just hanging down. She felt queasy at the sight of the blood, of the raw and open muscle, but she held herself together. Tió hadn't taken his eyes off her. Her reaction seemed to matter to him.

"We can't take him to a hospital. They'll be looking for us there."

"They'll be looking for us everywhere. He needs stitches."

"We can't stop. Not yet," Eddie said. His tone had changed. "It's really that bad?"

Carmen nodded, but said nothing more.

Eddie tapped the steering wheel heavily, thinking. "All right, but we need to get a good ways from here. Damn it."

"Don't be mad, Eddie," Tió pleaded.

"Is Lugert too far away?" Carmen asked.

Eddie looked back at her. "Why?"

"My father took us to the river there once. It's at the base of Quartz Mountain. There are old hunting shacks scattered about in the hills. We stayed in one. It might be a place to hide, a place for Tió to get better."

Eddie nodded. "Good. You remember how to get there?"

"Yes."

The tenseness in Eddie's shoulders relaxed. "All right. Hang on, Tió. Maybe there's a doctor in that town. Wrap his arm tight with the shirt, Carmen. Try to get the bleeding stopped. Make a tourniquet. You know what I mean?"

"I don't know what to do, Eddie," Carmen said as her stomach rolled with nervousness. "I'm not a nurse. I'm just a girl."

"Well, figure it out. Just fuckin' figure it out!"

There was no town where Carmen thought one should be. Just a lake. Eddie pulled the Model A over to the side of the road and looked out at a wide view. "You're sure this is the place?" he asked Carmen. There was a short fuse on the tip of his tongue, but he had not started yelling—yet.

"Yes. I'm certain. Or, I thought I was." She saw the same thing Eddie did. A big lake with rising hills surrounding it and mountains off in the distance. There wasn't a building to be seen. Not one sign of a town of any kind.

"How long ago were you here?" Eddie asked.

"I was just a little girl, Eddie. Seven or eight years ago. I'm not sure."

Eddie pulled the car forward, inching along the road, if it could be called that. It was more like a dirt path that butted up to the shore of the lake.

Carmen took her attention away from Tió, who was sleeping. He'd balled himself up in the corner of the seat after she'd gotten the bleeding to slow. She followed the point of the car and saw a man up ahead, standing ankle-deep in the water with a fishing pole in his hand.

Eddie stopped the car, turned off the engine, and shouted to the fisherman. "Hey, mister, can you tell me how to get to Lugert?"

The man turned around. He was gaunt, haggard, looked like he hadn't had a bath in a month. "You're sittin' in it."

"Ain't no town that I see," Eddie said.

"Was. Town was right here. Tornado came through in '27, flattened all but one building. The rest of them was reduced to nothing but sticks. Feds came in after that and dammed up the North Fork of the Red River. Got us a lake now."

Eddie looked out over the lake, sighed, and tapped the steering wheel. The drumming sound was like fingers on a chalkboard to Carmen. She wanted to yell at him to stop, but her fear of him was returning. It was her idea to come to Lugert, and now there was nothing around. There'd be a price to pay for that. She was sure of it.

"Ain't no doctor around, then?" Eddie asked. He slid his fingers around the steering wheel and gripped it tightly.

The man craned his neck toward the car but didn't take a step toward it. He looked wary of them. "Somebody in there hurt?"

Eddie shook his head. "We're thinkin' of settling down around here. Might need a doctor on occasion."

"You should drive up to Vinson, then. But there ain't much there these days, either. Just a whole lot of dust and broken dreams, just like everywheres else in this godforsaken state. Seems like everybody's on the move lookin' for a rainbow. FDR keeps promisin' relief, but all I see is black clouds and empty stomachs."

Eddie fidgeted in the seat, glanced over his shoulder to Carmen, who was watching—and listening—intently. "Nobody's much around then?"

"Here? No. Just travelers, on occasion, like you."

"Will this road take me on to Vinson then? Up through that pass?"

The fisherman shook his head. "Road ends into the lake. You want to go to Vinson you'll have to go back a piece and turn left at the first house you come to. That road'll take you straight into town."

"How do I get over the mountain then?" Eddie asked.

"Only one way that I know of and that's to walk. It's hard country. Not much there but thicket and lonesome wind these days."

"There was a time when there was some huntin' shacks up that way," Eddie said.

"Still are, as far as I know. They could've been used as firewood. Hard to say. I ain't been up that way in a coon's age. My gout's been a actin' up on me, and my days on that mountain are pretty much at an end. All's I can do is look at it these days. That and take some fish out of this lake. But even they're skinny and few and far between. We don't get more rain soon, it'll be empty and dead, just like everything else 'round here."

Eddie nodded. "Thank you for your help, then." He started the car and pulled away with a wave.

The fisherman waved back and stared after the car.

Carmen watched the man disappear out the back window and turned around once she realized that Eddie wasn't going to turn around and go back to Vinson. He was heading for the end of the road.

There was a small series of foothills at the base of Quartz Mountain. All brown, with scrub trees poking about and some bushes low to the ground. Anything that was tender and green had been chewed off by squirrels or deer, struggling to make a living just like every other creature in the world. All that was left were bare branches. It didn't look like anything could survive there for long, not even them.

"I think this is a bad idea," Carmen said. "We don't know where the shacks are. You heard the man. It's hard country. Tió's not up to this."

"He can stay here and die then." Eddie got out of the car, walked to the front of it, and stared at the mountain. "You'll recognize the place when you get up there."

"I was just a kid, Eddie," Carmen yelled after him. She looked over to

Tió, who was wide awake now. The bleeding had stopped, and he looked paler than he had before. "I don't think I can change his mind," she said softly.

Tió stared at Carmen, then reached across his belly with his good hand and opened the door. "I'm not gonna die *here*." He reached over the seat and grabbed the hood ornament, Mercury, from the Buick they had stolen in Shamrock, eased out of the car, found his footing, and made his way toward Eddie, using the car to steady himself as he went.

Carmen shook her head and got out the car on the other side, being careful of the glass.

Eddie stared at Tió, then looked back at the mountain. "What is that?" he asked, staring at the hood ornament.

"Mercury, our good-luck charm."

"Leave it," Eddie said.

"It's good luck, Eddie."

"Put it back in the car. I'll need it later."

Tió glared at Eddie, muttered something under his breath, then did as he was told.

Eddie eyed Tió angrily. "We'll go up, find a place, then I'll come back down and go into town and get some supplies. How's the arm?"

Carmen joined them. "It needs sewed up and cleaned up so infection won't set in."

"What do you know?" Eddie snapped.

"I know more than you think." Carmen used the same tone.

"Stop. Stop it, both of you," Tió yelled. "Kiss and make up. The girl is here to stay, Eddie. She knows how to sew. How to do things we don't. Leave her be, Eddie. We need her."

Eddie started to say something to Tió but held back. He slammed his fist into his own leg, turned, and headed back to the trunk of the battered Model A. "We have two bottles of Dr. Pepper and half a loaf of bread. That'll have to do you until I get back." He hoisted the two bottled drinks and the bread out of the trunk, slammed the lid, and stalked off toward the foothills. His pistol was sticking out of the back of his pants, the barrel jammed downward.

Carmen hesitated and looked at Tió, who was already struggling to catch up. She had no choice but to follow after the boys. She was sure Eddie would've shot her if she'd made a run for it. Besides, where would she go?

CHAPTER 22

Sonny stopped the truck behind Jonesy's car. There was another car in front of the sheriff's. One Sonny recognized immediately. It was Jesse's car. A sigh slipped out of his mouth, and Blue whined at the same time. "What's the matter, fella?" Sonny's feet became heavy, like they had cinder blocks tied to them as he opened the door and swung them out of the truck.

The dog stood up, wagged its tail, and stared at Sonny expectantly.

"Be a lot easier if you could talk." Sonny looked away from Blue then, past the two cars, out into the open field. The sheriff and Jesse were standing next to each other, staring down at the girl's body. Somebody had covered her with a sheet or a blanket.

Things were as they should be—the sheriff and a Ranger talking between themselves—but it bothered Sonny. Bothered him more than he ever thought it would—because it wasn't him standing there. Wouldn't have mattered if it was Jesse or a stranger. He had lost his place through no fault of his own, and his whole body itched, like he had rolled in a patch of prickly pear.

"You probably have to pee, don't you, boy? I'm sorry. I haven't owned a dog for a long time." Sonny motioned for Blue, and the dog obliged. He stopped at the edge of the seat, and looked at the ground like it was a tall cliff. Before the hound could think about jumping, injuring his bad leg even more, Sonny reached in with his left hand and scooped up Blue the best he could, easing him to the ground. The dog immediately hobbled off, found the closest dead bush, and raised his leg.

"Figured as much," Sonny said. He waited for Blue to finish, then walked out toward the sheriff and Jesse. "Come on, you can go with me this time. If the tall one growls at you, you can growl back. Won't hurt my feelings none at all."

Blue looked up at Sonny, then followed after him, a happy sway to his tail.

Aldo stayed behind. He sat in the bed of the truck with his head bent forward over his knees, like he was praying. The two men hadn't spoken since they'd left the Maxwell's place. There was nothing more to be said. Aldo wanted to wait another day.

Sonny slowed as he passed by Jesse's car, a year-old Plymouth with baby moon hubcaps. The hubcap on the rear wheel was missing. The windshield looked a rock had been thrown against it, or, upon closer inspection, it looked like Jesse had been shot at. It was a spider web shatter with a distinct pattern. A perfect hole at the very center of the cracks was unmistakable. The point of impact was about three inches off the mark.

He looked behind him. Blue was on his heels. The dog's loyal presence forced a smile to flash across his face. But it disappeared quickly when he looked up and made eye contact with Jesse.

It only took Sonny a second or two to reach the two men. "I hope that was a rock that came up and cracked your front glass," Sonny said.

Like every other Ranger, Jesse was not obligated to wear a uniform. He had on a pair of well-worn dungarees, a brown, short-sleeved work shirt, and a white Stetson on his head. There was a Cinco badge pinned over his heart, and a holster on his hip with the standard of the organization, a .38-caliber Smith & Wesson revolver, sticking out of it.

"Not a rock," Jesse said. "What are you doin' here?"

"Out for a stroll with my dog," Sonny answered smartly.

"And a Mexican." Jesse flipped his chin into the air, toward the truck.

"Didn't know that it was a crime to give a man a ride."

Jonesy remained quiet. He looked at the ground, just past the sheet-covered body, and pretended like he wasn't listening—but he was. Layton Jones didn't miss a thing. Not in front of him or two hundred yards away, on any day of the week.

Sonny stared at Jesse as the wind whipped up around and in

between them. The ferocity of the gusts had steadied out into a constant blow. Rocks kept the sheet from blowing away, cornered and put in the middle for stability. Only the girl's feet stuck outside of it. One foot had a shoe on it, sensible and scuffed, while the other was bare. The sole of her foot looked tender, stark white against the dirt and dead grass, like she had never gone barefoot a day in her short life.

Sonny shuddered and wondered where the other shoe was, then turned his back to the wind to keep from being pelted by the bits of sand. It was a lesson that he'd learned from horses and cows a long time ago. "Hugh Beaverwood's on his way, Jonesy."

Jonesy looked up and nodded. "That'd be fine. I figure by the time he gets here, she'll be stiff as a board."

Jesse glared at the sheriff, then looked away once he got the same look back.

"If it wasn't a rock, what was it?" Sonny asked Jesse.

"Just ran into a little trouble out by the state line, that's all. Can't really say more than that."

Jonesy wandered away and started to look for a new piece of grass to chew on. It hadn't been that long ago that the sheriff was fond of chewing on a cigar. Sonny couldn't remember a time when one of the half-smoked stogies wasn't angled out of the corner of the sheriff's mouth. But one day it wasn't there, and it hadn't been since. When Sonny had asked about it, Jonesy had said, "Had to give that up." And that was it. No more commentary other than that. The tone of the answer shooed Sonny off quicker than being told he was trespassing on land that wasn't hospitable.

Sonny squared his shoulders. "Looks like a bullet hole to me."

"I'd say you ought to know one when you see one."

There was a temptation bouncing in Sonny's mind to reach out and twist Jesse's ear as hard he could and cause the boy to crumble to the ground on his knees. Jesse'd always been a willful child and that was fine, Sonny could respect a man with an independent streak. But what he couldn't respect—and wouldn't tolerate—was a man who showed him no respect. Especially when that man was his one and only son.

The small pellets of sand and dirt that were being shotgunned out of the southwest finally convinced Jesse to turn his back to the wind so he was standing shoulder-to-shoulder next to Sonny.

"You going to tell me what your problem is?" Sonny eyed Jonesy, who was still within earshot.

Jesse looked into Sonny's eyes harshly and didn't say a word.

There were times when Sonny had completely forgotten what Martha looked like, how she had acted, how angry she was all her life, until he had the opportunity to look into Jesse's eyes. The boy had inherited a lot from his mother. More than her eyes, which Sonny found to be a damn shame.

"You've done what the sheriff asked you to," Jesse finally said.

Sonny didn't flinch. He grunted, "Um," and didn't blink, either. "You haven't seen Frank Hamer around these parts, have you?"

"Why would I?"

"Just asking."

"Last I heard he was in Dallas."

"Word of him comes around the office, you'll let me know?"

"Yes, sir, I'll be sure to do that."

Sonny studied Jesse's face and tense body language and knew right away that his son was lying to him. "All right, Blue, I suppose it's best to get you and Aldo home. There's a storm brewing, and I don't want to be caught out in it. Jonesy," he called out, "You know where I'll be if you need anything."

"Sure enough, Sonny. Thanks for callin' Hugh for me," the sheriff said, as he bit down on a short stalk of perfect grass, a dead seed head dangling at the end of it.

"You, too, as far as that goes," Sonny said to Jesse. "I'll be around if you need anything."

Jesse offered a grunt back, mocking Sonny's earlier response without offering anything else.

A sudden thrust of energy pulsed through Sonny's body, and, for a brief instant, he felt the tips of his right fingers. It was like he was clenching his hand into a fist but when he looked down there was nothing there. Phantom pains. Only now, he really wished his fist was there. Or at least, the back of his hand.

Instead of offering anything more, Sonny ignored the impulse and walked away. He headed directly into the wind, his head down so his eyes were safe from blowing dust. Blue followed along the best he could.

It didn't take long to reach the truck. "Get in the cab," he said to Aldo. "You don't need to be out in this crap any more than I do."

"*Sí.*" Aldo eased himself out of the bed of the truck and into the truck like he had been instructed. A person would have had to have been deaf to mistake the tone or offer an argument to Sonny of any kind.

The wind whistled and cut along the ground with a growing intensity. Sonny's pant legs flapped harder, and the sand and dust felt like insects stinging through the fabric. He opened the door, scooped up Blue, and helped him up to the seat as best he could. The dog hustled over and sat down next to Aldo without an ounce of hesitation.

"Let's get out of here," Sonny said, as he watched the sheet fly off the dead girl's body. It blew up into the air like it was a soul departing for heaven.

"This dust storm looks like it's going to get a lot worse before it gets any better," Sonny said, as he went through the motions of starting the truck.

They drove without speaking for a long time. Blue sat comfortably between Sonny and Aldo, staring straight ahead, turning his attention to them every once in a while, but mostly just content to be in the truck.

The wind had not subsided, nor had the dust storm that it had created. It was like driving inside a brown cloud. Sonny had his headlights on and could only see about a car length ahead of him. He drove very slowly.

"Your son looks like he is uncomfortable," Aldo finally said.

Sonny shrugged without taking his eyes off of the road. "He's just trying to do his job. I understand. Me and Jonesy go back a long way. Jesse is just trying to stake out his claim. I get it. My time is past."

"It is something we must all face."

Sonny looked over to Aldo. "Regret's a heavy burden to bear."

"*Sí*, it is. I've made plenty of mistakes with my *niños*." Aldo looked away, out the window, then back quickly. "I have a confession to make, *señor*."

Sonny focused his eyes on the road ahead even more than he already was. They were getting close to Aldo's house, and the Mexican knew that. There was no letup in the storm. The dust swirled around them like it was plentiful, here to stay, never leaving. There had been storms like this before, but not as long in duration. They were getting worse, lasting longer in Texas and Oklahoma, offering more misery than was necessary. He had nothing to offer Aldo. No forgiveness, no absolution, nothing. He had no power of any kind. If that was not evident to Aldo by now, then there was nothing Sonny could do to enlighten him.

"I have done some bad things in my life, *señor*. Things against the law. Man's law *and* God's law."

"We have all made mistakes, Aldo."

"No mistakes. I ran gin for a lot of years."

"But those days are over."

"*Sí*, they are. But there will be other ways to sell under the law. The Clever, Clever boys, they are runners, too. They will have to find another way to make a living now that Prohibition has ended. They are desperate."

"They've taken to armed robbery. The change has already come."

"A very bad thing. Especially since my Carmen is with them."

"If she is there because she wants to be, Aldo, it will be a problem. You know that, right?" Sonny looked as far ahead as he could and downshifted the truck. He had to nudge Blue out of the way. He turned slowly onto Aldo's road and missed the shift. The gears ground loudly, and the gearshift jumped away from Sonny's left hand. "Goddamn, it," he said, wrestling the handle back in place, while trying to orchestrate his foot on the clutch at the same time. It took a second or two, but the gear slipped into place, and the truck lurched forward to the third house on the road.

"I know, *señor*. It is because of me that Carmen is with them. She stole my recipe for gin and gave it to Eddie, the oldest. *Ella está enamorada*. She is in love. It was her way of showing me up, of getting even."

"And you forbade her from seeing him?"

Aldo nodded yes and held his head down. "I wanted to keep her away from him. I was very much like him when I was young. She could do better, my Carmen. Better than that *pandillero* and his half-wit brother."

"I don't have a good feeling about this, Aldo; I have to be honest." Sonny brought the truck to a stop in front of Aldo's and let the engine idle.

Just as suddenly as the dust storm appeared, it ended. The wall of brown dirt passed by, and the wind died down, like it had run out of energy, just plain tuckered itself out. There was dirt and sand everywhere—on the floorboard, in the seat, on the dash, even in Blue's ears. But the sight of everything had come back, and the sun shone again, beating down on the earth with the same ferocity as before the storm had come on. The sun looked like it was determined to burn up everything it touched—or crash into it, if it could break away from whatever was holding it back.

"I'll call around and see if I can't get ahold of Frank Hamer. My son's not going to be any help with that at all."

"You do not think it is too late?"

Sonny exhaled deeply, then looked at the floor between his knees. "Those boys have to pay for killing Tom Turnell, and your daughter might have punishment coming for her part in it, you know that. But there's a family out there, Aldo, that doesn't know their girl is dead. All they know, I imagine, is that she is missing, and they want nothing more than for her to return. When she does return, it will be in a pine box, and that will have to be enough. They will consider their regrets, just like you have," he paused, then looked directly into Aldo's eyes. "We'll bring your *chica* back home, Aldo. One way or another, we'll bring her back home. I promise you."

CHAPTER 23

The crows had gathered at the base of a dead sycamore tree. The wind-torn bark looked like white skin that had been violently peeled off the tree in spots, exposing dark brown bits of bone. Like a lot of things in this part of the world, the tree had most likely died of thirst, brought on by the unrelenting drought. The crows, on the other hand, weren't worried about finding drinking water. There was plenty of moisture to be found inside the carcass of a fresh kill or something that had died from natural causes. The birds were mostly worried about surviving the dust storm. Stray grains to the eye could permanently blind them, making it more difficult to hunt, to see danger coming their way. One-eyed crows never lived long.

As it was, they were all huddled together, a black apron of death around the trunk of the sycamore, waiting for the wind to subside. They were afraid. Being on the ground with their heads tucked down made them vulnerable. Coyotes, or a man, could sneak up on them unseen, unheard in the thrusts and groans of the wind. It would be too late for them to take to the air. They felt safe in the sky, nervous on the ground.

Fear was as unnatural to the crows as a white feather among all the black. They would do anything to get rid of it. Even kill one of their own, if it came right down to it, if it meant surviving another day. But for now, they had no choice. No choice but to wait and hope nothing came along with the intention of killing them, eating them, using their feathers to down a nest.

Carmen raced up the trail, hoping that her childhood memory was accurate, that there was a hunter's shack just over the rise. She couldn't be sure, since most of the markers she thought she could rely on were gone, but the high, rounded rock at the top of the trail looked vaguely familiar.

A quick glance over her shoulder didn't make Carmen feel any better. Eddie was struggling to keep Tió upright, on two feet. He was nearly dragging him. Tió looked pale and weak. The blood on his shirt was unmistakable in the bright overhead sun. Vultures circled to the west, inching closer with every rotation, and there had been no one on the trail. They hadn't seen anyone since they'd left the fisherman. It was like they were on the moon, or lost in the desert—alone, without any idea of what was waiting for them around the next bend. They could hope for water, but it would most likely be a mirage.

Carmen pushed on up the hill, carrying the two bottles of Dr. Pepper and what was left of the bread. She was out of breath, sweating, tired, and scared, but she had no choice but to continue to climb. Time had faded away. She wore no watch, had no idea how long it had been since they'd abandoned the beat up Model A at the base of Quartz Mountain. It seemed like hours, but it had probably been less than that.

She finally crested the rise of the hill, and, much to her dismay and disappointment, there was no shack. There was nothing but more hills to climb. A few trees along the path, mostly dead or dying. Nothing green. Nothing to offer her any hope—not even a shadow.

Fear shimmered through her entire body from head to toe. Carmen was afraid Eddie would be mad, would scream at her, hit her. She had seen what he had done to Tió when he'd crossed him. Tió's eye was still black from the hit he took from Eddie after they'd robbed Lancer's Market. Still, she stood and waited for the brothers to catch up to her.

Eddie was sweating as heavily as Carmen was, maybe more. His shirt was soaked all the way through, like he had stood out in the rain without an umbrella. His hair was wet and his bronze skin shiny, like it had been waxed. Any resemblance to an Aztec god had left him long before he stepped out from behind the steering wheel of the car. Tió looked pretty much the same, except that he was frail, looked like he was ready to surrender to the fight to stand, to breathe, to live.

"I can't go on. We have bad luck because we left Mercury behind," Tió said. He bent over and grabbed his knees. Every time his lungs heaved, more blood eased out of the wound on his arm.

"It's just a little farther, *me'jo*. That thing wouldn't have made a difference." Eddie looked over to Carmen questioningly. She lifted her shoulders slightly, offering a negative shrug, hoping Tió didn't see it—but he did.

"Maybe we are on the wrong trail," Carmen offered. "It's been a long time, and mostly it was my father in the lead."

"He was on a run, wasn't he?" Eddie asked.

"I didn't know it then, but probably. What do we know of vacations? People like us. We were barely lucky enough to have enough masa to make tortillas."

Eddie held onto Tió so he didn't teeter and fall forward. "We can only hope this is still a gin-running route. That there's still a trail through here. It's isolated enough. I see why Aldo was drawn to this place, used it. You have to figure out where we are, Carmen." There was concern in Eddie's voice. He was afraid for Tió. But there was a hard edge to it, too. The hint of the threat she feared.

Carmen closed her eyes and tried to remember the path to the shack. There was a round rock in her memory, a rock like the one at the top of the rise. "I am pretty sure it was here. But maybe it is farther up. I had little legs then, and I was afraid. I had never been to a place like this. But who knows? There was once a town below. Now there is a lake. Things change, Eddie."

Eddie stared at Carmen unfazed, then said, "Go on, go up and see what you can find. But leave me one of them bottles of Dr. Pepper."

Carmen handed him a bottle and the bread and thought about offering an encouraging word to Tió but said nothing. She marched away with her unopened bottle, looking straight ahead, hoping upon hope that she was right. Time was not on Tió's side. He couldn't last on the trail much longer, she was sure of it.

It didn't take long for Eddie and Tió to be out of sight. If she had ever thought of making a run for it, this was her chance. Except there was nowhere to run. Sooner or later, Eddie would find her. She knew that as certainly as she knew that the sun was nothing but a big, round rock, set afire for eternity. Eddie would be as persistent as the sun. He would rise tomorrow and the next day to find her if she ran. So she pushed on, her quest certain.

About ten minutes into her trek, she came to another rise and a similar rock formation. To her relief, a small shack sat in the shadow of a high outcropping. It was smaller than she remembered, but it was there—a place for them to hide, to recover, to figure out where to go next.

Before heading back to Eddie, Carmen made her way to the shack. The door was closed, and the windows were covered with dust and grime. It didn't look like anyone had been around for a long time. There weren't even any coon tracks to be seen around the door or under the windows. Which meant there was no food to be found, inside or out. A determined raccoon would have had no problem making its way into the shack if it really wanted to get in, if there was a smell of the smallest bite to eat. But then she thought, *maybe there's not coons up this far. What do I know?*

Carmen pushed her way inside the door, easing it open as carefully as she could. She held the remaining bottle of Dr. Pepper by the neck, like it was a miniature club.

There was no sign of life inside the shack, except maybe a startled spider. The window sills were lined with dead moths. Two bunk beds, an old Franklin stove with the exhaust pipe dangling from the wall, and a water pump next to a sink that looked like it had rusted up pretty much took up all of the room inside the small, one-room shack. A tall locker stood between the bunks. It looked like it was once used for storing clothes and guns. The shack smelled musty and a little pungent, like maybe something had crawled into it and died. But there was no sign of a skeleton or pelt to be seen. Carmen left the door open when she left to find Eddie and tell him the good news.

It didn't take long for her to the find the twins. They were right where she had left them. Tió looked a little stronger. The empty bottle of Dr. Pepper sat at his feet, and Eddie had refashioned the tourniquet on his arm.

Tió wobbled when he stood up, and Eddie was there to catch him if he fell, but he didn't. Tió walked the rest of the way to the shack on his own.

Once inside the shack, Eddie made sure that Tió was settled on the bottom bunk and stood back. "I'll be back as soon as I can."

Carmen put down the Dr. Pepper, and Eddie handed her the bread and a bottle opener. It was all they had. "I'll get things straightened up. I hope that water pump works," she said.

"I won't be gone long. Into Vinson and back. It'll be after dark." Eddie dug into his back, and pulled out the handgun. He offered it to Carmen. "Take this. You might need it."

She shook her head. "I don't want that. I never want to touch another gun in my life, Eddie."

Eddie stared at her hard and pushed the gun at her, pressed it barrel down against her chest. "You'll need to protect yourself."

"What if I killed that cop, Eddie? I'll go to jail. They'll electrocute me."

"You don't know if it hit him or not. Don't matter. Nobody'll find us. I promise."

"I don't like your promises, Eddie." Carmen couldn't restrain herself any longer. Tears rolled down her cheeks. Thick tears that had had time to build up and break the dam of her eyelids and fall to the dusty floor in a splatter.

Eddie pushed the gun harder into Carmen's chest, and she stumbled backward, coming to a stop at the threshold of the door. "Take it," he demanded.

Before Eddie could say another word, Tió jumped up from the bunk and put himself in between them. "Give me the gun, Eddie," he said. "Ain't the girl's job to look out for me. I'll shoot if I have to. You know that."

Eddie exhaled, let his own cheeks collapse from their tenseness, then pushed the gun at Tió. "Shoot to kill."

Tió took the gun and glanced over at Carmen. "Ain't nobody gonna need to get shot, 'cause ain't no one that knows where we are. But if they come lookin', I'll do what I have to. Ain't none of us goin' to jail."

Eddie nodded. "All right, then." He pushed by Carmen and walked out the door.

She said nothing, just looked at the floor and tried to pretend like she didn't exist as Eddie stalked by her.

There was little of use in the locker. A couple of old rags, a half-burned candle, an empty crate that had once held ammunition, and a bunch of cobwebs that disintegrated upon being touched. But luck had smiled on them with a few things that could be of use, most notably, outside of an old coat, was a box of safety matches and another small box that held a couple of spools of thread and a sewing needle.

Carmen smiled at the discovery. "I can try and sew up your arm, Tió."

He was sitting on the bed, stiff, alert at every noise. He had eaten nearly all of the bread. "Eddie can do it when he gets back."

"I won't hurt you." Carmen stood up and walked over to him carrying the thread in one hand and the matches in the other.

Tió stared at her for a long moment. "It stopped bleeding."

"Let me see."

He shook his head.

Carmen stared back at him, disappointed. "I won't hurt you," she repeated.

Tió sighed and looked away, out the door. "I know." It was nearly a whisper. He looked over at his shoulder, then slowly started to untie the tourniquet.

"I've never done this before, but I've sewed a lot of things. It'd probably be better if we had something to clean the wound with, but there's nothing."

"Dr. Pepper," Tió said.

"I guess it'll have to do," Carmen said. She found the bottle, then shook out a rag and beat it against her leg. Certain that it was as clean as it was going to get, she dabbed the syrupy drink onto it.

The skin on Tió's arm gaped open like someone had taken a very sharp knife and slit it open. But it wasn't a knife. It was a bullet. A bullet that had cut right across the muscle and kept on going. The wound was bloody and deep but not deep enough to show bone. Carmen was glad of that. She didn't know if sewing it up would help if that were the case.

She eased in and touched the wet rag to Tió's skin as gently as she could. "Does that hurt?"

He shook his head and looked away. "Go on."

"Okay." Carmen cleaned away what blood she could, then set a flame over the needle, sanitizing it as well as possible, then threaded it and pierced the first bit of skin, while holding it together with her other hand.

Tió flinched but said nothing. His jaw tightened, and Carmen could tell that he was biting his lip as hard as he could without puncturing it. "Should I stop?" she asked.

"Finish," Tió said. "Please."

Carmen went on with the sewing, piercing and looping as tight as she could. Her movement caused the wound to start bleeding all over again, and her hands were nearly as blood-covered as Tió's arm.

Finally, she drew in the last loop, pulled the thread in, and snipped it off. "Are you all right?"

Tió nodded. "Are you done?"

"For now. As long as it holds." Carmen touched the stitches as softly as she could, proud of her work.

She stood up, wiped her hands on her dress, and took a little swallow of the Dr. Pepper. There was only about half an inch left in the bottom.

Her stomach growled with hunger, and Tió must have heard it. He offered her what was left of the bread. "It's yours," he said.

Carmen took the bread, bit off a piece and walked to the door. She stood just inside it and stared out into the world. She wondered where

Eddie was, and, for the first time, hoped that he hadn't gotten himself in trouble. They needed him.

There were no clouds in the sky, and the wind had died away, vanished like it had worn itself out from blowing so hard. A coyote yipped in the distance, its lonely call soulful and frightening at the same time. Not only were they at risk from somebody finding them but from animals, too.

Carmen closed the door, bringing darkness inside the shack. The only light came in through the two windows.

"Leave it open," Tió said. "Just a little."

Carmen stopped, studied the look on his face, and said, "Are you afraid of the dark, Tió?"

He didn't answer. He pulled up his shirt sleeve, and lay down on the bed, his back to Carmen and to the door.

Sometime in the late afternoon, the door opened, rousing Carmen from her sleep. She looked over her shoulder and relaxed as soon as she saw a familiar silhouette standing just inside.

"Here," she whispered, "there's room for both of us."

He hesitated, then closed the door and made his way slowly to the bed. Carmen had her shift on and that was all. She scooted over to the wall, her back to him, and was glad for the presence in her bed.

He eased up next to her tepidly, fitting his body next to hers. They fit together like two puzzle pieces. That had always been the trouble with Eddie. He made her feel good, made her feel like she never had before. He always left her wanting him more.

"I was worried about you," she whispered. She couldn't help herself. His body felt good, pressing against her back. She rolled her hips slightly and pushed into him. His hot breath on her ear sent shimmers of electricity down her spine, not stopping until they found that special spot between her legs.

When he didn't respond, she pushed against him harder. He gasped, then ran his hand down her leg, kissed her on the base of her neck, then nuzzled into her.

Carmen could feel him getting hard, encouraging her not to stop moving. But she was cautious, kept her voice to herself even though it was difficult. She wanted to moan out loud when he ran his had up her leg and didn't stop at her thigh. He kept going and probed into her wetness with his finger, curious, gentle, but unrelenting. He knew just where to touch her.

She was vibrating now, lost in the feeling. Nothing that had happened in the last couple of days mattered. All that mattered was what was happening now. And that he continued to do what he was doing. "Don't stop."

Carmen reached around, and pulled up her shift, then felt his pants, rubbed the rock that was there, aching to escape. She easily undid each button, and with his help, freed him of all that had restrained him.

He found her wetness easily and slid into her but held back, then started to rock slowly, quietly. Time stopped ticking, the world stopped spinning, and when he finished and pulled out of her, Carmen smiled. She had known that it wasn't Eddie as soon as he had eased his finger into her. Eddie never touched her like that.

CHAPTER 24

All Sonny could taste was the sand in the back of his teeth. The promise to Aldo echoed in his mind, making the gritty flavor of Texas dirt even worse. He knew better than to make promises like that; *We'll bring your chica back home*. It was against every code he had abided by in his professional life. Every code, except the one he served now—the one that didn't exist. He was not beholden to any organization's rules. There was no state or local government laws to answer to. He was free to do and say what he wanted to. But that didn't matter. He had given the grieving man false hope, and, to Sonny's way of thinking, that was a crime within itself. He would have to apologize. It was as simple as that.

But the realization that he was held by no bounds felt like electricity running through his entire body. And the feeling stopped at his stump. There was no phantom pain, no wishes for a new arm that were impossible to fulfill.

Blue was sitting where he liked it best, next to the window so he could stick his head out of it. Aldo had disappeared back inside the house, and Sonny was left with the choice of going up to the door and making amends or going into town to see if he could find out where Frank Hamer was and how to get ahold of him—or going home and just leaving things be.

He wasn't going home, that was certain. And he wasn't going straight into town, even though he'd decided that talking to Hamer was a way to set things right with Aldo. But there was a stop he thought needed to make first, on the way.

With a confident combination of moves, Sonny mastered the

ballet of putting the truck into reverse. He eased it out into the lane, pointed the truck in the opposite direction of his house, and headed back toward Wellington.

Pete Jorgenson's house looked all buttoned up. Blinds drawn. Doors closed. No sign of a car or truck in the yard.

Sonny parked the truck in front of the porch and craned his neck to see if the one chicken that was there before was in the coop—and he couldn't tell. The nearest coop looked empty, giving Sonny a bad feeling and another reason for distaste in his mouth. *Was it possible that Pete and Lidde had packed up what they needed and run off?* It was a valid question to ask, and one that Sonny hoped he was wrong about, especially considering there was another dead girl to add to the sheriff's list.

Blue wagged his tail, and Sonny helped him out of the truck. It looked like the dog's limp was getting a little less painful, a little better—but that might have been nothing but wishful thinking. The broken bone had not had time to heal.

About halfway up to the house, Lidde walked out of the front door, a grim look on her round face and a broom held tightly in her hand. She started when she looked up and saw Sonny. "I didn't hear you pull up," she said, stopping in the center of the porch.

"Didn't mean to sneak up on you, Lidde." Blue bolted around Sonny and limped as quickly as he could up to see Lidde, his tail wagging like the pendulum of a clock gone haywire.

Lidde smiled and leaned down and petted the dog. "Looks like he's gonna be okay." There was always a hint of Sweden in her voice. Today it was especially noticeable. Her words were drawn out slow, with rolling syllables, hitting the high notes in odd places for most Texans.

Sonny stopped about fifteen feet from the woman. "He seems to like being around. Hasn't tried to run off, yet. Not that he could easily enough, but he just kind of accepted where he was at and made himself at home."

"That's good, Sonny. You needed a dog about you."

Sonny smiled, then let it quickly fade away. "Pete around? I'd kind of like to talk to him for a minute."

Lidde tilted her head. "He's out back in the barn. Making sure all is well. That there was some fierce dust storm. Likes of I haven't seen before, but expect to again, sad as that may be."

Sonny nodded. "Seems to be the way of things. You mind keeping an eye on Blue while I go talk to Pete?"

"Nah, nah, you go ahead. Me and Blue'll have us a visit. I'll teach him a trick or two if I have the time." She leaned and patted the dog's head. Blue seemed to like her. He barked and tried to jump up on her apron, but realized halfway up that it was going to hurt when he landed. He yelped slightly when the bandaged leg and paw came down on the porch floor. Lidde swept up the dog and cradled him like he was a newborn baby. "There, there, let's go see if I can find a good bone for you."

"I won't be long." Sonny walked off toward the barn. He felt bad for considering that Pete and Lidde might have had reason to run off, that they were involved in any of the three girls' murders. Seeing Lidde with Blue reminded him of her tenderness, and he was certain, at that moment, that she couldn't have been involved in the horror that was laying out in that field.

The barn was a long one, meant for dairy cows, but there wasn't much grass these days for cows to chew on, and Pete hadn't ever used it for that purpose, at least as far as Sonny could remember.

It smelled like all barns, a mixture of straw, rotting food, and mouse piss that somehow all combined into a pleasurable, expected odor. Light rushed in the door as Sonny pushed inside without any hesitation. All of the sashes were pulled to on the windows, not allowing the sun, or any dust, inside.

A feral cat scurried out of the way, and Sonny stopped just inside the door to get his bearings. He'd been in the barn countless times before, but never when it was dark inside. From what he could remember, there were old cars, tractors, and a heap of rusted old metal strung about, along with stalls full of crates and cages that held all sorts of critters.

Pete took in all kinds of animals, not just the domestic. If someone found an injured deer or fox out and about and didn't have the heart or inclination to shoot it, they'd bring it to Pete. So there were a variety of animals inside the barn. Cows, birds, even a three-legged coyote, along with various cats and dogs, either stray, or left behind by folks who just couldn't pay Pete for taking care of them.

It didn't take long for Sonny's eyes to adjust, and he saw the glow of a railroad lantern at the opposite end of the barn. "Hey, Pete, that you?" Sonny called out.

A response took a second to come back, but one came pretty quick. "Yah, yah, it's me. You stay right there. I'll be over in a second."

Not wanting to navigate the ins and outs of the barn without a light, Sonny did what he was told. He had no reason to be in a hurry.

Something moved about in the hayloft above him. Might have been a rat or a cat, it was hard to tell. Might've even been a barn owl out for an afternoon snack. Either way, Sonny stepped back, and reached around to the gun that was stuffed between his pants and undershirt. He didn't care for rats at all. Mice he could tolerate, but big rodents made him nervous.

"What brings ya out this way, Ranger Burton? Day's been as ugly as any I can remember." Pete Jorgenson appeared out of the darkness without the lamp. He had on work clothes, sleeves rolled up, and his left hand was covered with dried blood.

"Been a worse day for me," Sonny said. "What'd you get yourself into?" Nodding at Pete's hands.

"I was butcherin' a suckling pig when the storm blew up. I guess I forgot to clean myself up. Wasn't expectin' anyone to be out."

Sonny nodded. "They found another girl, Pete."

Pete exhaled and looked at the ground. "That why you're here?"

Sonny shrugged, stared at Pete to see if he could get a feeling one way or another about what was truly going on in the man's mind and heart. It was hard to tell. A steel curtain had fallen over the Swede's face; he looked like a carved bust sitting on some piano teacher's shelf.

Pete finally looked up and shook his head. "Lord have mercy on those poor girls' souls. Ain't never heard of such a thing in all of my life."

"You don't know anything about it then?"

"You official, yah?"

"Just curious."

"Jonesy done been out. More 'an once. Not today, of course, but now that I know there's been another killin', well, I 'spect to see him drive up. I'll have to tell Lidde. She frets about all them girls. This will break her heart for sure. We hoped it was just a tramp passin' through, you know, but this killer seems like he's gonna stay, along with all the rest of the bad news."

Sonny watched Pete's face intently. He'd always been a pretty good judge of the truth, or a lie, when he heard it. His judgment was clouded, though, because he liked Pete and Lidde. He would have never considered them suspects of something so heinous—but Sonny knew it was hard to know what a person was really capable of doing. He'd seen a lot of good people do bad things. "You haven't had a girl here lately?"

Pete shook his head. "Not since early spring. You got to understand, it ain't like we take appointments. They just show up at the door. Lidde, she takes them in, makes sure they eat right, rest, know how to care for a child if they want to keep it. Most don't. They want to leave it here like such a thing never happened and get on with their lives. Sometimes, they come with a note and money pinned by their momma, grandmother, asking for us to make this trouble go away as soon as we can, but we can't do that. We have to wait out the time, you understand."

"Take care of it," Sonny said, recalling the pool of blood underneath the girl's dress.

"End the life. You know what I mean."

"I was just making sure."

Both men took a breath and let any words they were thinking just pass on by. Whatever had been moving in the hayloft above them had scurried away and taken to hiding again. Silence returned to the barn.

"We don't have nothing to do with killing any creature. Not by oath or creed but by what is right. Only to end the sufferin', that's all.

I've spent my life tryin' to ease the pain of all living things. Killin' a child or its mother is something that only a monster could do. And that's not me. I've said the same thing to Jonesy, and I'll say it to you: Lidde and I had nothin' to do with any of this foul business. We help girls. We don't kill them. And for anyone to think such a thing, well, it offends us greatly. But we understand, yah, why we would be the first ones to come to mind."

"I'm sorry, Pete. I shouldn't have come by."

"I'm glad you did." Pete stepped forward and put his big hand on Sonny's shoulder. "Come on, I think Lidde has some iced tea ready. Be a fine thing to share with you and speak of pleasanter things. If you've got time."

"I've got time."

They headed out the door and were halfway to the house when a car pulled in and parked behind Sonny's truck.

It was a familiar car, one with a spiderweb windshield. It was Jesse.

Jesse Burton's face was red with restrained rage as he jumped out of the black sedan and slammed the door. The windshield cracked a little more and threatened to cave in, but it didn't. The glass just shook like it had been touched by the finger of an earthquake.

"What the hell are you doing here?" Jesse demanded, stalking straight up to Sonny and Pete.

Sonny could smell old coffee on his son's breath. "I stopped by for a visit."

"Sure you did."

"Do you think you could excuse us both a second, Pete. I need to have a discussion with my son here for a moment. Seems he's lost a bit of his manners."

"Sure, sure thing." Pete nodded to them both, then hurried up to the porch and dashed inside the house without looking back.

The curtains fluttered in the window next to the door, and Sonny surmised that it was Lidde, seeing who else had arrived and what the shouting was all about. "You've got no call to speak to me like that in front of Pete. You've got no call to speak to anyone like that."

"The hell, I don't," Jesse said. His face had grown even redder, and if there was ever any question that the boy was Martha's and her hot-headed kin, there was no mistaking it now. "You've got no badge, no jurisdiction, and no reason to be talking to Pete Jorgenson. He's a suspect, Pa, a suspect in an ugly, brutal string of murders that needs to be stopped."

"And how's that working out for you and Jonesy?" Sonny couldn't restrain himself any longer.

"What's that supposed to mean? We're doing just fine, thank you. We have people of interest that we're keeping an eye on. And I certainly don't need you steppin' in and trying to act like you're capable of helping when you're not hardly capable of feeding yourself."

"You mean I'm not whole because I don't have both arms, both hands?"

All of the air had got sucked out of the world at that very moment, and there was nothing around Sonny that he could hear past his own rising anger. He couldn't hear his own beating heart. It was like it had stopped. If Martha had always confounded Sonny, then Jesse had always challenged him—challenged him not to just haul off and smack the boy's mouth when he deserved it—which, over the years, was, more often than not, every time they were in each other's company.

"You said it," Jesse answered. "Now go on. Go home. This is Ranger business. Stay out of it."

If Sonny had a right hand, he would have balled up his fist and punched Jesse square in the mouth—which, at the moment, probably would have landed him in jail. But he didn't have a hand, or a fist, and he had no feeling at all there.

Instead, Sonny exhaled deeply and stepped back. He was glad to see Lidde walk out the door with Blue at her heels. Pete wasn't far behind. They all three stopped at the top of the porch steps.

"Blue be ready to go home now, Sonny," Lidde said. She had a brown paper bag in her left hand and held it out to him. "Here's some bones for him, and another for your next bit of beans."

Sonny understood; he was being shooed off. They both knew what was coming. They'd been through it before. He nodded, walked up to the porch, and took the bag. "You need me, you call, you hear?"

Pete and Lidde nodded in unison, like they were connected by the same wire and operated off the same motor. "We'll be fine," Pete said.

"Come on, Blue, let's go." Sonny turned and walked toward his truck. The dog followed loyally behind him, struggling to keep up.

"I meant what I said, Pa. Stay out of this," Jesse said, as Sonny walked by him.

Sonny didn't answer; he just stared straight ahead, helped Blue in the truck, and drove off, doing his hale and hearty best not to miss a shift as he sped away.

CHAPTER 25

The afternoon tilted toward evening and the temperature reached for its peak. Sonny was glad to enter a building to escape the glare of the day, if only for a moment. The local Texas Ranger office was in the basement of the Collingsworth County courthouse, and it was always a few degrees cooler there. Not that Sonny ever enjoyed being behind a desk, but in the depths of summer, the office had been a retreat.

Headquarters for Company C, on the other hand, the division of Rangers who covered the Panhandle and collection of counties south, was located down in Lubbock, nearly a hundred and eighty miles away, in a three-story building that held heat like an oven. It had been a long time since Sonny had ventured to headquarters, well on over a year. He didn't even know who the captain was these days. It didn't matter much to him. He'd never kept up with the politics of the organization. His father had been a captain, and the ghost of that office had followed Sonny throughout his entire career, like he wouldn't have accomplished anything if he didn't match his father's rise as a commanding officer. Leadership had never interested Sonny. He just wanted to do his job the best he could. The basement office in Wellington with one secretary had suited him just fine.

The drive into town from Pete and Lidde Jorgenson's was a blur. He was so mad he could've kicked a cow. Jesse warning him off the Jorgenson's place was above and beyond any of his powers. But the boy was insecure, there was no question about that. Ambition showed on Jesse from the shine on his shoes to the stiffness of his gait. He held himself like a general going into battle no matter what the circumstance was. There was no question in Sonny's mind that there would be another Captain Burton on the Ranger scrolls, etched to stand the time before it was all said and done. Jesse had always wanted to be in charge. Always. That was part of their tangle.

Sonny gunned the Model A truck into one of the many slanted parking spots that surrounded the courthouse and hit the brakes just before hitting the curb. Blue nearly fell off the seat. "Sorry about that, boy," Sonny said, realizing what he had allowed his anger to do, or almost do. He couldn't imagine hurting the dog—again—and the thought made his stomach roll. Blue squared himself in the seat and wagged his tail.

The courthouse took up a full city block and served as the center of Wellington, with businesses surrounding the square, some successful but most not. The Depression had brought a load of new boards to the windows of the store fronts. The butcher, hardware store, grocery, and Ritz Theater had hung on, but nearly all the other stores had been forced to close. People just didn't have money for anything extra—other than movies and newsreels.

Sonny tried to ignore the theater as he stepped out of the truck, but he couldn't keep himself from looking over his shoulder at the red brick building. It was impossible not to see the image of Bonnie and Clyde sauntering out of the Ritz, arm in arm, like they were just two young lovers on an innocent date. But it was more than that. It had been a distraction, the dark movie house a place to hide for a brief moment. Everything had changed after that—for them and for Sonny. *And the town, too*, Sonny thought, as he stepped out of the truck.

It was after the shootout with Bonnie and Clyde that the murders had started. Three nameless girls dead in a matter of a year. No clue to the identity of the killer, just two of the nicest people in the world as suspects, as persons of interest—Pete and Lidde Jorgenson. That didn't settle well with Sonny. Hadn't since he'd found out that they were the focus of suspicion—they had the means, but there was no motive and no evidence, at least that Sonny knew of. But that was not why he was at the courthouse. Not this time. Not yet. He had a wrong to right first, a friend to help, a girl to rescue, if that were possible.

"You stay here, Blue." The dog stood at the window, which Sonny had left rolled down about six inches so the breeze could pass through it. Blue ran his nose up and down the window, trying to figure a way out, so he could go, too. "Not this time. I won't be long," Sonny said.

The sun had started to fall to the other side of the earth, and it was the hottest part of the day. Clouds were as rare as a fat jackrabbit, and the wind had subsided for the moment. The air was as still as the inside of a kettle. Sonny wasn't keen on leaving Blue in the truck in the heat, but he had no choice. The animal wasn't welcome inside the courthouse. They barely tolerated children. He hoped he was telling the dog the truth, that he wouldn't be too long.

Sonny looked straight up at the courthouse and pushed away the image and any more thoughts about Bonnie and Clyde. His concern now was the Clever, Clever boys and Carmen, a girl, little more than a child, who had fallen into their grasp. At least, that was the way Aldo told it.

On the whole of things, the hows and whys of the girl's residence with the boys didn't matter much. What mattered was bringing her home. Sonny really didn't know if that was possible. His gut told him she was a lost cause. His time would be better spent trying to prove that Pete and Lidde were innocent.

He entered through two double doors and stood in the foyer of the building as the doors clanked closed behind him. The rub of the metal latches echoed upward to the open ceiling after bouncing off the marble floors.

The courthouse smelled institutional, but not sterile like the hospital. It smelled of paper, wax, and books, books that were stuffed into the walnut barrister bookcases that stood in every office, niche, and corner where one could fit. If law and order had a smell, then the inside of the courthouse fit that bill.

Sonny had walked in and out of the courthouse doors a million times in his long life. Once to get his marriage license, another time to get a death certificate, but mostly, just back and forth to work and to the courts to settle matters of justice, civil and criminal, depending on the matter that he had been involved in.

People came and went, paying Sonny little mind as he stood there taking in the scope of the courthouse, with its mezzanine, many doors and hallways, and high ceiling. He was a fixture in the courthouse, almost as permanent as the brass door handles.

He hadn't been inside the building since he'd left the Rangers, since he'd had to turn in his badge and gun.

The small of his back arched at the thought, so that he felt his own gun now, carried out of sight, just like any authority he thought he might possess—which, according to his son, was exactly zero.

He turned left and started to head toward the door that led down to the basement, to the Ranger office, but it opened with a hard push before he got there. To his surprise, Sonny found himself face-to-face with Frank Hamer.

"Well, if it ain't Sonny Burton. I was just askin' Faye about you," Hamer said. He was a hair shorter than Sonny, but with his wide-brimmed hat on they looked to be about the same height. Hamer was nearly fifty years old, clean-shaven, and had a hard-set jaw that was common among men who chose law enforcement as a profession—and some who did not. You could tell he had been a thin man when he was young, but age had put some weight on him. He didn't look fat, just full, filled out. There were a few people who said Hamer favored the gangster John Dillinger, but never to his face. That would have been a mistake for any man, or woman as far as that went, to make. Such a comment would provoke a harshness that would belie any kindness and prove the swagger he walked with to be true and not just bluster.

Sonny nodded and stepped back as Hamer's right hand flinched up, then fell quickly back to his side, uncertain what to do with the customary handshake.

"It's all right, Frank," Sonny said.

Hamer exhaled, then looked away from the pinned sleeve that had once held Sonny's right arm. "Sorry how things worked out for you, Sonny."

"You got them. That's what matters."

"It is. Hey, I got that Remington Model 8 out in the car I used in the shoot-out. You want to see it?"

"No, that's all right; I'll pass."

"It's a dandy. Petmecky, in Austin, got me a custom fifteen-round clip. Boy, it's got balance, but a little man'll carry a bruise for a month if he doesn't hold the dang thing right."

"I'm sure it's a fine weapon, Frank." Sonny nodded in appreciation of J. C. Petmecky and the gunsmith's notorious skill, and he was a little envious, too. He'd always wanted to own a custom-made gun from the shop in Austin but could never afford one.

Sonny was glad to see the usual gregariousness that accompanied Frank Hamer, but it seemed a little overdone, like the man was forcing his enthusiasm; he was nervous or uncomfortable, Sonny couldn't tell which. "I was hoping to get a call into you, that Faye would know how to get ahold of you. What brings you up this way?"

Hamer's shoulders stiffened, and he stepped in so he was nearly nose-to-nose with Sonny. "Jonesy called a week ago, but I had my hands full and couldn't make it up this way. Your boy put out a call, too. A few things are heatin' up, and he needs some help, so I thought I better set aside the unnecessariness and see what the deal was up here. I know they haven't been the same since you . . . um, had to leave."

"Good, I'm glad to hear he called the right man. There's a lot going on."

"How much do you know?"

"Not much. I've been laying low since . . . Since, well, you know. I figured it was best to stay out of the way."

"But you couldn't help yourself, right? Am I right or am I wrong? I'm right aren't I?"

"Sure, Frank. Right as rain. You're right as rain. I couldn't help myself."

Hamer leaned in and whispered, "These murders've got everybody on edge. We think it's the same bastard doin' the deed. Add in the string of robberies and upstairs is afraid there's gonna be another set of outlaws to track down. The whole affair blasted out in the papers to make us all look bad, like we can't do our jobs protectin' the citizenry."

Sonny lowered his head, as if in prayer. "I was there, at the robbery.

That's why I wanted to talk with you. I think there was a young girl doing the driving. She's got caught up in something that's out of her league, over her head."

Hamer listened intently, and he watched Sonny closely, never taking his eyes off of him. "Let me guess. The girl's folks have come to you and asked for help."

"Her father. How'd you know?"

"Happens. I'd come to you, too, if I was from 'round here. How old is this girl?"

"Sixteen."

Hamer shook his head in disgust. "Just a baby."

"Exactly. Not old enough to know what she's done to the rest of her life."

"None of us know about consequences at that age."

"True. So, what do you think?"

"Well, I don't think these murders got anything to do with these kids and their tirade, but I could be wrong about that. Gut says I'm not. Two different things. But I've been wrong before, so you never know."

Sonny shifted his weight and was aware of people coming and going, in and out of the courthouse, eyeing them, leaning in trying to hear the words being spoken as they hurried by. "After they killed Tom Turnell, they hit a place outside of Shamrock and then, earlier this morning, I'm certain that Jesse got into a shoot-out with them at the state line. He wouldn't say so, that's just a guess."

"It's a good guess," Hamer said, then paused. "Bad thing about all this is that goddamn Clyde Barrow and his ways. And, of course, the newspapers are guilty, too, for puttin' every inch of their strategies in the paper. Barrow liked to jump in and out of states to let things cool off. My guess is, these three'll come back, but venture up or down only a few roads. They won't come back on the same roads they left out on, be afraid we're watchin' for them, and they'd be right about that. Maybe tomorrow or the next day. It won't be long. That's tough country over in Oklahoma. Not much there for them. They'll come back around here, especially if they got kin here. Mark my word. They'll come in around midnight, or dawn, when they think everybody'll be asleep. I'll be right, you'll see."

"I'm sure you will be."

"I'll talk to Jonesy, see if we can't set something up. I'll let you know when and where, if you'd like. It's the least I can do. These are good folks, right?"

"Yes, I think so."

"All right, then, you take care of yourself, Sonny." Hamer tapped him on the left shoulder, then turned to walk away but stopped a few feet from the door, and said, "I'm sorry I didn't get those two sooner, Sonny. If I would've, you'd still be in the company. Did your boy give you the shell I sent up?"

Sonny nodded and had little to say other than a mute thank you. He'd never been fond of souvenirs.

Satisfied, Frank Hamer turned and bolted out the door of the courthouse, leaving a swirl of dust in the wake of his exit.

There was nothing left for Sonny to accomplish at the courthouse. Going down to see Faye, stepping foot into the office, would just make things more difficult.

Blue was glad to see Sonny, and Sonny was glad he didn't have to stay inside the courthouse any longer than he had. The inside of the truck was as hot as a brick oven.

The day was getting on, and it had been a full one. All Sonny wanted to do was go home, have a little dinner, and settle down for some rest. All of this running around had tired him out. He wasn't used to it.

Still, there was one more stop he wanted to make before he left town.

He drove straight over to the hospital, got out, and walked up to the door without any hesitation. That didn't come until he went to open it. He drew in a deep breath, like he was sucking up courage, and then walked inside, head up, heart racing, like he was on a mission that couldn't be aborted.

Betty Maxwell looked up from her desk with a surprised expression on her face. "Mr. Burton, I wasn't expecting to see you." It looked like she was putting things in order, readying to leave for the day.

"I didn't expect to be here today, either."

"Is there something I can help you with?"

Sonny nodded, his mouth went dry.

Nurse Betty stood up. "Are you all right?"

"I am, ma'am. I was just wondering if you could . . ." He stopped, and felt like an inexperienced young man, afraid of what he was about to set in motion.

"You've got me a little concerned," she said.

Sonny shook his head. "No, no, there's nothing wrong. I was just wondering if you could help me?"

"Help you with what?"

"With that thing. The hook. Help me put the prosthetic on? Help me to know how to use it."

CHAPTER 26

Betty Maxwell led Sonny into an examining room. "We have one around here, somewhere," she said.

Sonny was already regretting asking for help with the prosthetic. It felt like a foolish thing to do, but the last few days had accumulated certainties in his mind that he couldn't avoid. He wasn't going to put a gun to his head anytime soon. Suddenly, he had things to do, promises to keep, and, most importantly, a point to prove to his son. He might not be full-bodied, but his mind was whole and still of use. The rebuke from Jesse stung deep. He still felt the anger of the harsh words, could hear them ringing in his mind, and he knew the feeling wasn't going to go away anytime soon.

The examining room was a little bigger than a closet and held a table with a big light angled over it, a chair for the doctor, a cupboard full of medicines, and a closet. A single window, with the blind closed, allowed some diffused light into the room.

Nurse Betty turned on the big light and headed to the closet.

The room smelled clean, like it had been mopped and washed down with bleach recently. The cleanliness of it stung Sonny's nose, giving him more reason to not want to be there.

"Close the door behind you," Nurse Betty said, as she opened the door to the closet. It was full of boxes and things that Sonny had no clue what their use, or name, was. Metal rods, beakers of all sizes, blankets, sheets, and more utensils that looked like they were designed to inflict pain not heal anyone. Hospitals had always made him nervous.

He did as he was told and closed the door. But he remained there, watching Betty Maxwell make her way through the closet like she was on the most important mission in the world.

She was shapely and easy to look at. Sonny liked her, found her pleasant to be around, if not a little too direct, kind of like her son, Leo, now that Sonny thought about it.

"Ah," Betty said, "here it is." She pulled a box out of the closet, put it on the examining table, opened it, and laid the fake arm on the table, gently, like it was real.

The prosthetic was much like the one at home; a tangle of leather straps, wood painted to look like hard flesh, with a shiny hook attached to the end.

"Didn't we fit you with one before you went home?" Betty asked.

"I refused," Sonny said. He couldn't take his eyes off the hook.

"Oh, yes, I remember. Doc Meyers was not happy with me at all when I told him. I figured you'd eventually come around. It just took you a little longer than I thought it would."

"I'm not sure this is a good idea."

"Sure it is. Take off your shirt, Mr. Burton. I think you'll find this will be an improvement to your life, not a detriment." Nurse Betty smiled at him, but Sonny couldn't find it in himself to return the gesture. "Come on, now, no need to be bashful. I've seen men who came back from the war and plenty more."

"That was a long time ago."

"I'm a little older than you might think. But some of those men have had long, productive lives, just like you. They catch colds, too. Now, go on, take it off."

Sonny nodded. "I suppose you're right." He reached over with his left hand, and fumbled with the top button.

Nurse Betty stepped toward him, like she was going to help, but he shook his head. She relented, stopped without saying anything else.

It took a minute, but Sonny was able to unbutton the shirt and pull it off, leaving him standing there with his undershirt still tucked into his pants, and a sock pulled up on his stump. The sock nearly went all the way to his shoulder. He only had about five inches of his arm left.

"You can leave your undershirt on," Betty said. "Do you mind if I take the sock off and put a fresh one on? I want to see how you've healed."

Sonny nodded. It was quiet outside the room. The day had gotten long, the comings and goings for appointments had pretty much come to an end. A ceiling fan whirled overhead, offering a little relief in the room. But he was still hot, uncomfortable. It wouldn't have mattered what the temperature was in the room.

Betty stepped up and carefully peeled the sock off his stump. She smelled like a garden of freshly cut lilacs.

"It looks like it's healed nicely." She tossed the sock on the table and went to the cupboard to retrieve another one.

Sonny watched her intently. It was then that something struck him as odd. As foggy as it was, he remembered back to their first meeting, when Aldo had driven him home. If he remembered right, he thought Betty had looked like she was pregnant or had just had a baby. Aldo had said, "She has problems." Funny thing was, there was only her son at the house. When Sonny had gone inside to use the phone to call Hugh Beaverwood for Jonesy, there was no sign of a baby at all. Nothing. The house was quiet as a church and neat as a pen.

It might not have meant anything, but it suddenly felt . . . odd, like seeing something out of place, that didn't quit fit. There were all kinds of possibilities, mostly tragic, as Sonny toyed with the thought of her earlier condition, but mostly, he decided, none of them were any of his business at all.

Betty came back, the smile still on her face, and slipped the fresh white sock on his stump. It fit better, like it was made to fit a stump instead of a foot.

"What's the matter? You look glum," Nurse Betty said.

"Nothing, I was just thinking."

"All right." She picked up the prosthetic and pulled the strap out, then adjusted a buckle at the end of it into a loop. "Here," she said, holding out the loop, "put your left arm through here." Sonny straightened his arm and eased his hand through the loop. As he did, Betty pulled the arm to the other side. "Now, ease your arm into the hole."

Sonny hesitated, stared directly into Nurse Betty's cornflower blue eyes.

"You're doin' fine, Mr. Burton."

He nodded, then aimed his stump into the end of the prosthetic. It fit perfectly, and it moved when he did.

"Now, pull the other buckle tight, and there you are."

"That's all there is to it?"

Nurse Betty smiled. "Yes. That's it. You'll need some time to adjust to it, figure out how to move the elbow up and down." She pulled the hook up, then pushed it down again gently. "It'll just take some force, either with your hand, or on the wall, your chest, the gearshift. You'll see. In a few days, you'll wonder how you got along without it."

"If you say so."

"I do. Why don't you go ahead and try to put your shirt back on."

"How do I get this thing off?"

"Same way you put it on. Unbuckle it, pull it off, then take the loop on your other arm off. You can do this," Nurse Betty said. Her voice was strong as steel. There was no arguing with her.

"All right." Sonny picked up his shirt, slid the hook through the sleeve, stood up, then reached around and pulled the other sleeve to him. In a second he had his shirt on and was buttoning it with his left hand. The prosthetic felt heavy. Heavier than a real arm. It would take a while to get used to having something there, to finding a balance to it, but to his surprise the arm wasn't as uncomfortable as he thought it would be.

"Well, look at you," Nurse Betty smiled. "How's it feel?"

"All right, I suppose. It'll take some getting used to." He started to unbutton his shirt.

"What are you doing?" Betty asked.

"Taking it off, giving it back."

She shook her head. "You can keep it for a while. Try the one you have at home. See which one feels better, then bring me one back. There's no rush. I want you to be comfortable."

"Are you sure?"

"Of course." She walked up to him and straightened his shirt at the shoulders. A big smile flashed across Betty Maxwell's face. "You look fine. Just fine," she said, as she headed for the door, preparing to leave; her job finished.

"I was out at your house a little bit ago," Sonny said, still standing.

Betty had her hand on the knob but let it fall away. She tensed up, then turned around. "Leo's not in any trouble, is he?"

"Not that I know of," Sonny said. "He was decent enough to let me use the phone."

Betty exhaled, relaxed a little bit, though she stared at Sonny curiously, obviously trying to figure out what the problem was. "He can be a handful, sometimes."

"There's nothing to worry about."

"Okay, then why bring it up?"

"Just figured I ought to tell you."

"What'd you need the phone for?"

"Sheriff needed me to make a call."

"Where to?"

"Rather not say. Not my place to spread news before it gets out."

Betty Maxwell walked up to Sonny and stopped about a foot in front of him. "You're bein' awful coy, Mr. Burton. I know things about half the people in this town that nobody else knows just by the benefit of where I sit and the job I do. Privacy is part of my job. It's not an expectation; it's a demand. Do you understand?"

"I do, ma'am. It's just that it was for police business, so I'd best not say much more. You'll be able to piece things together come tomorrow," Sonny said. He was eyeing her as intently as she was him. It was easy to tell that he had upset her, and he felt bad about doing that, but there was something in him that he couldn't stop—the curious investigator, the Texas Ranger, all focused on that poor dead girl laying out in the field.

"I'll read the paper tomorrow, then." Betty turned away again.

"I guess I was expecting to see a child at your house," Sonny said. He felt bad as soon as he said it.

She stopped and spun around. "I only have one child, thank you very much, Mr. Burton. And I don't see what business it is of yours." Tears suddenly welled up in Betty Maxwell's eyes, and the room felt like the inside of an oven.

The bad feeling got worse, like Sonny had just made a horrible mistake. He was embarrassed, ashamed. He pushed by her, hardly able to breath. "I'm sorry," he said. "I don't know what I was thinking. I should go."

Betty Maxwell didn't say a word. She just let him pass by—but Sonny heard her break into a sob as he hurried out the front door. The depth of her cries echoed behind him like those of a grieving mother of a dead soldier, standing over her son's grave for the last time. Sonny had been to too many of those kind of funerals. He knew that kind of pain when he heard it.

CHAPTER 27

Silence sat between Carmen and Tió like a giant boulder fallen squarely in the middle of the hunter's shack. They could hardly look at each other. Soft candlelight lit the inside of the shack, exposing floating dust that looked like the sparkle had fallen off an old flapper's skirt—small pinpoint diamonds of no value that hung suspended in the air like prom decorations. Beauty and tenderness had been replaced by fear and guilt.

The bread was gone, and only a swig of Dr. Pepper remained in the bottom of the bottle. Tió had offered it to Carmen, but she'd refused.

There was no sign of Eddie. It was like he had vanished, ran off, and left them there without the intention of returning. Each new sound outside the shack caused Carmen to jump with anticipation. She knew he would come back. He had to. He just had to.

Tió, who had been sitting on his bunk, finally stood up. "We need water."

"The lake's too far away. You're not up to it." The blood had dried on his shirt. It looked like a big brown spot, like Tió had rolled in a deep puddle of mud and just left it there on the shirt that had come from the donation bin at St Michael's.

"It only hurts a little," he said.

"I don't want to be here alone."

"We need water." Tió was a little more stern. "I have the gun. I can kill a rabbit."

"Have you ever killed a rabbit?"

"Just chickens. We were hungry. Like now. We are hungry. We shouldn't have left Mercury behind."

"But you didn't like killing the chicken," Carmen said. It wasn't a question.

Tió shook his head, then made his way to the door. It was open so the air could pass through the shack, offering whatever comfort it chose to bring. "I won't go too far. If there's a lake, there's a stream somewhere close. We need water."

"If it's not dried up."

Tió stared at Carmen for a long second, like he wanted to say goodbye or remember how she looked. Even with his bloody, torn shirt and the dirt that had collected on his skin, he still looked innocent to Carmen, like a little boy trying to do the best he could without having all of the moving parts. God, she thought, what had I been thinking?

The words were obviously lost in Tió's mind, and he walked away silently, disappearing into the night as easily as he had slipped into her bed.

The loneliness of the shack was almost immediate. Carmen fell back on the tiny bed, pulled the sheet up and hugged it tight, like it was another human being or a teddy bear like the one her father had won at the carnival and given to her proudly. That was a long time ago.

Hugging the sheet gave her no comfort. Tears came to her eyes, and she let them fall, did nothing to restrain them. Or the sobs that soon followed. She cried heartily. Cried until she fell back to sleep, back to the land of dark nothingness where she longed to stay—safe from the realities of the world and the two boys who orbited around her.

Heavy footsteps on the plank floor startled Carmen awake. She opened her eyes, blurred by sleep. In the light from the still-burning candle, it only took her a second to realize that it was Eddie. His near-perfect boots, blue work pants, and St. Christopher medal that dangled from his neck made him unmistakable, hard to confuse with Tió. There was no way she could do that now.

Carmen sat straight up in the bed, tossing the sheet to the side—the smell of her and Tió's tryst along with it. "Where have you been?" It wasn't a demand or anger but concern. At least, that's what she wanted Eddie to hear—sweetness and concern.

"It took longer than I thought," Eddie said. He had an open box tucked under his right arm. It was full of food—a loaf of bread, a bottle of milk, and some canned goods that Carmen could see. "There were cops everywhere. I had to hide until the middle of the night, then try and sneak back here without bein' seen." He sat the box down next to the bed, then leaned in and kissed Carmen. She kissed back, but not as hungrily as he obviously expected her to. Eddie pulled away instantly, an odd look crossing his face as he stood up straight.

"I was worried about you," Carmen said.

"You're sure?"

Carmen nodded.

"Where's Tió?" Eddie asked, looking around, his eyes stopping on Tió's unmade bunk.

Carmen didn't answer. She didn't have to.

"I'm right here," Tió said from behind Eddie, standing on the door stoop just outside the shack. He had a Dr. Pepper bottle full of water in his left hand. His right hand dangled free.

Eddie strode over to Tió and tapped the toe of his boot against Tió's. "I told you not to leave her."

"I went after water, Eddie. We didn't know if you was comin' back. I was scared and thirsty. There weren't no rabbits, Carmen."

Eddie drew back. "Carmen? You call her Carmen now?"

"It's her name, Eddie."

"You have never acknowledged her presence, Tió. You wouldn't call her anything. You didn't want her here." Eddie spun around to face Carmen. "What'd you do to him?"

She didn't answer.

Eddie lunged toward the bed, reached out to grab Carmen's foot, but she scurried back out of his reach, cowering in the corner like a trapped animal.

"Nothing. I didn't do nothing, Eddie. I swear. I swear to God," Carmen said.

Eddie stood up at the end of the bed and kicked the box of food, sending it crashing into the wall. It tipped sideways. Cans rolled across the uneven floor and the lid pushed off the milk, spilling it like a faucet of white water had been fully opened.

"You're a liar, Carmen. A goddamned liar. I always knew you were nothin' but a little whore."

Carmen pushed herself into the corner, burying her head in her arms. She couldn't see Eddie or Tió. "I want to go home," she whimpered. "I just want to go home."

Eddie crawled up on the bed, enraged like a tiger on the attack. "Look at me, you little bitch. Look at me and swear to God you didn't do nothin' to him." He pulled her arms apart, and Carmen screamed. Screamed so loud it hurt her own eardrums.

But Eddie didn't relent. "Tell me!" he screamed. "Tell me what you did!"

Carmen couldn't answer. Tears poured out of her eyes, and she was hyperventilating, couldn't catch her breath. Her lungs burned like they were on fire, and her nose was clogged. She thought she was going to suffocate. She couldn't tell him what had happened. She just couldn't.

When no answer came, Eddie slapped her, slapped her as hard as he could.

At first, it stung, like he had electrocuted her with the tips of his fingers. Then her head hit the wall and the pain came, followed by teetering wooziness. Her stomach lurched, and, since it only had bread and Dr. Pepper in it, the puke was minimal, almost like a dry heave.

"What did you do!" Eddie screamed again. A shadow crossed her face, like he was reloading, pulling his hand back to hit her again.

But the strike never came.

A gunshot echoed inside the tiny room.

Carmen blinked her eyes open, could taste the gunpowder. Tió was just inside the door, with the gun that Eddie had given to him before he'd left pointed at the ceiling. The Dr. Pepper bottle was on the floor, water draining, mixing with the milk.

Eddie stood over Carmen on his knees, arm cocked back, frozen like he was posing for a statue. "Put the gun down, Tió," Eddie said, lowering his voice so he was calm. But it was also an order, a command that Carmen had heard Eddie use a hundred times.

Tió shook his head. "You shouldn't hit girls, Eddie. Momma always said that. You know why."

"I know why. Poppa hit her and she didn't like it." He slung his leg off the bed.

"Don't," Tió said. "Put up your other hand, Eddie. This is a stick-up."

Eddie glared at Tió and finally did what he was told when Tió dropped the gun from the ceiling, pointed it straight at him, and nudged the barrel upward.

"Did you steal my girl, Tió?" Eddie said.

"Didn't steal nothin', Eddie. She was nice to me."

"I bet she was."

"Don't be mean, Eddie. I don't like it when you're mean." Tió stepped toward Eddie. "Keep your hands up. I'm not as stupid as you think I am."

Carmen wiped her eyes clear with the back of her hand, then wiped off her face with the sleeve of her dress. She could hardly believe what she was seeing; Tió standing up to Eddie. He never had before. Never.

The small, single-room shack suddenly felt hotter. All Carmen wanted to do was run, run as far away as she could. But she was trapped. Eddie and Tió blocked her way out.

Tió stopped a foot in front of Eddie and raised the gun to his brother's head. "How's it feel now, Eddie? You think you should have shot me a long time ago? Put me out of your misery?"

"I was mad, Tió. I didn't mean it when I said those things. Come on, *me'jo*. I am your brother, what are you thinking? We're a team, me and you. The Clever, Clever boys, that's us." There was an unmistakable tremor in Eddie's voice.

"You're the clever one. It should have been Clever and Stupid. It was always like that."

Eddie didn't answer straight away. "I didn't mean it," Eddie whispered. A third fluid mixed with the other two. Fear had propelled Eddie to lose control of his bladder.

"Just like you didn't mean to hit Carmen?"

Tió pressed the gun against Eddie's temple, then leaned in and said, "You're not so tough now, are you, Eddie?" He pulled the hammer back. The click of it sounded like dynamite had gone off in the small room.

Carmen shook, tried to scream at Tió, tell him not to shoot. *Stop.* But the words were stuck in her throat. She couldn't speak. By the time the one word—"Stop!"—came out, it was too late.

Tió pulled the trigger.

CHAPTER 28

Night covered the world in a welcome blanket of darkness. Relief from the brightness of the sun was one thing, but the arrival of coolness was completely another.

Sonny slept with the window open. A soft breeze fluttered the curtains, a mix of the oscillating fan and the air from the outside, all making it comfortable in the bedroom.

Sleep had come easily to Sonny after a long day, and Blue had made his way back to the foot of the bed, staking out his spot.

The moonlight was dim, offering a patch of soft light in the window, but the rest of the house was dark. The mantle clock ticked, and the radio was off. Water dripped at a slow rate from the faucet of the water pump, and even the mice in the walls had quieted down. Roaches came and went, still feasting on what had been left out for them to scavenge, but they were silent about their work. Sonny had vowed to start cleaning up the place the next day.

Two prosthetic prehensors lay on the table, almost identical. One was a little more comfortable than the other.

When the phone began to ring, the sudden arrival of the clanging bell and the unexpectedness of it, startled Sonny awake immediately.

He got to the phone on the fourth ring, determined to quiet it down, hoping like hell that it was a wrong number. Good news never came in the middle of the night.

Blue had padded after Sonny and stood at his feet.

"Hello," Sonny said into the receiver.

"Did I wake you, Ranger Burton?"

Sonny recognized the voice straight away. It was Frank Hamer. "It's the middle of the night, Frank."

"Sorry about that, but news of a robbery came in from Vinson. No money, just food. Sounds like our trio. I think they're goin' to get desperate out there, just like I said."

"What can I do for you, Frank?"

"We're goin' to set up at a few spots by the state line at dawn, just in case they try and make their way back. Gonna meet at Lancer's Market in an hour. I said I'd call you."

"I'll be there. Thanks for calling, Frank."

The line went dead, and Sonny stood there making sure he was awake and hadn't dreamed the whole conversation.

The abandoned hunter's shack had smelled like death warmed over from the very beginning. Now it was worse. Eddie lay on the floor on his back, unblinking eyes staring at the ceiling, his face adorned with ribbons of blood that were quick to dry. The flies had already found their way inside the door.

Silence had returned to the lonely night, after the echo of the gunshot had advanced out into the world, fading away around Jupiter or Mars. The stars pulsed in the sky, offering the only hint of life, and the sliver of moon looked frozen in place, like it was staring down, unable to comprehend what it was seeing.

The only sound that pierced the silence at any time was a dry wretch, the sound of a body flailing, toes to tongue, from the inside out. Carmen couldn't stop puking even though nothing came out of her mouth. Knees on the ground, palms of her hands forward, she crouched like a dog unsure of where to go next. She had fallen, stumbled out of the shack, unable to collapse all of the way.

The ground was hard and pebbles dug into her hands, but she didn't care. She was numb to physical pain of any kind. It was her mind and heart that were on fire. Particles of gunpowder and smoke coursed through her veins, unable to destroy, unable to hurt. It was like they were looking for a home. The invisible cause of the pain was unbearable.

Eddie was dead. Had died instantly. With one pull of the trigger, Tió had ended twenty years of rage, of being second-best, abused, threatened, beat-up, and pushed around. He had screamed like a banshee and chased the echo of the gunshot out the door, disappeared into the darkness, fleeing his own action of madness, his own fears, and the ultimate realization that was yet to come: He was alone now. Alone and lost.

Carmen heaved again and allowed the guttural pain to escape from her mouth. It sounded like a wail, a grieving barred owl, a coyote trapped in a narrow pass, unable to free itself. Nothing solid escaped her lips, only drool and spittle that tasted like three-week-old milk that had been left out in the sun.

She didn't know how long she had crouched there, but she knew if she fell the rest of the way to the ground she would just lie there, refuse to get up, drift off, and hope to awake to find that this was all a nightmare, not real. She would become more vulnerable than she already was, an easy meal for any predator that happened by.

If she stood up, then she would have to admit that she was on her own, too. Just as lost as Tió. In charge of her own destiny. She would have to decide what to do next, what to do with Eddie's body, what to do about Tió, where to go from here.

The darkness of night would not last forever. Morning would break and shine new light on the world, exposing the deeds and crimes of the night, just like it did every day. There was no escaping the light, the truth. Carmen knew that much, even though she was just a girl.

So she stayed that way, on all fours, half-human, half-animal, until she could stay no more, until her body threatened to disobey her mind, her will. She stood up when she no longer had a choice.

Carmen's eyes had adjusted to the dark as best they could, but her heart skipped a beat when she saw Tió standing by the door of the shack, leaning on the weathered clapboards with all of his weight, head down, the pistol dangling in his right hand. She froze in place, hoping he hadn't heard her, seen her. But it was too late. He raised his head and looked straight at her.

Even in the dim light of the fingernail moon, she could see that his face was soaked with tears, like a sheen of oil had been painted across his perfect Aztec-god-like cheeks and forehead—a warrior returning from the battle. Tió glowed with sadness and doom. He was not an angel arriving to save her. His eyes were caught in a deep struggle, one of many that had accumulated over the years. Slights and fights and bites that were beyond Carmen's knowledge or desire to know, all boiling up in the quick pull of a trigger.

She didn't know if she was safe, if she should run from him—or to him.

"We have to leave, Carmen," Tió said. His voice sounded like a trumpet on the radio, wavering with a plunger at the end of the horn, slow and sad, not fast and happy. There would be no dancing on this night.

Carmen hesitated, studied Tió the best she could. There was no escaping him. There had been no escaping from either of them, the Clever, Clever boys, from the moment she had climbed down the tree with her pillowcase of clothes and gotten into the car with them. The joyride had turned bloody, doomed from the start. She had been too young to know then what she knew now. The arrival of death is a quick teacher.

"We can't just leave," Carmen said. She stepped forward slowly, like she was walking on a winter pond, the ice thin and uncertain.

A burst of light suddenly flared in front of Tió. He had struck a match on the sole of his boot. "I have fire."

Carmen stopped in her tracks. Tió held the safety match at his chest. Hot, orange light glowed outward, making the dirt and rock formations that surrounded the shack look like an alien planet, an imaginary place where fanged, blood-hungry monsters lurked in the shadows. And the light glowed upward, glinting off Tió's shiny face, making him look twisted and strange, like maybe one of those alien monsters had consumed his soul. That would explain everything. But

Carmen knew this was no radio play, no made up drama. The twist in Tió's face was real.

"We can see, that's good, Tió," Carmen said.

He shook his head. "I can burn the shack. Set it on fire."

"Somebody will see it."

"We'll be gone," Tió said. "It won't matter."

"Where are we going, Tió?"

"I'm going to take you home, Carmen. Isn't that what you've wanted to do all along?" Tió said, tossing the match inside the shack, onto the bed that he and Carmen had shared, onto the bed covered with Eddie Renaldo's blood. It didn't take long for the flame to turn into a blaze.

CHAPTER 29

It felt strange to Sonny to be in the truck without Blue. The dog had been a constant companion since they had come together, but on this night Sonny thought the dog should remain behind, at home, inside where it was safe. He had no idea how the hound would react to gunfire—if there was any. Frank Hamer seemed certain of his plan, so there was little doubt that the seat next to him would not be the place for a lame dog.

Instead of Blue, the seat held his .45, a fully loaded gun belt, three boxes of shells for the 12-gauge Winchester repeating shotgun that sat wedged between the seat and the door, and a ten-inch Bowie knife that had been his father's. He figured he'd need every bit of ammunition from his personal armory to face the Clever, Clever boys.

Whether it was a smart thing to do or not, Sonny had taken the time to put on the prosthetic. It had felt far more comfortable than he had expected, and it gave him a sense of balance on his feet that had been lacking since the amputation. Suddenly, he had more equilibrium, stood up straighter. He had even used the hook, for the first time, to shift gears, from first to second. It was a start, and the gear slid into place perfectly, allowing Sonny to keep his good hand on the steering wheel, and his eyes—mostly—on the road.

The truck's headlights cut into the darkness like hundred-candle torches, showing him the way to Lancer's Market. A skunk had scurried across in front of him, leaving a foul smell in its wake, but that was the only creature of the night that Sonny had seen. He was glad he hadn't hit the thing.

The night sky was clear, and there was no hint, yet, of the day to come. It was just a little after four o'clock in the morning. Dawn would start to break in another hour.

Six vehicles sat in Lancer's parking lot—Jonesy's car, another sheriff's car next to it, a black Ford sedan that Sonny figured belonged to Frank Hamer, Jesse's sedan, Bertie Turnell's delivery truck, and the truck that served as Hugh Beaverwood's ambulance and hearse. It was a full lineup, one that Sonny had expected and dreaded. He knew Jesse would be none too happy to see him.

Sonny pulled up next to Jonesy's brown-and-tan Chevrolet and sat for a second. Eight men stood on the porch of Lancer's Market, two of them that Sonny didn't recognize. They must have been with Frank or were county deputies that he'd never met. That was possible, since he'd been out of the field for a while.

It had been a long time since he'd been part of a gang like this, a posse of sorts, and even though it was still the middle of the night for most folks—and most creatures—he felt more awake than he had in a long time.

He didn't have to wait long to face Jesse. The Ranger was at his door before Sonny could grab up his gun belt and step foot into the parking lot.

Jesse rapped on the window with his knuckle as hard as he could. "What the hell are you doing here?"

Sonny stared at his son, his face all bound up in anger and dissatisfaction, and he barely recognized him. "You better ask him," Sonny said through the window, motioning to Frank Hamer, who had come up on Jesse without being noticed.

Jesse turned to see Hamer, and Sonny pushed out the door.

"I called him here, Ranger Burton," Frank Hamer said, standing as tall and straight as one of those new oil derricks that were starting to pop up across the Texas landscape. "You have a problem with that?"

"I do. He's a liability. He can hardly take care of himself, much less fire a gun. And he's only got one arm."

"Looks like he's got two to me," Hamer said, nodding toward Sonny's full sleeve and hook.

"What the hell?" Jesse said.

Sonny slapped on his gun belt, pulled it through the buckle, and tightened it on his hip. Luckily, it went off without a hitch—or any practice. Adrenaline and pride made for a viable combination. "No 'what the hell' about it, boy," Sonny said. "Where do you want me, Frank?"

"You can ride with me, Sonny, if that suits you?"

"Suits me just fine. Just fine."

The road dipped just before the state line, and the ditch beside it was deep enough to put a car into. It was Jesse's place, out of sight to watch for the car that had shot at him. He had a flashlight to signal Frank Hamer, Sonny, and Jonesy. The other deputies, along with Bertie Turnell, were on a road over, armed with an old Navy flare gun, just in case the boys came that way.

Of course, there was no telling if the Clever, Clever boys would come this way, or be in a different car. It was all a hunch based on Frank Hamer's experience. No one was going to argue the plan, not even Jesse.

Hamer and Sonny were off the side of the road, the black Ford sedan hidden behind some scrub trees and some brush they'd pulled over and covered the shiny parts of the car with. Jonesy was hidden in the same fashion, down the road about twenty yards, and Hugh Beaverwood's ambulance was down another parcel, sitting on the side of the road. The coroner wasn't armed.

There had been no traffic since they had all got in place. A thin line of gray light was just starting to break along the eastern horizon, and a lone robin had whistled once or twice, hoarse like a bluebird, like it was just practicing, just waking up.

"Might be a few of these kind of mornings," Frank Hamer said. "If they don't show. Evenings, too."

"You sound certain they'll come back, and come back soon," Sonny said.

"These boys, from what I can tell, are small-time. Something set Bonnie and Clyde off. Might have been the papers and the radio. Once they got a taste of fame, they wanted more. These fellas, they ain't got the marquee that those two had. Pretty blonde out for a joyride with a bad boy."

"There's a girl with them."

"Jonesy will give them a chance, Sonny."

"I know, but . . ." He let his words trail off.

"They're Mexican, Sonny. Now, I don't have nothin' against them for that, but a lot of folks do. Be hard to overcome in this county and in this state. You know how those things go. There's no mercy for a greaser, especially two that are thieves and killers. Plain and simple."

Sonny nodded and stared in the distance toward Jesse. A pair of headlights crested the hill, cutting into the darkness like a beacon set against a fresh set of mirrors. There was no time to dispute what Hamer had just said.

Not that he would have anyway—but he was concerned about the welfare of the girl, of Carmen Hernandez. He was pretty sure Frank Hamer couldn't care less if she lived or died. But Sonny did. Not only had he made Aldo a promise, but Carmen was just sixteen, a year away from being a little girl. He didn't think he could live with himself if he killed a child—unless he was forced to—in self-defense. If she shot first. Then there would be no choice. He would have to save himself and the rest of the men who had come out to see justice served for Tom Turnell's cold-blooded murder.

Sonny held his breath and waited for the signal.

When it came, three quick flashes from Jesse's light, Frank Hamer raised his rifle—the same Remington Model 8 that he'd used to kill Bonnie and Clyde—aimed it at the car, and put his finger on the trigger.

Sonny said nothing. He followed suit, with one exception. He lifted the shotgun, slid his hook against the metal trigger, and lodged the butt of the gun up against his right shoulder—where it belonged. The action clinked slightly, like a funeral bell had been rung miles away.

CHAPTER 30

Tió slowed the car as he came over the hill, and then, without a reason why, he brought it to a stop. The Model A's engine idled roughly, a piston missing on occasion. He had never had the time to make the car run faster, boost the performance. From the sound of things, they were lucky it had got them this far.

"What's the matter?" Carmen said. She was sitting as close to the door as she could. Mercury sat on the floorboard. Up until that moment, it would have been easy to believe that the hood ornament really was a good luck charm. They had hardly seen a car on the road since leaving Oklahoma—and the burning shack—behind.

"I thought I saw a light."

Carmen looked around and saw nothing but darkness. Dawn was breaking on the horizon, and she hoped she would be home, in her own bed, by daylight. She wanted to leave the night and everything that had happened behind. She pushed the burning shack, with Eddie's body inside, as quickly out of her mind as she could. "I don't see anything."

Tió acted like he hadn't heard a word she said. He stared straight ahead, past the reach of the headlights, into the night that still existed, like he was lost and looking for his way. After another long second, he put the car back into gear and inched forward.

Two seconds later, a pair of headlights appeared in the middle of the road ahead of them. A car had stopped and was sitting in the middle of the road, pointing right at them. It blinked the lights three times. Fast. A warning. Carmen was certain of it.

Tió slammed his foot on the brake and glanced in the rearview mirror. "Uh-oh. Bad trouble."

Her stomach fluttered at the first sign of the headlights. She was praying to make it home. They were close, so close she could almost run there from where they were and climb in her bed like she had never been gone.

Carmen looked behind them, over her shoulder, and slipped her hand on the door handle at the same time.

There was another car back there. It had appeared out of nowhere, just like the first, its lights directly on them. This car had a spotlight attached to the driver's door, and it suddenly lit up, illuminating the inside of the Model A like it was the middle of the day. The other car set a red flare in the road. They were trapped.

Panic flashed in Tió's brown eyes. "We gotta get out of here."

"Get out of the car, and you will not be hurt," a voice, amplified by a bullhorn, demanded from behind them.

Tió shook his head. "Not going to jail. You can't go home, Carmen. Not now."

Tió switched his foot from the brake pedal to the accelerator and slammed it down as far as it would go.

The tires spun into motion and the car lurched forward, throwing Carmen back against the seat. She hadn't been expecting the move. Her hand fell away from the door handle. She lost any chance she might have had of jumping out and making a run for it.

Tió wrenched the steering wheel and turned left off the road, jumping over the berm, bouncing them both around like they were on an out-of-control carnival ride. Carmen held on to the seat as tight as she could, but she rolled sideways, toward Tió.

Over the clatter of the engine and the bounce and bump of the car making a path off the road, Carmen heard what she thought was distant thunder. But there were no clouds in the sky, only stars and a widening gray horizon, offering more light to the world by the second.

Metal ripped through metal, and the thunder was not thunder at all. It was a gunshot.

The first bullet slammed into Carmen's leg and went right through it like it was nothing but a piece of paper. She barely had time to scream before the passenger window shattered and shards of glass rained down on her.

The smell of gunpowder infiltrated Sonny's nose, and for a moment he thought he was at war, in a battle, transported back to France one more time. Except no one was shooting back. It had been a problem since he'd returned from the distant shores, mistaking where he was, jumping at the sound of a gunshot. But the shock of the war, of all he had seen and done, had worn off over the years. He knew it was because this was fresh. He'd been off of his feet and without a gun in his hand for a long time.

Frank Hamer had a fifteen-round clip on his Remington, and he was firing one shot after the next. Sonny eased the hook off of the shotgun's trigger and stood back.

Hamer noticed and stopped shooting. "What's the matter, Burton?"

"They're not shooting back."

The last shot from the Remington echoed over the hill, but there was still firing. It was Jesse. Orange flashes popped out of the end of his rifle, exposing his position.

As dawn ate away the night, the Ranger car in the ditch would become more and more visible. Grayness covered half the sky. Daylight was coming on fast.

Sighting the beat-up Model A was easier, clearer. It had careened off the road, gaining speed, and was just about out of range when it came to a sudden stop. The car teetered on its side like it had struck something unseen.

Frank Hamer eased the rifle down onto the hood of his car. They had stood behind it for protection. He picked up a flashlight and blinked it on and off three times. Cease fire. "We might have got them," he said.

"There's no need to pulverize them," Sonny said. Hamer shot him a harsh look, and Sonny almost regretted saying it but offered nothing to retract the statement.

There was no question that Bonnie and Clyde had needed to be stopped when they were. They would've just kept on with their killing spree. No man who wore a badge within three states would have been safe. But what Sonny had learned of the shoot-out troubled him then—and now. He saw no need to overdo it. And he still held out hope to rescue Carmen. At least save her from the same fate as Bonnie Parker.

"All right, let's see what they do." Hamer set the flashlight down, produced a pair of binoculars, and directed his attention to the Model A. "No movement. Doesn't look like the car's going anywhere soon. The axle's broke. We got 'em stopped at the very least."

The second shot had barely missed Tió, but it might as well have hit him. Once Carmen screamed, Tió began to wail and tremble. He drove wildly across the field, trying to dodge unseen bullets but to no avail. The car was a target.

All hell broke loose. The windows shattered. Mercury's head flew off, deflecting the bullet. It whizzed by Carmen's ear. If it hadn't have been for the hood ornament, the bullet would have slapped her between the eyes ... but she was hardly aware of that. Once she had taken the first shot in the leg, she had slid to the floor and buried herself as tight against the firewall as she could. After that, shock came fast. She was slightly aware of where she was, that she was still alive. Pain was the only confirmation of her mortality.

The air was filled with all kinds of noises. Mechanical groans as the car sped across a hard field, gunshots, thunder, glass breaking, Tió yelling, crying, babbling. And then the car came to sudden stop, like it had hit a wall. It jerked and then slammed down, a great breaking sound coming from underneath it.

The gunshots kept on peppering the metal doors, the roof, the radiator. The smell of steam, gas, and blood all mixed together, but Carmen couldn't puke—there was nothing left in her stomach to vacate. She couldn't breathe, couldn't move. She felt like she was going to lose consciousness, pass out. Maybe this was her death, what it felt like to die. The angels were coming for her. Tears drained down her cheeks, but she couldn't even hear herself cry.

Then silence came, and to her surprise she was still alive, still awake. She could feel the pain in her leg growing worse, blood rushing from her body. The bullets had bounced around her, but had not hit her anywhere else.

Tió was slumped against the door, his eyes open, staring straight ahead, bloodier than anything she had ever seen.

Carmen knew that Tió was dead. The agony of living, of knowing what he had done to his brother, to her, was over for him. He would be second-best no longer. There had never been anything she could have done to save him. Something deep inside told her she should have tried harder.

They approached the Model A carefully, taking cover at every step, guns drawn, fingers on their triggers.

The sky was white, like a blank canvas, waiting for the rest of the day and weather to arrive. There seemed little question that a storm of any kind was going to blow up any time soon. The air was still and the clouds were high and thin, barely perceptible against the same-colored sky. Once again, darkness had lost the battle against light—but there would be another time for that, as the sun turned away from the earth for just a blink. The war would never end as long as the world kept spinning.

Sonny eased up alongside Frank Hamer, taking each step hopefully but sensing all of his hope had been wasted. It didn't look like anyone could survive what had just happened.

The morning light made the land more navigable, snake holes more defined, and movement in the car—which remained still—clearer.

Jesse had pulled his car down to the spot where the Model A had turned off the road. Jonesy and Hugh Beaverwood had come up, too, bringing their vehicles with them.

A flare, cutting into the soft white sky like a glowing red worm, had been shot to alert the deputies on the other road that they were needed at this scene.

Sonny saw the boy slumped by the steering wheel from ten feet away. He could see the rest of the seats—the back door had popped open on impact—and there was no one there. It was empty. *There should be three of them*, he thought, but didn't say.

Frank Hamer knew that, too, and saw the same thing that Sonny did. He motioned for Sonny to stop, then crouched down and slid up the door of the car, the barrel of his gun leading the way.

"There's only one of them and a girl." Hamer stood back and waved at the road.

Sonny turned and saw the tall, lanky Hugh Beaverwood jump into action and pull a gurney out of the back of the ambulance.

Hamer rushed around to the other side of the car and yanked the door open. "Looks like this one's still alive, but she's been hit."

Sonny followed, happy at Frank Hamer's announcement. Upon seeing Carmen, there was no question that she was Aldo's daughter—she looked just like him, only younger, softer.

There had been no time to alert Aldo during the night about Hamer's plan. The Mexican probably would have been unwelcome among the posse, but Sonny still wished that Aldo was there to see his daughter . . . just in case she died before she got to the hospital.

Both doors at the back of the ambulance stood open. Hugh Beaverwood pulled the gurney up over the berm as Jesse pushed it up from the back.

Sonny had hurried alongside Carmen the best he could. She hadn't spoken a word, was not conscious. Her eyes were closed.

Dawn was gone, and morning had arrived with a pure brightness that made it difficult not to see everything clearly, There was no mistaking the blood on Carmen's leg.

Hugh Beaverwood had fashioned a tourniquet to slow the bleeding, but anyone with any battlefield experience at all knew there was little chance that Carmen was going to survive. It looked like an artery had been severed.

With a yank and a pull from both men, the gurney lurched over the berm.

Beaverwood and Jesse hurried to the ambulance and slid Carmen inside. Sonny never left her side, nearly pushing Jesse out of the way from the door.

The sun had popped over the horizon, casting even more light on the cars and the surrounding landscape. The inside of the ambulance was lit up like it had klieg lights on the inside of it.

Carmen's face was pale, and she had yet to move. She was covered up to her neck with a white blanket, like a mummy about to be set into a tomb.

Hugh Beaverwood stood back, closed the door on his side, then looked at Sonny expectantly—who was standing in the way of the other door being closed.

Sonny was focused on Carmen, on the interior of the ambulance.

"Every second counts, Ranger Burton," the coroner said.

"Right," Sonny answered, a little distracted. He stood back and slammed the door.

Hugh Beaverwood hurried out of sight, and in a matter of seconds, the ambulance sped away, toward the hospital in Wellington.

Sonny didn't move. He stood in the middle of the road, watching the ambulance disappear down the road.

"What's the matter, Pa?" Jesse had sidled up next to Sonny, followed by Frank Hamer.

Sonny shrugged. "Nothing. I don't think. But maybe something."

"What?" Hamer said.

Sonny shook his head. "There was a shoe in the back of the ambulance."

"A shoe?" Jesse said. There was a tone of recognition, of coming trouble in his voice.

"Yes, a shoe. One shoe. Sensible and slightly scuffed," Sonny said.

"Just like the girl in the field was wearing," Jesse answered, turning toward his car. "Damn it. I knew it."

"That's it. Just like the girl in the field was wearing. Son of a bitch. He's been standing in front of us the whole time. One shoe was missing." Sonny followed after Jesse and jumped into the passenger seat of his car—leaving Frank Hamer in the dust, with a confused look on his face.

CHAPTER 31

The crows were startled awake by the gunshots, roused from the safety of their roost earlier than normal. The sky had been black, black as their wings, but they lifted away from their resting spot in search of safer limbs.

It didn't take long for all of them to figure out that they were not the target of men's guns.

The conflict, the hunt, was man after man, or in this case men after a boy and a girl. What was apparent to the birds, though, was that there would be blood left about, drops to draw other things to the ruckus.

So they stayed close. Watched from a distance and became even more hopeful when they saw the two-legged one that was most like them. The first one to always show up when there was human blood, death, opportunity.

If the man had wings, he'd be their leader, a member of the gang, and they would be all the better for it—rich in food beyond their wildest dreams.

He was dark like them, and they wondered what stories there were about men like him, men with eyes as black as a thousand falling crows.

Jesse punched the accelerator and gripped the steering wheel so hard his knuckles turned red.

"You knew?" Sonny asked.

"Don't start, Pa." Jesse's eyes were focused on the road. There was no sign of the ambulance.

"Hugh Beaverwood," Sonny said, with a frustrated exhale.

"Maybe. Yes. I didn't have a clue until late yesterday."

Sonny looked at Jesse, then back at the road. There was still no sign of the ambulance. "You best tell me what you know."

Jesse set his jaw, gritted his teeth, fought off whatever he was feeling. "Betty Maxwell called me after you left the hospital yesterday. She was nearly hysterical, afraid."

Sonny immediately recalled the conversation with Nurse Betty and felt bad all over again. "I was rude," he said.

"You were. You saw that she was pregnant, or had been, and then there was no child, no baby to show for it. That's what set her off, got her thinking."

"What's this have to do with Hugh Beaverwood, Jesse?" Sonny looked up the road, and in the distance he saw a plume of dust rising in the air. "That it might be him?"

Jesse nodded, then looked over at Sonny. "She's a grown woman with a son, single, and under enough scrutiny as it is, just for that. Working at the hospital gives her a little bit of credibility in this town, but folks are uncomfortable with their secrets bein' known. If she came up pregnant and not married, she'd lose what she had. She didn't have a choice."

"A choice?" Sonny pulled the .45 out from his back and held it in his left hand.

"She had to take care of it," Jesse said.

Sonny didn't say anything. They were still a good distance from the ambulance—which was driving at its flat-out speed—but it was no match for Jesse's newer-model sedan. "So, she went to Hugh Beaverwood?"

"Seems that way. She asked me about the two dead girls, if they'd been pregnant. I confirmed that and told her about the third girl, and it was like the lights just came on. She told me everything then, that it was Hugh Beaverwood who took care of the girls that came to town and didn't go out to the Jorgensons to have their babies."

Jesse shot Sonny a terse glance, then let it fade it away as quickly as it had come on. "She didn't know, Pa. She didn't understand the consequences of silence. None of us do until it's too late to change things."

"I rushed out of there and started asking him questions, and he denied everything. He wasn't nervous at all. Just went about his business, closed everything up, and went inside. Just left me there, feeling like I had insulted him. I was going to go to the judge first thing this morning for a search warrant, but Hamer's call came in. Things happened so fast I didn't have time."

Sonny chambered a round in the .45. "You rattled him. He knew you were on his scent."

Jesse glanced over to Sonny, then back to the road. "Hold on, there's a dip comin'."

Sonny braced himself by jamming his wood arm into the door, letting go of the .45, and gripping the seat with his left hand. It was a hard bounce, and the gun fell to the floorboard, but he maintained his balance.

Sonny reached down to get the gun, then sat back up. When he did, he saw the rear end of the ambulance about two hundred yards ahead of them.

Jesse maintained control of the sedan and pressed down the accelerator even more, demanding as much as he could from the V-8. "Hugh talked to Betty on occasion. He didn't have a whole lot of friends. She had known for a long time that girls went to Hugh, but she never thought it was something she would do. She understood that those things happen. It wasn't any of her business. She turned her head because nobody was getting hurt, and those girls were getting a second chance at life. At least, that's what she thought. She was just keepin' one more secret. It was a habit to look the other way."

Sonny bounced in the seat and let his mind wander away from Jesse's voice for a second, then said, "We might have a bigger problem than the one that's right before us, if that's the case," Sonny said. "If you're on the money about Hugh Beaverwood."

"What?" There was panic in Jesse's voice.

"Have you talked to Betty since you went to talk to Hugh?"

Jesse shook his head. "No."

"I was afraid you were going to say that."

Jesse's lip quivered. "He went after Betty?"

"I'm afraid he might have, Jesse," Sonny said. "I'm just afraid he might have, if he thought Betty tipped you off."

CHAPTER 32

There was no way the ambulance was going to outrun Jesse's Plymouth sedan. In the blink of an eye, they were on the bumper of the vehicle, giving Sonny little time to think things through, even though he knew what he had to do—he just wasn't sure how he was going to do it.

"He knows it's us," Jesse said.

"He's not going to stop." Sonny leaned forward with the prosthetic and put the hook on the dashboard. Metal against metal, jostled about by the forward motion of the vehicle, the hook slid off, and there was no way to stop it. "Damn it."

Jesse looked over to Sonny. "What are you doing?"

"Trying to figure out how to get a good shot." Sonny made another attempt, only this time, he leaned into the dashboard and butted the hook against it. With the wood arm extended, it was like a steady bridge.

Hugh Beaverwood was driving erratically now, outmaneuvering Jesse at every turn. The coroner was good at playing cat and mouse, anticipating the Ranger's intentions to go around him.

Sonny let his wood-arm relax, leaned over, swaying and dodging the whole time, and rolled down the window. "Get up alongside him," he said to Jesse.

"I'm tryin', Pa." Jesse's face was drawn tight with focus and frustration at the same time.

There was no way that Sonny couldn't see the child in the man, trying and failing, but refusing to give up. One thing about Jesse, he had never cried when he fell off a horse, off of old Snag. He dusted himself off and climbed back up on the saddle. That determination had served him well as a man—mostly.

Sonny wedged the hook into the dashboard, picked up the .45, and leveraged it over the wood bridge, so that it was as stable as it could be. "Go on, dodge right, dodge right again, then veer left as fast as you can, and pull up next to him so I can get a shot into the cab."

Jesse glanced over at Sonny and started to say something, but held back. He did what he was told.

Sonny hung on, tensing his lower back the best he could, so his trunk only swayed slightly. He had a hard grip on the .45 and aimed the barrel directly out the window.

Beaverwood fell for the ruse. Not that it was much of a ploy. It wasn't like they were on a mountain road. There were flat, dry fields on both sides of the road, room to maneuver—it was just a matter of time before the cat, before Jesse, won the game.

Jesse sped up, trying to get next to the ambulance.

Sonny could see Hugh Beaverwood's thin frame hunched forward over the steering wheel, like he was trying to urge the truck on, make it go faster. But that was impossible. He was going as fast as he could. The coroner looked over his shoulder frequently, worried, afraid, then turned back to the road.

"Shoot the tires," Jesse yelled.

Sonny shook his head. "Carmen's in there. We can't risk it if he wrecks."

Jesse nodded, then leaned into the steering wheel, just like Beaverwood, trying to will the sedan to go faster than it could.

They were halfway up to the driver's door of the ambulance when Sonny started shouting, "Pull over! Pull over!"

There was no response. Sonny might as well have been yelling at a wall. He hooked his finger around the trigger, felt the familiar touch of the metal, and didn't hesitate. He pulled the trigger with as much certainty as he ever had—shooting at Bonnie and Clyde; in France at an unknown German; as a little boy, the gun bigger than his head, standing next to his father, firing for the very first time. Every bit of skill Sonny had acquired over the years was in that one pull.

The boom echoed inside the sedan and was more deafening than Sonny thought it would be. The smell of gunpowder lingered for a second, then the burst of smoke whooshed out the window and was gone with the speed of the car.

Glass shattered and fell in on Hugh Beaverwood. The ambulance lurched right, then straightened out, back under control.

Sonny had not shot to kill, or to even to maim. He had shot to warn, to show that he was serious. He wanted to take Hugh Beaverwood alive.

"What are you doin'?" Jesse yelled.

Sonny ignored him and shot again, this time blowing out the windshield in front of the steering wheel. The ambulance wobbled a little bit—then did something that neither Sonny nor Jesse expected: Hugh Beaverwood slammed on the brakes of the ambulance. It came to a sudden stop in a big cloud of dust.

It took Jesse a second to react, but he hit the brakes, too, sending the sedan into a sudden slide sideways on the hard dirt road.

Pebbles and small rocks flew into the window and pelted Sonny like buckshot. For a second, he was afraid he'd been shot. One of the rocks was of decent size and hit him in the chest. It bounced off him and fell into his lap. He almost laughed in relief, but there was nothing funny at the moment.

Jesse was out of the car before the dust cleared.

Sonny looked over his shoulder, blinked, and watched, trying to ascertain the situation. He saw a fully capable figure running—tall, black, almost like he was trying to gain speed to fly. But he wasn't quick enough, and there was no place to run. The flat Texas land was Hugh Beaverwood's enemy now.

"Stop, in the name of law," Jesse yelled, giving the man the opportunity to prove them wrong, to claim innocence.

Hugh Beaverwood didn't stop running. He ran faster, his eyes focused on a distant spot on the horizon. If he heard Jesse, he offered no sign of it.

Jesse yelled again, "Stop!" and got the same response. This time he leveled his rifle and took down Hugh Beaverwood with one shot.

Jonesy, Frank Hamer, and the other deputies appeared out of nowhere, surrounding Jesse and Sonny like members of a pack of wolves come to inspect a kill and fight for their rightful place around the table. But Hugh Beaverwood wasn't dead. Jesse had shot him in the leg, behind the knee, making sure he wasn't going to run anywhere any time soon.

The coroner was still breathing, unconscious but breathing, piled up face-first on the ground, like he had been tossed there and left for dead, left for the scavengers to have their way with him. It looked like he had hit his head on a rock in the fall. Blood ran out of his ear. Flies paid no attention to the circle of men. They found a way in, around, above, below, desperate for a taste and a place to deposit a bit of themselves, lay eggs, and move on.

A crow cawed in the distance not too far away, calling others as the wind gusted about, carrying every sound of opportunity to the farthest reaches of the field and beyond.

Jesse looked at Sonny. "Damn it, he can't talk."

"It's all right," Sonny said. He turned to Frank Hamer. "You need to get that girl to the hospital, pronto, and this monster, too. We need him to talk." Then he spun around without any other explanation and hurried back toward Jesse's car.

"Where you goin'?" Hamer yelled out.

Jesse realized what Sonny was up to and ran to join up with him.

There was no time to explain, no time to hand-wring over what was right and what was wrong, all Sonny could think of was Betty Maxwell and her son, Leo.

He hoped his gut was wrong. He hoped they were still alive. "We need to go find a nurse," Sonny answered over his shoulder.

The Maxwell house looked no different than it had the last time Sonny had seen the property. Except the screen door stood open, battering against the frame with a steady beat.

The wind had picked up again, out of nowhere, offering no promise of rain but of another dust storm, another bitter cloud that dropped nothing of sustenance on the land, just more of the same—dirt, sand, and misery.

Sonny and Jesse hurried out of the car, both with their pistols pointed upward, fingers on the triggers.

"Betty!" Sonny called out as he hurried up the porch steps. "Are you here? Leo?"

No answer came, and the bad feeling that Sonny had in the pit of his stomach grew bigger, darker, sadder. He had seen what Hugh Beaverwood had done to girls he didn't know. He couldn't imagine what he would do to Betty Maxwell, all things considered.

The front room was a mess. Chairs turned over. Broken glass on the floor. And blood. One blot, and several dots leading to the kitchen. There was no question there'd been a struggle of some kind. Sonny's heart sank at the realization that he'd been right about Hugh Beaverwood.

Jesse said nothing; he just followed the trail of blood like a dog on a scent. Sonny stayed behind him, in his shadow, listening, hoping somehow that he was wrong.

The house was silent. Sonny heard nothing past his own heartbeat and Jesse's footsteps. There was nothing alive under the roof, not even a mouse dared move about, contributing to the dread Sonny felt.

The kitchen was empty.

"I'll check upstairs. You clear the downstairs," Jesse said, as he pushed by Sonny.

Sonny agreed with a nod. It was a good plan. Now was not the time to jockey for power or control. *Let the boy be*, Sonny thought. *He's good at what he does. Don't act surprised.*

Jesse hurried up the stairs, and the sound carried though the house like a man yelling in a canyon.

Sonny checked the larder, the closet, the parlor, and a single bedroom on the first floor. They were empty. Jesse checked all the rooms overhead, and then hurried back downstairs, shaking his head. "Nothing here. Let's check the cellar."

Jesse ran out to his car, rummaged for a flashlight, then hurried back to the side of the house. He called out for Betty and Leo again, then pushed down the stairs that led to the cellar. Sonny was on his heels, at the ready, the .45 comfortable in his left hand.

Jesse yanked open the door, shined the light all around, and called out again. There was no one inside the dark cavern, and it didn't look like there had been for a long time. Cobwebs dangled in the doorway.

"Damn it," Jesse said.

Sonny sighed. "Maybe he took them somewhere."

"Maybe. But where?"

"Only one place that I can think of," Sonny said.

"The funeral home in Wellington?"

"That's what I was thinking."

Normal life pulsed on the streets of town. Cars and trucks came and went from the stores and the courthouse on the square. People walked on the sidewalks like it was a perfect day—and it might have been—for them. A bus sat in front of the Ritz Theater, waiting to depart.

Wind blew dust around, but it didn't look like it was going to manifest into a big storm. There was no indication that anything was wrong outside of town. News of the shoot-out and capture of Hugh Beaverwood hadn't reached anyone yet, and the weather was just an accepted way of life in this part of Texas.

Jesse hurried the sedan though town and made his way to the one and only funeral home in Wellington. He parked in the back, where Hugh loaded and unloaded bodies.

"Looks locked up tighter than a drum," Jesse said, as he got out of the car.

Sonny followed Jesse up to the door. "You realize we need a warrant."

Jesse stared at Sonny and shrugged. "I see blood on the ground, don't you?"

Sonny looked at his feet and didn't see a thing. "Sure, if you say so."

"I say so." Jesse checked the door to see if it was locked. It was. He didn't hesitate. He kicked it in.

The inside of the funeral home was dark. It smelled musty and old inside. Like a library with the added aroma of embalming fluid—formaldehyde and methanol. Sonny's eyes stung and began to water, making everything in his line of vision wavy, like he was underwater.

"You ever been back here before?" Jesse asked Sonny.

"Once or twice. This is a receiving room, then there's a room where Hugh does his work, and the chapel or whatever you call it behind that. He keeps coffins in the basement."

Jesse looked at Sonny curiously.

"I had to go down there and pick one out for your mother," Sonny said.

"Where's the door?"

"Past the embalming room."

"This place gives me the creeps even in the daytime."

Sonny ignored Jesse, and his ear perked up. "You hear that?"

Jesse cocked his head. "Yes." A hopeful look crossed his face, and he hurried down the hall and stopped at the first door. He kicked in the door and swept inside with the barrel of his gun. Sonny backed him up.

There was just enough light to see Leo tied to a chair and gagged, his eyes wide with fear and relief at the same time.

Jesse hurried to the boy and pulled off the gag. "Where's your mother?"

"I don't know. Downstairs maybe. I heard him drag something down the steps. Find her, please. Just find her," Leo cried.

Both men bolted for the door, but Sonny stopped and looked back at the boy. "Don't worry; you're safe now. We'll be back for you."

"What about him!"

"Hugh Beaverwood can't hurt anyone anymore. Don't you worry, son," Sonny said.

Jesse was already down the stairs and into the basement by the time Sonny made it to the top of the stairs.

"Betty, Betty, are you down here?" Jesse called out.

Sonny heard a thump, thump, thump, like somebody was beating on a drum. He hurried down the stairs, his heart racing like it never had before.

Jesse had turned on the overhead lights, illuminating the basement like it was daylight.

By the time Sonny reached the bottom of the stairs, the thumping had stopped. There was a sea of coffins, mostly unfinished. It smelled like raw wood and varnish mixed with death.

Jesse stood over a plain walnut coffin with the lid up. "It's her, Pa. She's alive. Beaten up. But alive."

CHAPTER 33

Sonny downshifted the truck as he pulled into the Jorgenson's drive. The house looked like the oasis it was in the soft morning light. Lidde had worked hard to green some zinnias in front of the house, and they were watered and blooming. It looked like a rainbow of colors—reds, yellows, and oranges—had fallen from the sky and stayed there. More than one chicken pecked at the ground. There were six or seven from what Sonny could tell. Fences were mended, and a few cages back by the barn had dogs in them. They barked as the truck rolled to a stop.

Pete and Lidde were standing on the porch, waiting, expecting them. There was no slouch in Pete's shoulders, and Lidde had a wide, welcoming smile on her face. Her hands were clasped at her ample waist, against her ever-present freshly bleached apron.

Sonny drew in a deep breath and looked over at Blue, who was on all fours, standing up, thumping his tail against the seat. He knew where he was. "Calm down, boy, you can go in a minute." He looked past the dog to Carmen. There was no mistaking the small bulge in her stomach, like she had slid a ball under her dress. "Are you ready?"

Carmen shook her head.

"They're good people," Sonny said. "Lidde will help you like no one else can."

"I don't want to give him up," Carmen said in Spanish, staring out the window. She eased her hand down to her belly and touched it gently. "He will need me." A tear dripped down her cheek.

"No one said you had to give up the baby," Sonny said. "You can decide when the time comes."

"I have already decided."

There was steel in Carmen's eyes and voice that Sonny couldn't—wouldn't—dispute. He nodded, opened the truck door, and stood up out of it.

Blue followed, easily jumping to the ground. The splint and bandage had come off, leaving the hound with a noticeable limp—but it did nothing to deter him. He ran straight up to Lidde, wagging his tail, nuzzling into her as she leaned down to greet the dog.

Aldo was already out of the back of the truck, waiting on Sonny and Carmen.

Like the house, and the Jorgensons, Aldo looked a little refreshed, but a little older, weathered by the past events. He looked at Carmen with sadness and love, though it was easy to see that he was hesitant around her, tepid, like he was afraid he would scare her off at any second.

Carmen sat in the truck, her teeth set tight, her eyes distant, her cheeks wet with fresh tears.

Aldo leaned inside the driver's door. "It is not a jail," he said.

"I know," Carmen answered. "They are strangers. Anglos. What do they know of me?"

Sonny stood back, stoic, waiting, trying not to listen, but there was no way to avoid it.

"Your momma would be here if she could. This is the best place for you and the baby," Aldo said.

"They won't take him?"

"No one will take him, I promise. *Señor* Burton promises."

Carmen looked at Sonny, who nodded again, reassuring her.

Sonny was surprised that they both were convinced that the baby was a boy, but said nothing. That was not any of his business.

Carmen nodded, then pushed out of the truck.

A smile crept across Aldo's face. He reached into the bed of the truck, and pulled out a small suitcase.

"She doesn't know how lucky she is," Sonny said to Aldo.

"No, I don't think so. She could be in jail. Probably would be if she were older," Aldo said. "I am thankful she is alive, here. That is all that matters. The baby has no crime to his name."

Sonny nodded and remained where he stood. Aldo met Carmen, and they walked up to the house together.

Lidde met them at the stoop and allowed Aldo to make the introduction. Pete smiled down at Carmen and took the suitcase from Aldo.

"Come on," Lidde said, wrapping her arm around Carmen, "let's go look at your room, yah? I've made it extra comfortable, just for you. You'll like it, you'll see."

Carmen looked at Aldo, who nodded, then leaned in and kissed her on the cheek. "You will be fine. You'll see. I will stop in every day on my way home from work. You will not be alone here."

"Promise?" Carmen asked.

"Yes, I promise," Aldo said.

Carmen nodded. Lidde smiled. And they disappeared into the house. Blue followed, walked through the open door like he was welcome, like he lived there, too. No one noticed, or if they did, they didn't object.

Aldo watched, then turned, walked back to the truck, and climbed into the bed without saying a word to Sonny or Pete.

Sonny walked up to the porch and Pete set the suitcase down.

"Thanks for taking her in, Pete."

"Our pleasure," he said. "It's the last of that business for a while. How is your son? I haven't seen him for a while."

Sonny sighed. "He went back to Brownsville for a little while to take care of some business. Once that's done, he'll be back up here permanent."

"Gonna stay north with the company in your place?"

"I think it's a good thing. The trial'll be coming up soon, and Jesse'll need to be here anyway."

Pete Jorgenson shook his head in disgust. "I never was comfortable around Hugh Beaverwood, but I always suspected that it was because he smelled like death, because of what he did for a livin'. But I guess all those tales about him was true after all. He was a bad man. Hurt more than he helped."

"More will come out, I suppose," Sonny said. "But I saw enough, know enough. I'm happy to leave all that to Jesse, now. He can handle it."

"I think he can," Pete offered with a smile, reaching out to tap Sonny's right shoulder like he would any old friend. He stopped as soon as he realized what he had done. A stricken look crossed Pete's face, replacing the ease and comfort that had been there seconds before.

"It's okay, Pete," Sonny said, raising the hook. "I don't feel much pain anymore, and I'm getting used to it more and more every day. Why, just this morning, I tied my shoes with it." He looked down at his feet, proud of himself.

Pete smiled. "I'm glad to hear it."

"Well," Sonny said, "I best get Aldo back home. I suppose you've got work to do."

"Always that," Pete said. He reached down and picked up the suitcase.

Sonny whistled for Blue, and in a matter of seconds the dog came running out the door. "I'll be seeing you, Pete," he said, stepping off the porch, heading to the truck.

"Stop by any time, Sonny. There's always a cup of coffee for you here."

Sonny waved and walked to the truck, then opened the door for Blue to jump in. The dog dove straight inside the cab and settled into his spot by the passenger window. Sonny slid into the driver's seat and started the truck like he'd been doing it all his life.

He smiled as he drove away from the Jorgensons'. It was the first time he could ever remember Pete calling him anything but Ranger Burton.

The crows watched and waited, hoping for another two-legged one to walk the world. The other one had vanished, but they knew it would only be a matter of time before another one would come along, leading them in the darkness to blood, to opportunity, to a silent festival of crows.

AUTHOR'S NOTE

Bonnie Parker and Clyde Barrow's visit to Wellington, Texas, is based on actual events, but it has been shaped to fit the fictional narrative of this novel by the author. People, places, and timelines have been eliminated, meshed, and moved for the sole purpose of story-telling, not to rewrite history. Any mistakes are my own.

Readers interested in the Texas Rangers and Bonnie and Clyde in the 1930s should look to these books for further reading: *Lone Star Lawmen: The Second Century of the Texas Rangers* (Berkley, 2008) by Robert M. Utley, *Time of the Rangers: Texas Rangers: From 1900 to the Present* (Forge, 2010) by Mike Cox, and *Go Down Together: The True, Untold Story of Bonnie and Clyde* (Simon & Shuster, 2009) by Jeff Guinn.

ACKNOWLEDGMENTS

This novel wouldn't have been possible without the encouragement of Matthew P. Mayo and David Cranmer. They selected my short story, "Shadow of the Crow," for an anthology they edited, *Beat to a Pulp: Round Two*, giving me the belief and encouragement that there was more to Sonny Burton's story to tell. Thank you both.

Luckily, I have had the pleasure and opportunity to spend quality time around American crows. Liz and Chris Hatton rehab injured wild birds and also use them to educate the general public about their existence and why the birds are so important to us all. It is a privilege to be in the company of a wild animal, and I'm grateful for the opportunity and the lessons I have learned. Thank you, Liz and Chris, this book wouldn't have been the same without spending time with you and the crows.

Special thanks goes to Dan Mayer, for your enthusiasm for this story, and to the entire Seventh Street Books team that sees my books to the shelves. Also, to my longtime agent, Cherry Weiner, who believed in this book from start and never gave up on it (a recurring theme).

Finally, thank you to my wife, Rose. You constantly amaze me with your wit, intelligence, and genuine heart. I am able to do what I do because of your continued belief and encouragement. Thank you.

ABOUT THE AUTHOR

Larry D. Sweazy (www.larrydsweazy.com) is a two-time WWA (Western Writers of America) Spur Award winner, a two-time, back-to-back, winner of the Will Rogers Medallion Award, a Best Books of Indiana award winner, and the inaugural winner of the 2013 Elmer Kelton Book Award. He was also nominated for a Short Mystery Fiction Society (SMFS) Derringer award in 2007 (for the short story, "See Also Murder"). Larry has published over sixty nonfiction articles and short stories and is the author of ten novels, including six novels in the Josiah Wolfe western series (Berkley), two novels in the Lucas Fume western series (Berkley), *The Devil's Bones*, a thriller set in Indiana (Five Star), and one novel (*See Also Murder*) in the Marjorie Trumaine Mystery series (Seventh Street Books), with two more planned for the future. He currently lives in Indiana with his wife, Rose.